Dedicated to Earl Bettinger,
the husband who . . .

The Cat Who Went Into The Closet

Read ALL the CAT WHO mysteries!

THE CAT WHO COULD READ BACKWARDS: The world of modern art is a mystery to many—but for Jim Qwilleran and Koko it turns into a mystery of another sort . . .

THE CAT WHO ATE DANISH MODERN: Qwill isn't thrilled about covering the interior design beat for *The Daily Fluxion.* Little does he know that a murderer has designs on a local woman featured in one of his stories . . .

THE CAT WHO TURNED ON AND OFF: Qwill and Koko are joined by Yum Yum as they try to solve a murder in an antique shop . . .

THE CAT WHO SAW RED: Qwill starts his diet—*and* starts a new gourmet column for the *Fluxion.* It isn't easy—but it's not as hard as solving a shocking murder case!

THE CAT WHO PLAYED BRAHMS: While fishing at a secluded cabin, Qwill hooks onto a murder mystery—and Koko develops a strange fondness for classical music . . .

*TURN THE PAGE FOR MORE
CAT WHODUNITS . . .*

THE CAT WHO PLAYED POST OFFICE: Koko and Yum Yum turn into fat cats when Qwill inherits millions and moves into a mansion. But amid the caviar and champagne, Koko starts sniffing clues to a murder!

THE CAT WHO HAD 14 TALES: A delightful collection of feline mystery fiction from the creator of Koko and Yum Yum!

THE CAT WHO KNEW SHAKESPEARE: The local newspaper publisher has perished in an accident—or is it murder? That is the question . . .

THE CAT WHO SNIFFED GLUE: After a rich banker and his wife are killed, Koko develops an odd appetite for glue. To solve the murder, Qwill has to figure out why . . .

THE CAT WHO WENT UNDERGROUND: Qwill and the cats head for their Moose County log cabin for a relaxing summer—but when a handyman disappears, Koko must dig up the buried motive for a sinister crime . . .

THE CAT WHO TALKED TO GHOSTS: Qwill and Koko try to solve a haunting mystery in a historic farmhouse.

THE CAT WHO LIVED HIGH: A glamorous art dealer was killed in Qwill's new high-rise apartment—and he and the cats are about to reach new heights in detection as they try to find out whodunit . . .

THE CAT WHO KNEW A CARDINAL: The director of the local Shakespeare production dies in Qwill's orchard—and the stage is set for a puzzling mystery!

THE CAT WHO MOVED A MOUNTAIN: Qwill moves to a new home in the beautiful Potato Mountains. But when a dispute between local residents and developers boils over into a murder case, he has to keep his eyes open to find the culprit!

THE CAT WHO WASN'T THERE: Qwill's on his way to Scotland—and on his way to solving another purr-plexing mystery!

And turn to the back for a special excerpt from . . .

THE CAT WHO CAME TO BREAKFAST: Peaceful Breakfast Island is turned upside-down by real-estate developers, controversy—and murder. It's up to Qwill and the cats to find out whodunit . . .

Available in hardcover
from G. P. Putnam's Sons

The Cat Who Went Into The Closet

Lilian Jackson Braun

JOVE BOOKS, NEW YORK

This Jove Book contains the complete
text of the original hardcover edition.
It has been completely reset in a typeface
designed for easy reading and was printed
from new film.

THE CAT WHO WENT INTO THE CLOSET

A Jove Book / published by arrangement with
the author

PRINTING HISTORY
G. P. Putnam's Sons edition published April 1993
Jove edition / March 1994

ISBN: 0-515-11332-8

A JOVE BOOK®
Jove Books are published by The Berkley Publishing Group,
200 Madison Avenue, New York, New York 10016.
JOVE and the "J" logo
are trademarks belonging to Jove Publications, Inc.

PRINTED IN THE UNITED STATES OF AMERICA

10 9 8 7 6 5 4 3 2 1

ONE

THE WPKX RADIO announcer hunched over the newsdesk in front of a dead microphone, anxiously fingering his script and waiting for the signal to go on the air. The station was filling in with classical music. The lilting "Anitra's Dance" seemed hardly appropriate under the circumstances. Abruptly the music stopped in the middle of a bar, and the newscaster began to read in a crisp, professional tone that belied the alarming nature of the news:

"We interrupt this program to bring you a bulletin on the forest fires that are rapidly approaching Moose County after destroying hundreds of square miles to the south and west. Rising winds are spreading the

1

scattered fires into areas already parched by the abnormally hot summer and drought conditions.

"From this studio in the tower of the courthouse in Pickax City we can see a red glow on the horizon, and the sky is hazy with drifting smoke. Children have been sent home from school, and businesses are closed, allowing workers to protect their families and dwellings. The temperature is extremely high; hot winds are gusting up to forty miles an hour.

"Traffic is streaming into Main Street from towns that are in the path of the flames. Here in the courthouse, which is said to be fireproof, preparations are being made to house the refugees. Many are farmers, who report that their houses, barns, and livestock are totally destroyed. They tell of balls of fire flying through the air, causing fields to burst into flame. One old man on the courthouse steps is proclaiming the end of the world and exhorting passersby to fall on their knees and pray."

The newscaster mopped his brow and gulped water as he glanced at slips of paper on the desk. "Bulletins are coming in from all areas surrounding Pickax. The entire town of Dry River burst into flames an hour ago and was completely demolished in a matter of minutes . . . The village of New Perth is in ashes; thirty-two are reported dead . . . Pardon me."

He stopped for a fit of coughing and then went on with difficulty. "Smoke is seeping into the studio." He coughed again. "Pineytown . . . totally destroyed. Seventeen persons running to escape . . . killed as the flames overtook them . . . Volunteer firefighters who went out from Pickax are back. They say . . . the fire is out of control."

His voice was muffled as he tried to breathe

through a cupped hand. "Very dark here! Heat unbearable! Wind is roaring! . . . Hold on!" He jumped to his feet, knocking his chair backward, and crouched over the mike with a gasping cry: "Here it comes! A wall of fire! Right down Main Street! *Pickax is in flames!*"

The lights blacked out. Coughing and choking, the announcer groped for a doorknob and stumbled from the studio.

Music blared from the speakers—crashing chords and roaring crescendoes—and the studio audience sat motionless, stunned into silence until a few started to applaud. The initial clapping swelled into a tumultuous response.

Someone in the front row said, "Gad! That was so real, I could feel the heat!"

"I swear I could smell smoke," another said. "That guy is some actor, isn't he? He wrote the stuff, too."

Most of the onlookers, gripped by emotion, were still speechless as they glanced once more at their programs:

The Moose County Something
presents
"THE BIG BURNING OF 1869"

- An original docu-drama based on historic fact
- Written and performed by James Qwilleran
- Produced and directed by Hixie Rice

The audience is asked to imagine that radio existed in 1869, as we bring you a simulated newscast covering the greatest disaster in the history of Moose County. The scene on the stage repre-

sents a broadcasting studio in the tower of the
county courthouse. The action takes place on October 17 and 18, 1869. There will be one intermis-
sion.

PLEASE JOIN US FOR REFRESHMENTS
AFTER THE PERFORMANCE

The audience, having struggled back to reality,
erupted in a babble of comments and recollections:

"I had an old uncle who used to tell stories about a
big forest fire, but I was too young to pay any attention."

"Where did Qwill get his information? He must
have done a heck of a lot of research."

"My mother said her great-great-grandmother on
her father's side lost most of her family in a big forest
fire. Makes you want to hit the history books, doesn't
it?"

More than a hundred prominent residents of Moose
County were attending the performance in the ballroom of a mansion that Jim Qwilleran was renting for
the winter months. Most of them knew all about the
middle-aged journalist with the oversized moustache
and doleful expression. He had been a prize-winning
crime writer for major newspapers around the United
States. He was the heir to an enormous fortune based
in Moose County. He wrote a much-admired column
for the local daily, *The Moose County Something*. He
spelled his name with a Qw. He liked to eat but never
took a drink. He was divorced and thought by women
to be highly attractive. His easy-going manner and jo-
cose banter made him enjoyable company. He was a

close friend of Polly Duncan's, the Pickax librarian. He lived alone—with two cats.

The townspeople often saw the big, well-built man walking or biking around Pickax, his casual way of dressing and lack of pretension belying his status as a multi-millionaire. And they had heard remarkable stories about his cats. Now, sitting in rows of folding chairs and waiting for Scene Two, the spectators saw a sleek Siamese march sedately down the center aisle. He jumped up on the stage and, with tail importantly erect, proceeded to the door where the radio announcer had made his frantic exit.

The audience tittered, and someone said, "That's Koko. He always has to get into the act."

The door, upstage right, was only loosely latched, and the cat pawed it until it opened a few inches and he could slither through. In two seconds he bounded out again as if propelled by a tap on the rump, and the audience laughed once more. Unabashed, Koko licked his left shoulder blade and scratched his right ear, then jumped off the stage and walked haughtily up the center aisle.

The house lights dimmed, and the radio announcer entered in a fresh shirt, with another script in his hand.

"Tuesday, October 18. After a sleepless night, Pickax can see daylight. The smoke is lifting, but the acrid smell of burning is everywhere, and the landscape is a scene of desolation in every direction. Only this court-house and a few isolated dwellings and barns are miraculously left standing. The heat is oppressive—110 degrees in the studio—and the window glass is still too hot to touch.

"Crews of men are now fanning out through the

countryside, burying bodies that are charred beyond recognition. Because so many families lived in isolated clearings, we may never have an accurate count of the dead. More than four hundred refugees are packed into the courthouse, lying dazed and exhausted in the corridors, on the stairs, in the courtroom and judge's chamber. Some have lost their feet; some have lost their eyes; some have lost their senses, and they babble incoherently. The groans of badly burned survivors mingle with the crying of babies. There is no medicine to ease their pain. Someone has brought a cow to the courthouse to provide milk for the youngest, but there is no food for the others . . ."

Before the dramatic presentation of "The Big Burning of 1869," the historic calamity had been quite forgotten by current generations intent on land development, tourism, new sewers, and the quality of TV reception. Qwilleran himself, playwright and star of the production, had never heard of the disaster until he rented the old mansion on Goodwinter Boulevard and started rummaging in closets. The furnishings were sparse, but the closets were stuffed to the ceiling with odds and ends— a treasure trove for an inquisitive journalist. As for his male cat, he was cat enough to risk death to satisfy his catly curiosity; with tail horizontal he would slink into a closet and emerge with a matchbook or champagne cork clamped in his jaws.

The mansion was constructed of stone and intended to last down the ages, one of several formidable edifices on the boulevard. They had been built by lumber barons and mining tycoons during Moose County's boom years in the late nineteenth century. A pioneer shipbuilder by the name of Gage had been responsible for the one Qwilleran was renting. One feature made the Gage mansion unique: the abundance of closets.

Shortly after moving in, Qwilleran mentioned the closets to his landlord. Junior Goodwinter, the young managing editor of the *Moose County Something,* had recently acquired the obsolete building as a gift from his aging grandmother, and he was thankful to have the rental income from his friend and fellow-staffer. The two men were sitting in Junior's office with their feet on the desk and coffee mugs in their hands. It was three weeks before the preview of "The Big Burning."

Junior's facial features and physical stature were still boyish, and he had grown a beard in an attempt to look older, but his youthful vitality gave him away. "What do you think of Grandma's house, Qwill? Does the furnace work okay? Have you tried lighting any of the fireplaces? How's the refrigerator? It's pretty ancient."

"It sounds like a motor boat when it's running," Qwilleran said, "and when it stops, it roars and snarls like a sick tiger. It frightens the cats out of their fur."

"Why was I dumb enough to let Grandma Gage unload that white elephant on me?" Junior complained. "She just wanted to avoid paying taxes and insurance, and now I'm stuck with all the bills. If I could find a buyer, I'd let the place go for peanuts, but who wants to live in a castle? People like ranch houses with sliding glass doors and smoke detectors . . . More coffee, Qwill?"

"Too bad the city won't re-zone it for commercial use. I've said it before. You could have law offices, medical clinics, high-class nursing homes, high-rent apartments ... Parking would be the only problem. You'd have to pave the backyards."

"The city will never re-zone," Junior said. "Not so long as old families and city officials live on the street. Sorry about the lack of furniture, Qwill. The Gages had fabulous antiques and paintings, but the old gal sold them all when she relocated in Florida. Now she lives in a retirement village, and she's a new person! She plays shuffleboard, goes to the dog races, wears elaborate makeup! On her last trip here, she looked like a wrinkled china doll. Jody says she must have met one of those cosmetics girls who drive around in lavender convertibles."

"She may have found romance in her declining years," Qwilleran suggested.

"Could be! She looks a lot younger than eighty-eight!"

"Answer one question, Junior. Why are there so many closets? I've counted fifty, all over the house. It was my understanding that our forefathers didn't have closets. They had wardrobes, dressers, highboys, china cabinets, breakfronts, sideboards ..."

"Well, you see," the editor explained, "my great-great-grandfather Gage was a shipbuilder, accustomed to having everything built-in, and that's what he wanted in his house. Ships' carpenters did the work. Have you noticed the woodwork? Best on the boulevard!"

"By today's construction standards it's incredible! The foyer looks like a luxury liner of early vintage. But do you know the closets are filled with junk?"

"Oh, sure. The Gages never threw anything away."

"Not even champagne corks," Qwilleran agreed.

Junior looked at his watch. "Time for Arch's meeting. Shall we amble across the hall?"

Arch Riker, publisher and CEO of the *Moose County Something,* had scheduled a brainstorming session for editors, writers, and the effervescent promotion director, Hixie Rice. None of the editorial staff liked meetings, and Qwilleran expressed his distaste by slumping in a chair in a far corner of the room. Hixie, on the other hand, breezed into the meeting with her shoulder-length hair bouncing and her eyes sparkling. She had worked in advertising Down Below—as Pickax natives called the major cities to the south— and she had never lost her occupational bounce and sparkle.

Similarly Qwilleran and Riker were transplants from Down Below, having grown up together in Chicago, but they had the detached demeanor of veteran newsmen. They had adapted easily to the slow pace of Pickax City (population 3,000) and the remoteness of Moose County, which claimed to be 400 miles north of everywhere.

Riker, a florid, paunchy deskman who seldom raised his voice, opened the meeting in his usual sleepy style: "Well, you guys, in case you don't know it, winter is coming . . . and winters are pretty dull in this neck of the woods . . . unless you're crazy about ten-foot snow drifts and wall-to-wall ice. So . . . I'd like to see this newspaper sponsor some kind of diversion that will give people a topic of conversation other than the daily rate of snowfall . . . Let's hear some ideas from you geniuses." He turned on a tape recorder.

The assembled staffers sat in stolid silence. Some looked at each other hopelessly.

"Don't stop to think," the boss admonished. "Just blurt it out, off the top of your head."

"Well," said a woman editor bravely, "we could sponsor a hobby contest with a thrilling prize."

"Yeah," said Junior. "Like a two-week all-expenses-paid vacation in Iceland."

"How about a food festival? Everyone likes to eat," said Mildred Hanstable, whose ample girth supported her claim. She wrote the food column for the *Something* and taught home economics in the Pickax school system. "We could have cooking demonstrations, a baking contest, an ethnic food bazaar, a Moose County cookbook, nutrition classes—"

"Second it!" Hixie interrupted with her usual enthusiasm. "And we could promote neat little tie-ins with restaurants, like wine-and-cheese tastings, and snacking-and-grazing parties, and a Bon Appetit Club with dining-out discounts. *C'est magnifique!*" She had once studied French briefly, preparatory to eloping to Paris.

There was a dead silence among the staffers. As a matter of newsroom honor they deplored Hixie's commercial taint. One of them muttered a five-letter word in French.

Junior came to the rescue with an idea for a Christmas parade. He said, "Qwill could play Santa with a white beard and a couple of pillows stuffed under his belt and some flour on his moustache."

Qwilleran grunted a few inaudible words, but Hixie cried, "I like it! I like it! He could arrive in a dogsled pulled by fifteen huskies! Mushing is a terribly trendy winter sport, you know, and we could get national publicity! The networks are avid for weatherbites in winter."

Riker said, "I believe we're getting warm—or cold, if you prefer. Snow is what we do best up here. How can we capitalize on it?"

"A contest for snow sculpture!" suggested Mildred Hanstable, who also taught art in the public school system.

"How about a winter sports carnival?" the sports editor proposed. "Cross-country skiing, snowshoe races, ice-boating, ice-fishing, dog-sledding—"

"And a jousting match with snow blowers!" Junior added. "At least it's cleaner than mud wrestling."

Riker swiveled his chair around. "Qwill, are you asleep back there in that dark corner?"

Qwilleran smoothed his moustache before he answered. "Does anyone know about the big forest fire in 1869 that killed hundreds of Moose County pioneers? It destroyed farms, villages, forests, and wildlife. About the only thing left in Pickax was the brick courthouse."

Roger MacGillivray, general assignment reporter and history buff, said, "I've heard about it, but there's nothing in the history books. And we didn't have a newspaper of record in those days."

"Well, I've found a gold mine of information," said Qwilleran, straightening up in his chair, "and let me tell you something: We may be four hundred miles north of everywhere, but we've got a history up here that will curl your toes! It deserves to be told—not just in print—but before audiences, young and old, all over the county."

"How did you discover this?" Roger demanded.

"While snooping in closets, hunting for skeletons," Qwilleran retorted archly.

Riker said, "If we were to put together a program, what would we do for visuals?"

"That's the problem," Qwilleran admitted. "There are no pictures."

The publisher turned off the tape recorder. "Okay, we've heard six or eight good ideas. Kick 'em around, and we'll meet again in a couple of days . . . Back to work!"

As the staff shuffled out of the office, Hixie grabbed Qwilleran's arm and said in a low voice, "I've got a brilliant idea for dramatizing your disaster, Qwill. *C'est vrai!*"

He winced inwardly, recalling other brilliant ideas of Hixie's that had bombed: the Tipsy Look-Alike Contest that ended in a riot . . . the cooking demonstration that set fire to her hair . . . the line of Frozen Foods for Fussy Felines, for which she expected Koko to make TV commercials . . . not to mention her aborted elopement to France. Gallantly he said, however, "Want to have lunch at Lois's and tell me about it?"

"Okay," she said. "I'll buy. I can put it on my expense account."

TWO

THE ATMOSPHERE AT Lois's Luncheonette was bleak, and the menu was ordinary, but it was the only restaurant in downtown Pickax, and the old, friendly, decrepit ambiance made the locals feel at home. A dog-eared card in the window announced the day's special. Tuesday was always hot turkey sandwich with mashed potatoes and gravy, but it was real turkey sliced from the bird; the bread was baked in Lois's kitchen by a white-haired woman who started at five A.M. every day; and the mashed potatoes had the flavor of real potatoes grown in the mineral-rich soil of Moose County.

Qwilleran and Hixie ordered the special, and she said, "I hear that you're not living in your barn this winter." He had recently converted a hundred-year-old apple barn into a spectacular residence.

"There's too much snow to plow," he explained, "so I'm renting the Gage mansion on Goodwinter Boulevard, where the city does the plowing." He neglected to mention that Polly Duncan, the chief woman in his life, lived in the carriage house at the rear of the Gage property, and he envisioned cozy winter evenings and frequent invitations to dinner and/or breakfast.

"All right. Let's get down to business," Hixie said when the plates arrived, swimming in real turkey gravy. "How did you find out about the killer fire? Or is it a professional secret?"

Qwilleran patted his moustache in self-congratulation. "To make a long story short, one of Junior's ancestors was an amateur historian. He recorded spring floods, sawmill accidents, log jams, epidemics, and so on, based on the recollections of his elders. In his journals, written in fine script with a nib pen that blotted occasionally, there were firsthand descriptions of the 1869 forest fire in all its gruesome detail. The man was performing a valuable service for posterity, but no one knew his accounts existed . . . So what's your brilliant idea, Hixie?" Qwilleran concluded.

"What would you think of doing a one-man show?"

"Isn't a one-man show based on a three-county forest fire a trifle out of scale?"

"Mais non! Suppose we pretend they had radio stations in the nineteenth century, and the audience sees an announcer broadcasting on-the-spot coverage of the disaster."

Qwilleran gazed at her with new respect. "Not bad! Yes! Not bad! I'd go for that! I'd be glad to organize the material and write the script. If Larry Lanspeak would play the announcer—"

"No! If we're going to sponsor the show, we should keep it in our own organization," she contended. "Actually, Qwill, I was thinking about you for the part. You have an excellent voice, with exactly the right quality for a radio announcer . . . Stop frowning! You wouldn't have to learn lines. You'd be reading a script in front of a simulated mike." She was talking fast. "Besides, you're a local celebrity. Everyone loves your column! You'd be a big attraction, *sans doute.*"

He huffed into his moustache. At least she had the good taste to avoid mentioning his local fame as a multi-millionaire, philanthropist, and eligible bachelor.

She went on with contagious enthusiasm. "I could take care of production details. I could do the bookings. I'd even sweep the stage!"

Qwilleran had done some acting in college and enjoyed working before an audience. The temptation was there; the cause was a good one; the story of the great fire cried for attention. He gave her a guarded glance as his objections began to crumble. "How long a program should it be?"

"I would say forty-five minutes. That would fit into a school class period or fill a slot following a club luncheon."

After a few seconds' contemplation he said grimly, "I may regret this, but I'll do it."

"Merveilleux!" Hixie cried.

Neither of them remembered eating their lunch. They discussed a stage setting, lighting, props, a sound system, and how to pack everything in a carrying case, to fit in the trunk of a car.

Hixie said, "Consider it strictly a road show. My budget will cover expenses, but we'll need a name for the project to go into the computer. How about Suitcase Productions?"

"Sounds as if we manufacture luggage," Qwilleran muttered, but he liked it.

Returning home from that luncheon with a foil-wrapped chunk of turkey scrounged from Lois's kitchen, Qwilleran was greeted by two Siamese who could smell turkey through an oak door two inches thick. They yowled and pranced elegantly on long brown legs, and their blue eyes stared hypnotically at the foil package until its contents landed on their plate under the kitchen table.

With bemused admiration Qwilleran watched them devour their treat. Koko, whose legal title was Kao K'o Kung, had the dignity of his thirteenth-century namesake, plus a degree of intelligence and perception that was sometimes unnerving to a human with only five senses and a journalism degree. Yum Yum, the dainty one, had a different set of talents and qualities. She was a lovable bundle of female wiles, which she employed shamelessly to get her own way. When all else failed, she had only to reach up and touch Qwilleran's moustache with her paw, and he capitulated.

When the Siamese had finished their snack and had washed their whiskers and ears, he told them, "I have a lot of work to do in the next couple of weeks, my friends, and I'll have to shut you out of the library. Don't think it's anything personal." He always addressed them as if they understood human speech, and more and more it appeared to be a fact. In the days that followed, they sensed his preoccupation, leaving him alone, taking long naps, grooming each other interminably, and watching the autumn leaves flutter to the ground. The grand old oaks and maples of Goodwinter Boulevard were covering the ground with a tawny blanket. Only when Qwilleran was an hour late with their dinner did the cats interrupt, standing outside the library, rattling the door handle and scolding—Koko with an authoritative baritone "Yow!" and Yum Yum with her impatient "N-n-now!"

Qwilleran could write a thousand words for his newspaper column with one hand tied behind his back, but writing a script for a docu-drama was a new challenge. To relieve the radio announcer's forty-five-minute monologue, he introduced other voices on tape: eye witnesses being interviewed by telephone. He altered his voice to approximate the bureaucratese of a government weather observer, the brogue of an Irish innkeeper, and the twang of an old farmer. With their replies sandwiched between the announcer's questions, Qwilleran was actually interviewing himself.

Once the script was completed, there were nightly rehearsals in the ballroom of the Gage mansion, with Hixie cueing the taped voices into the live announcing. It required split-second timing to sound authentic. Meanwhile, Polly Duncan returned home each evening to her apartment in the carriage house at the rear of the property and saw Hixie's car parked in the side drive. It was a trying time for Polly. As library administrator she was a woman of admirable intelligence and self-control, but—where Qwilleran was concerned—she was inclined to be jealous of women younger and thinner than she.

One evening Arch Riker attended a rehearsal and

was so impressed that he proposed a private preview for prominent citizens. Invitations were immediately mailed to local officials, educators, business leaders, and officers of important organizations with replies requested. To Riker's dismay, few responded; he called an executive meeting to analyze the situation.

"I think," Hixie ventured, "they're all waiting to find out what's on TV Monday night."

"You've got it all wrong," said Junior Goodwinter, who was a native and entitled to know. "It's like this: The stuffed shirts in this backwater county never reply to an invitation till they know who else is going to be there. You've got to drop a few names."

"Or let them know you're spiking the punch," Qwilleran suggested.

"We should have specified a champagne afterglow," Hixie said.

Junior shook his head. "Champagne is not the drink of choice up here. 'Free booze' would have more impact."

"Well, you should know," said Riker. "The rest of us are innocents from Down Below."

"Let me write a piece and splash it on the front page," the young editor said. "I'll twist a few political arms. They're all up for re-election next month."

Accordingly, Friday's edition of the paper carried this news item:

MOOSE COUNTY DESTROYED BY FIRE . . . IN 1869

History will come to life Monday evening when civic leaders will preview a live docu-drama titled "The Big Burning of 1869." Following the private premiere at the Gage mansion on Goodwinter

Boulevard, the *Moose County Something* will offer the show to schools, churches, and clubs as a public service.

There followed the magic name of Jim Qwilleran, who was not only popular as a columnist but rich as Croesus. In addition, the mayor, council president, and county commissioners were quoted as saying they would attend the history-making event. As soon as the paper hit the street the telephones in Junior's office started jangling with acceptances from persons who now perceived themselves as civic leaders. Furthermore, "live" was a buzz word in a community jaded with slide shows and video presentations. Hixie went into action, borrowing folding chairs from the Dingleberry Funeral Home, renting coatracks for guests' wraps, and hiring a caterer.

On the gala evening the Gage mansion—with all windows alight—glowed like a lantern among the gloomy stone castles on the boulevard. Flashbulbs popped as the civic leaders approached the front steps. The publisher of the newspaper greeted them; the managing editor checked their wraps; the political columnist handed out programs; the sports editor directed them to the marble staircase leading to the ballroom on the lower level. The reporters who were providing valet parking carried one elderly man in a wheelchair up the front steps and wheeled him to the elevator, which was one of the mansion's special amenities.

Meanwhile, Qwilleran was sweating out his opening-night jitters backstage in the ballroom—a large, turn-of-the-century hall with Art Deco murals and light fixtures. More than a hundred chairs faced the band platform, where musicians had once played for the waltz and the turkey trot. The stage set was minimal: a plain wood table and chair for the announcer with an old-fashioned upright telephone and a replica of an early microphone. Off to one side was a table for the "studio engineer." Cables snaked across the platform, connecting the speakers and lighting tripods to the control board.

"Do they look messy?" Qwilleran asked Hixie.

"No, they look high tech," she decided.

"Good! Then let's throw a few more around." He uncoiled a long yellow extension cord that was not being used and added it to the tangle.

"Perfect!" Hixie said. "It gives the set a certain *je ne sais quoi.*"

A sweatered audience filed into the ballroom and filled the chairs. Pickax was a sweater city in winter—for all occasions except weddings and funerals. The house lights dimmed, and the lilting notes of "Anitra's Dance" filled the hall until the announcer rushed onstage from a door at the rear and spoke the first ominous words: "We interrupt this program to bring you a bulletin . . ."

Forty-five minutes later he delivered the final message: "No one will ever forget what happened here on October 17, 1869." It was an ironic punch line, considering that few persons in the county had ever heard of the Big Burning.

Climactic music burst from the speakers; the audience applauded wildly; and the mayor of Pickax jumped to his feet, saying, "We owe a debt of gratitude to these talented folks from Down Below who have made us see and hear and feel this forgotten chapter in our history."

The presenters bowed: Hixie with her buoyant smile and Qwilleran with his usual morose expression. Then, as the ballroom emptied, they packed the props and mechanical equipment into carrying cases.

"We did it!" Hixie exulted. "We've got a smash hit!"

"Yes, it went pretty well," Qwilleran agreed modestly. "Your timing was perfect, Hixie. Congratulations!"

A small boy in large eyeglasses and a red sweater, who had been in the audience with his father, stayed behind to watch the striking of the set. "What's that yellow wire for?" he asked.

Qwilleran replied with overblown pomposity, "That, young man, happens to be the major power conduit used by our engineer for operating our computerized sound and light system."

"Oh," the boy said. Then, after a moment's puzzled contemplation, he asked, "Why wasn't it connected?"

"Why don't you go upstairs and have some cookies?" Qwilleran countered. To Hixie he muttered, "Kids! Always asking questions! Not only that, but they're notorious carriers of the common cold. If we're taking this show on the road, I can't afford to be laid up."

"I predict we'll be swamped with bookings," she said.

"Undoubtedly. Moose County can't resist anything that's free."

"Should we extend our territory to Lockmaster County?"

"Only if they pay for it ... Now let's go upstairs and get some of that free grub." After the excitement of a first night and after forty-five minutes of intense concentration on his role, Qwilleran felt empty and parched.

On the main floor the guests were milling about the large, empty rooms, admiring the coffered paneling of the high ceiling and the lavishly carved fireplaces. They carried plates of hors d'oeuvres and glass cups of amber punch. The Siamese were milling about, too, dodging feet and hunting for dropped crumbs. Koko sniffed certain trousered legs and nylon-clad ankles; Yum Yum eluded the clutches of a young boy in a red sweater.

Qwilleran pushed through the crowd to the dining room, where a caterer's long table was draped in a white cloth and laden with warming trays of stuffed mushrooms, bacon-wrapped olives, cheese puffs, and other morsels too dainty for a hungry actor. There were two punch bowls, and he headed for the end of the table where Mildred Hanstable was ladling amber punch into glass cups.

"Cider?" he asked.

"No, this is Fish House punch made with two kinds of rum and two kinds of brandy," she warned him. "I think you'll want the other punch, Qwill. It's cranberry juice and Chinese tea with lemon grass."

"Sounds delicious," he grumbled. "How come no one is drinking it?"

Polly Duncan, looking radiant in a pink mohair sweater, was presiding over the unpopular bowl of pink punch. "Qwill, dear, you were splendid!" she said in her mellow voice that always gave him a frisson of pleasure. "Now I know why you were so totally preoccupied for the last two weeks. It was time well invested."

"Sorry to be so asocial," he apologized, "but we'll

make up for it. We'll do something special this weekend, like bird watching." This was a gesture of abject penitence on his part. He loathed birding.

"It's too late," she said. "They've gone south, and snow is predicted. But I'm going to do roast beef and Yorkshire pudding, and I have a new Brahms cassette."

"Say no more. I'm available for the entire weekend."

They were interrupted by a cracked, high-pitched voice. "Excellent job, my boy!" Homer Tibbitt, official historian for the county, was in his nineties but still active in spite of loudly creaking joints. He was pushing a wheelchair occupied by Adam Dingleberry, the ancient and indestructible patriarch of the mortuary that had lent the folding chairs.

Homer said to Qwilleran, "Just want to congratulate you before going home to my lovely young bride. Adam's great-grandson is on the way over to pick us up."

"Yep, he's bringin' the hearse," said old Dingleberry with a wicked laugh.

Homer delivered a feeble poke to Qwilleran's ribs. "You son-of-a-grasshopper! I've been scrabbling for information on that blasted fire for thirty years! Where'd you find it?"

"In some files that belonged to Euphonia Gage's father-in-law," Qwilleran replied. He neglected to say that Koko pried his way into a certain closet and dragged forth a scrap of yellowed manuscript. It was a clue to a cache of hundred-year-old documents.

A valet was paging them. "Car for Mr. Dingleberry! Mr. Tibbitt!"

As the elderly pair headed for the carriage entrance, Qwilleran was approached by a cordial man in a black cashmere sweater. "Good show, Mr. Q!" he said in a smooth, professional voice.

"Thank you."

"I'm Pender Wilmot, your next-door neighbor and Mrs. Gage's attorney."

"Too bad she couldn't be here tonight," Qwilleran said.

"I daresay this old house hasn't witnessed an event of this magnitude since Harding won the presidential election. How do you like living on the boulevard?"

"I find it somewhat depressing. There are seven for-sale signs at my last count."

"And I'd gladly make it eight," the attorney said, "but our property has been in the family for four generations, and Mrs. Wilmot is sentimental about it, although she might be swayed by a juicy offer."

"There'll be no juicy offers until the boulevard is re-zoned."

"It is my considered opinion," Wilmot said, "that the city will approve re-zoning in the year 2030 . . . Mr. Q, this is my son, Timmie." The boy in the red sweater, having failed to catch the slippery Yum Yum, was now clutching his parent's hand.

"And how did you like the show, young man?" Qwilleran asked him.

Timmie frowned. "All those houses burned down, and all those people burned up. Why didn't the firemen get a ladder and save them?"

"Come on, son," his father said. "We'll go home and discuss it."

They walked toward the front door just as Hixie dashed up, followed by the owner of the Black Bear Café. Gary Pratt's muscular hulk and lumbering gait and shaggy black hairiness explained the name of his restaurant. Excitedly Hixie announced, "Gary wants us to do the show at the Black Bear."

"Yeah," said the barkeeper, "the Outdoor Club meets once a month for burgers and beer and a program. They have a conservation guy or a video on the environment. They've never had a live show."

"How many members?" Qwilleran asked.

"Usually about forty turn out, but it'll be double that if they know you're coming."

"Okay with me. Go ahead and book it, Hixie."

Qwilleran moved through the crowd, accepting congratulations.

Susan Exbridge, the antique dealer, gave him her usual effusive hug. "Darling! You were glorious! You should be on the stage! . . . And this house! Isn't it magnificent? Euphonia gave me a tour before she sold the furnishings. Look at the carving on that staircase! Look at the parquet floors! Have you ever seen chandeliers like these? If you'd like a live-in housekeeper, Qwill, I'll work cheap!"

Next the Comptons paid their compliments. "You were terrific, Qwill," said Lisa, a cheerful, middle-aged woman in a Halloween sweater. "Everything was so professional!"

"It's my engineer's split-second timing that gives the show its snap," Qwilleran said.

"You guys ought to do the show for grades four to twelve," said Lyle Compton, superintendent of schools. "It would be a great way to hook the kids on history."

Qwilleran winced, having visions of a schoolful of carriers circulating respiratory diseases.

"Believe it or not," Lisa said, "I used to come to this

house to take 'natural dance' lessons from Euphonia. She had us flitting around the ballroom like Isadora Duncan. It was supposed to give us grace and poise, but we all thought it was boring. I really wanted to take tap."

Her husband said, "You should have stuck with Euphonia. She's in her late eighties and still has the spine of a drum major, which is more than I can say for any of us."

"I met her only once," Qwilleran said. "I came here to interview her for an oral history project and found this tiny woman sitting on the floor in the lotus position, wearing purple tights. She had white hair tied back with a purple ribbon, I recall."

Lisa nodded. "She used to tell us that purple is a source of energy. Junior says she still wears a lot of it and stands on her head every day."

"When she lived in Pickax," said Lyle, "she drove a Mercedes at twenty miles an hour and blew the horn at every intersection. The police were always ticketing her for obstructing traffic. All the Gages have been a little batty, although Junior seems to have his head on straight."

As Junior Goodwinter joined them, Lisa changed the subject. "Have you ever seen an autumn with so many leaves on the ground?"

"According to hizzoner the mayor," said Junior, "Lockmaster County is shipping truckloads of leaves up here every night under cover of darkness and dumping them on Pickax."

"I'll buy that," Lyle said. "We should send them some of our toxic waste."

They discussed the forthcoming football game between Pickax High and their Lockmaster rivals, and then the Comptons said goodnight.

Junior gazed ruefully at the empty rooms, faded wallcoverings, and discolored rectangles where large paintings had once hung. "Grandma had some great stuff! Susan Exbridge can tell you how valuable it was. Everything was sold out of state. Sorry there's no TV, Qwill. Why don't you bring one over from your barn before snow flies?"

"I can skip TV. It amuses the cats, but they can live without it. Would your grandmother have liked our show tonight?"

"I doubt it. She never likes anything that isn't her own idea."

"She sounds a lot like Koko. Is it true she used to give dancing lessons?"

"Way back, maybe forty years ago," Junior said. "Before leaving for Florida she asked me to videotape one of her dances. Yikes! It was embarrassing, Qwill—this woman in her eighties, in filmy draperies, cavorting around the ballroom like a woodland nymph. She was limber enough, and still kind of graceful, but I felt like a voyeur."

"What happened to the video?"

"She took it to Florida. Do you think she plays it on a VCR and dreams old dreams?"

"It's not a bad idea," Qwilleran said. "When I'm her age I'd like to watch myself sliding into first base."

"I saw you talking to Pender Wilmot. How did he like the show?"

"He was quite enthusiastic. By the way, Junior, I'm surprised your grandmother doesn't take her legal work to Hasselrich Bennett & Barter."

"They're too stuffy for her taste. She likes younger

people. She feels young herself. It's my guess that she'll outlive us all . . . Well, it looks like everyone's leaving. Sure was a success! I can't believe, Qwill, that you did all those voices yourself!"

Only a few members of the hungry and thirsty press remained to drain the two punch bowls. They mixed the contents of both and declared it tasted like varnish, but good!

Qwilleran said to Hixie, "Did you see the guy in a suit and tie? He was with a blonde—the only ones not in sweaters."

"That was a wig she was wearing," Hixie informed him. "Who were they?"

"That's what I was going to ask you."

"I say they were spies from the *Lockmaster Ledger,*" she said. "They steal all our good ideas. Do you suppose she had a tape recorder under that big wig? I'm glad we copyrighted the script; we can sue."

Arch Riker and Mildred Hanstable were almost the last to leave. The publisher was beaming. "Great job, you two kids! Best PR stunt we could spring on this kind of community!"

"Thanks, boss," said Qwilleran. "I'll expect a raise."

"You'll be fired if you don't start writing your column again. The readers are screaming for your pellucid prose on page two. Consider your vacation over as of tomorrow."

"Vacation! I've been working like a dog on this show! And I haven't seen anything that looks like a bonus!"

This sparring between the two old friends was a perpetual game, since the *Moose County Something* was backed financially by the Klingenschoen Foundation, established by Qwilleran to dispose of his unwanted millions.

Riker drove Mildred home, and Qwilleran told Polly he would escort her to her carriage house in the rear. "I'll be right back," he told the Siamese, who were loitering nearby and beaming questioning looks in his direction.

"I've missed you, dear," Polly said as they walked briskly hand in hand through the chill October evening. "I thought I had lost my Most Favored Woman status. Bootsie missed you, too."

"Sure," Qwilleran replied testily. He and Polly's macho Siamese had been engaged in a cold war ever since Bootsie was a kitten.

"Would you like to come upstairs for some real food and a cup of coffee?"

Qwilleran said he wouldn't mind going up for a few minutes. When he came down two hours later, he walked slowly despite the falling temperature, reflecting that he was happier than he had ever been in his entire life—not that the pursuit of happiness had concerned him in his earlier years. What mattered then was the excitement of covering breaking news, working all night to meet a deadline, moving from city to city for new challenges, hanging out at press clubs, and not caring about money. Now he was experiencing something totally different: the contentment of living in a small town, writing for a small newspaper, loving an intelligent woman of his own age, living with two companionable cats. And, to cap it all, he was on the stage again! Not since college days, when he played Tom in "The Glass Menagerie," had he known the satisfaction of creating a character and bringing that character to life for an audience.

At the side door of the mansion he was greeted by the scolding yowls and switching tails of two indignant Siamese, whose evening repast was late.

"My apologies," he said as he gave them a crunchy snack. "The pressure is off now, and we'll get back to normal. You've been very understanding and cooperative. How would you like a read after I've turned out the lights? The electric bill is going to be astronomical."

Despite his affluence, Qwilleran was frugal about utilities. Now he went from room to room through the great house, flipping off switches. The Siamese accompanied him, pursuing their own special interests. In one of the large front bedrooms upstairs he noticed a closet door ajar and a horizontal brown tail disappearing within. Minutes later, Koko caught up with him and dropped something at his feet.

"Thank you," Qwilleran said courteously as he picked up a purple ribbon bow and dropped it in his sweater pocket. To himself he said, If Euphonia's theory is true, Koko sensed a source of energy. Cats, he had been told, are attracted to sources of energy.

The three of them gathered in the library for their read, a ritual the Siamese always enjoyed. Whether it was the sound of a human voice, or the warmth of a human lap and a table lamp, or the simple idea of propinquity, a read was one of their catly pleasures that ranked with grooming their fur and chasing each other. As for Qwilleran, he enjoyed the company of living creatures and—to be perfectly honest—the sound of his own voice.

"Would anyone care to choose a title?" he asked.

In the library there were a few hundred books that Mrs. Gage had been unable to sell, plus a dozen classics that Qwilleran had brought from the barn along with his typewriter and computerized coffeemaker. Koko sniffed the bindings until his twitching nose settled on *Robinson Crusoe* from Qwilleran's own collection.

"Good choice," Qwilleran commented as he sank into a leather lounge chair worn to the contours of a hammock. Yum Yum leaped lightly into his lap, settling down slowly with a sigh, like a motor vehicle with hydraulic suspension, while Koko arranged himself on a nearby table under the glow of a 75-watt lamp bulb.

They were halfway through the opening paragraph when the telephone on the desk rang. "Excuse me," Qwilleran said, lifting Yum Yum gently and placing her on the seat he had vacated. He anticipated another compliment on "The Big Burning" and responded with a gracious "Good evening."

Arch Riker's voice barked with urgency. "Hate to bother you, Qwill, but I've just had a call from Junior. He's flying to Florida first thing in the morning. His grandmother was found dead in bed."

"Hmmm . . . curious!" Qwilleran murmured.

"What do you mean?"

"A few minutes ago Koko brought me one of her hair ribbons."

"Yeah, well . . . that cat is tuned in to everything. But why I'm calling—"

"And everyone at the party tonight," Qwilleran went on, "was mentioning how healthy she was."

"That's the sad part," Riker said. "The police told Junior it was suicide."

THREE

THE NEWS OF Euphonia Gage's suicide was surprising, if not incredible. "What was her motive?" Qwilleran asked Arch Riker.

"We don't know yet. We'll run a died-suddenly on the front page of tomorrow's paper and give it the full treatment Wednesday. Junior is drafting an obit on the plane and will fax it when he arrives down there and gets a few more details. Meanwhile, will you see if you can dig out some photos? Her early life, studio portraits—anything will be useful. She was the last of the Gages. Junior says she left some photo albums in the house, but he doesn't know exactly where."

As Qwilleran listened to the publisher's directive,

he felt a fumbling in his pocket and reached down to grab a paw. "No!" he scolded.

"What'd you say?"

"Nothing. Yum Yum was picking my pocket."

"Well, see what you can find for Wednesday. Usual deadline. Sorry to bother you tonight."

"No bother. I'll give you a ring in the morning."

Before resuming the reading of *Robinson Crusoe,* Qwilleran added the purple ribbon bow to what he called the Kao K'o Kung Collection in a desk drawer. It consisted of oddments retrieved by one or more cats from the gaping closets of the Gage mansion: champagne cork, matchbook, pocket comb, small sponge, pencil stub, rubber eraser, and the like. Yum Yum left her contributions scattered about the house; Koko organized his under the kitchen table, alongside their water dish and feeding station.

As the day ended, Qwilleran felt a welcome surge of relief and satisfaction; "The Big Burning" had been successfully launched and enthusiastically received. He slept soundly that night and would not have heard the early-morning summons from the library telephone if eight bony legs had not landed simultaneously on tender parts of his supine body.

Hixie Rice was on the line, as bright and breezy as ever. *"Pardonnez-moi!* Did I get you out of bed?" she asked when Qwilleran answered gruffly. "You sound as if you haven't had your coffee yet. Well, this will wake you up! We have two bookings for our show, if the dates are okay with you. The first is Thursday afternoon at Mooseland High School. That's a consolidated school serving the agricultural townships."

"I'm not keen about doing the show for kids," he objected.

"They're not kids. They're young adults, and they'll love it!"

"Of course. They love anything that gets them out of class, including chest X-rays," he said with precoffee cynicism. "What kind of facility do they have?"

"We'll be doing the show in the gym, with the audience seated in the bleachers. The custodian is constructing a platform for us."

"What's the second booking?"

"Monday night at the Black Bear Café. It's the annual family night for the Outdoor Club, and they were going to have a Laurel and Hardy film, but Gary urged them to book 'The Big Burning' instead."

"Maybe we can play it for laughs," Qwilleran muttered.

"At the high school we're scheduled for the sixth period, and we should get there at one o'clock. I'll be out in the territory, so I'll meet you there. It's on Sandpit Road, you know . . . And would you be a doll, Qwill, and glue my cuesheet on a card, *s'il vous plaît?* It'll be sturdier and easier to handle . . . See you Thursday afternoon. Don't forget to bring the complex computerized sound and light system," she concluded with a flippant laugh.

A grunt was his only reply to that remark. As he hung up the receiver he felt certain misgivings. Performing for a hand-picked audience of civic leaders had been a pleasure, but a gymful of noisy, hyperkinetic "young adults" from the potato farms and sheep ranches was a different ballgame. He pressed the button on his coffeemaker and was comforted somewhat by the sound of grinding beans and gurgling brew.

Meanwhile, he fed the cats, and whether it was the

soothing sight of feline feeding or the caffeine jolt of his first cup, something restored his positive attitude, and he tackled Riker's assignment with actual relish.

It was not as easy as either of them supposed. There were no photos of Euphonia Gage in the desk drawers. The closet in the library was locked. In the upstairs bedroom where Koko had found the purple ribbon, the closets were stuffed with outdated clothing, but no photographs. Returning to the library he surveyed the shelves of somber books collected by several generations of Gages: obsolete encyclopedias, anthologies of theological essays, forgotten classics, and biographies of persons now unknown. Sitting in the worn leather desk chair, he swiveled idly, pondering this mausoleum of the printed word.

It was then that he glimpsed a few inches of brown tail disappearing behind a row of books at eye level. Koko often retired to a bookshelf to escape Yum Yum's playful overtures. He failed to appreciate aggressive females, preferring to do the chasing himself. So now he was safely installed in the narrow space behind some volumes on nutrition, correct breathing, vegetarian diet, medicinal herbs, Hindu philosophy, and similar subjects of interest to the late Mrs. Gage.

Qwilleran smoothed his moustache, suspecting why Koko preferred these books to the Civil War histories on the same shelf. Could it corroborate the theory about cats and energy? Could Euphonia's innate verve have rubbed off on these particular bindings? In earlier years he would have scoffed at such a notion, but that was before he knew Koko. Now Qwilleran would believe anything!

Out of curiosity he opened the book on herbs and

found remedies for acne, allergies, asthma, and athlete's foot. Hopefully he looked under F but found nothing on football knee, which was his own Achilles' heel. He did find, however, an envelope addressed to Junior and mailed from Florida, casually stuck between a new book on cholesterol and an old book on mind power. He opened it and read:

Dear Junior,

Ship all my health books right away. I teach a class in breathing twice a week. These old people could solve half their problems if they knew how to breathe. Also send my photo albums. I think they're on the shelf with the Britannica. I'll pay the postage. Thank you for sending the clippings of Mr. Q's column. I like his style. No one down here has the slightest knowledge of how to write. Perhaps you should start a subscription to the paper for me. Send me the bill.

—Grandma

The letter, dated two weeks previously, hardly sounded like a potential suicide, and Qwilleran wondered, Had something drastic happened to change her lifestyle or her outlook? It could be sudden illness, sudden grief, personal catastrophe . . .

Two photo albums were exactly where she had said they would be, and he turned the pages to find the highlights of her life, all captioned and dated as if she expected some future biographer to publish her life. He found a tiny Euphonia in a christening dress two yards long, propped up on cushions; a young girl dancing on the grass in front of peony bushes; a horsewoman in full habit, with the straightest of spines; and a bride in a high-necked wedding dress with an armful of white roses. In none of the photos was there a glimpse of her bridegroom, daughter, parents, or grandchildren—only an unidentified horse.

Qwilleran narrowed the collection down to ten suitable pictures and telephoned Riker at the office. "Got 'em!" he announced. "How about lunch?"

At noon he walked downtown and tossed the photos on the publisher's desk. Riker shuffled through the pack, nodded without comment, and said, "Where shall we eat?"

"First I want to use your gluepot," Qwilleran said. "Do you have a five-by-seven index card?"

"No. What for?"

"Never mind. Just give me a file folder, and I'll cut it down. I want to paste Hixie's cuesheet on a card for durability."

"Apparently you're expecting a long run," the publisher said with satisfaction.

"Yes, and I'm charging the paper for mileage."

They drove in Riker's car to the Old Stone Mill on the outskirts of town, the best restaurant in the vicinity.

"Have you heard from Junior?" Qwilleran asked.

"Give him a break! His plane left only an hour ago." They were passing the impressive entrance to Goodwinter Boulevard. "How do you and the cats enjoy rattling around in that big house?"

"We're adaptable. Actually, I live in three rooms. I sleep in the housekeeper's old bedroom on the main floor. I make coffee and feed the cats in a huge antiquated kitchen. And I hang out in the library, which still has some furniture—not good, but not too bad."

"Is that where you found the dope on the forest fire?"

"No, it was in an upstairs closet. The house is honeycombed with closets, all filled with junk."

"That's the insidious thing about ample storage space," Riker said. "It sounds good, but it turns rational individuals into pack rats. I'm one of them."

"But Koko is having a field day. Old doors in old houses don't latch properly, so he can open a closet door and walk in."

Riker—who had once had a house and wife and children and cats of his own—nodded sagely. "Cats can't stand the sight of a closed door. If they're in, they have to get out; if they're out, they want in."

"The Rum Tum Tugger syndrome," Qwilleran said with equal sagacity.

In the restaurant parking lot they crossed paths with Scott Gippel, the car dealer. "I heard on the radio that old Mrs. Gage died down south. Died suddenly, they said. Is that true? Suicide?"

"That's what the police told Junior," Riker said.

"Too bad. She was a peppy old gal. I took her Mercedes in trade on a bright yellow sports car. She had me drop-ship it to Florida."

When they entered the restaurant, the hostess said, "Isn't that sad about Mrs. Gage? She had so much style! Always came in here wearing a hat and scarf. The barman kept a bottle of Dubonnet just for her . . . Your usual table, Mr. Q?"

The special for the day was a French dip sandwich with skins-on fries and a cup of cream of mushroom soup. Riker ordered a salad.

"What's the matter?" Qwilleran inquired. "Aren't you feeling well?"

"Just trying to lose a few pounds before the holidays. Do you have plans for Christmas Eve?"

"That's two months away! I'll be lucky if I survive Thursday afternoon at Mooseland High."

"How would you like to be best man at a Christmas Eve wedding?"

Qwilleran stopped nibbling breadsticks. "You and Mildred? Congratulations, old stiff! You two will be happy together."

"Why don't you and Polly take the plunge at the same time? Share the expenses. That should appeal to your thrifty nature."

"The chance to save a few bucks is tempting, Arch, but Polly and I prefer singlehood. Besides, our respective cats would be incompatible ... Have you broken the news to your kids?"

"Yeah, and right away they wanted to know how old she is. You know what they were thinking, that she'll outlive me and collect their inheritance."

"Nice offspring you begot," Qwilleran commented, half in sympathy and half in vindication. For years Riker had chided him for being childless. "Are they coming for the wedding?"

"If the airport stays open, but I doubt it. Fifty inches of snow are predicted before Christmas."

The two men talked about the forthcoming election (the incumbent mayor had a drinking problem) and the high cost of gasoline (when one lives 400 miles north of everywhere), and a good place for a honeymoon (*not* the New Pickax Hotel).

When coffee was served, Qwilleran brought up the subject that was bothering him. "You know, Arch, I can't understand why Mrs. Gage would choose to end her life."

"Old folks often pull up stakes and go to a sunny climate away from family and friends, and they discover the loneliness of old age. My father found it gets harder to make new friends as years go by. Mrs. Gage was eighty-eight, you know."

"What's eighty-eight in today's world? People of that age are running in marathons and winning swimming meets! Science is pushing the lifespan up to a hundred and ten."

"Not for me, please."

"Anyway, when Junior phones, ask him to call me at home."

The call from Junior came around six o'clock that evening. "Hey, Qwill, whaddaya think about all this? I can't believe Grandma Gage is gone! I thought she'd live forever."

"The idea of suicide is what puzzles me, Junior. Was that just a cop's guess?"

"No, it's official."

"Was there a suicide note?"

"She didn't leave any kind of explanation, but there was an empty bottle of sleeping pills by her bed, plus evidence that she'd been drinking. Her normal weight was under a hundred pounds, so it wouldn't take much to put her down, the doctor said."

"Did she drink? I thought she was a health nut."

"She always had a glass of Dubonnet before dinner, claiming it was nutritious. But who knows what she did after she started running with that retirement crowd in Florida? If you don't sow your wild oats when you're young, my dad told me, you'll do it when you're old."

"So what was the motive?"

"I wish I knew."

"Who found the body?"

"A neighbor. Around Monday noon. She'd been dead about sixteen hours. This woman called to pick her up for lunch. They were going to the mall."

"Have you talked with this neighbor?"

"Yes, she's a nice older woman. A widow."

"Yow!" said Koko, who was sitting on the desk and monitoring the call.

"Was that Koko?" Junior asked.

"Yes, he's always trying to line me up with a widow who'll make meatloaf like Mrs. Cobb's . . . So, what happens now, Junior?"

"I'm appointed as personal rep, and Pender Wilmot has told me what to do. She'd sold her condo and was living in a mobile home in a retirement complex called the Park of Pink Sunsets."

"Very Floridian," Qwilleran remarked.

"It's a top-of-the-line mobile home. She bought it furnished from the park management, and they'll buy it back, so I don't have that to worry about. I have to get some death certificates, round up her personal belongings, and ship the body to Pickax. She wanted to be buried in the Gage plot, Pender says."

"When do you expect to be home?"

"Before snow flies, I hope. Sooner the better. I don't care for this assignment."

"Let me know if you want a lift from the airport."

"My car's in the long-term garage, but thanks anyway, Qwill."

Qwilleran replaced the receiver slowly. No known motive! The news was a challenge to one who was tormented by unanswered questions and unsolved puzzles. He had known suicides motivated by guilt, depression, and fear of disgrace, but here was a healthy, spirited, active, well-to-do woman who simply decided to end it all.

"What happened?" he asked Koko, who was sitting on the desk, a self-appointed censor of incoming phone calls. The cat sat tall with his forelegs primly together and his tail curved flat on the desktop. At Qwilleran's question he shifted his feet nervously and blinked his eyes. Then, abruptly, he jerked his head toward the library door. In a blur of fur he was off the desk and out in the hallway. Qwilleran, alarmed by the sudden exit, followed almost as fast. The excitement was in the kitchen, where Yum Yum was already sniffing the bottom of the back door.

Koko's tail bushed, his ears swept back, his whiskers virtually disappeared, and a terrible growl came from the depths of his interior.

Qwilleran looked out the back window. It was dusk, but he could make out a large orange cat on the porch, crouched and swaying from side to side in a threatening way. The man banged on the door, yanked it open and yelled "Scat!" The intruder swooshed from the porch in a single streak and faded into the dusk. Yum Yum looked dreamily disappointed, and Koko bit her on the neck.

"Stop that!" Qwilleran commanded in a gruff voice that was totally ignored. Yum Yum appeared to be enjoying the abuse.

"Treat!" he shouted. It was the only guaranteed way to capture their immediate attention, and both cats scampered to the feeding station under the kitchen table, where they awaited their reward.

Returning to the library, Qwilleran phoned Lori Bamba, his free-lance secretary in Mooseville, who not only handled his correspondence but advised him on feline problems. He described the recent scene.

"It's a male," Lori said. "He's a threat to Koko's territory. He's interested in Yum Yum."

"Both of mine are neutered," he reminded her.

"It makes no difference. The visitor probably sprayed your back door."

"What! I won't stand for that!" Qwilleran stormed into the phone. "Isn't there some kind of protection against marauding animals, invading and vandalizing private property—an ordinance or whatever?"

"I don't think so. Do you have any idea where he lives?"

"When I chased him, he headed for the attorney's house next door. Well, thanks, Lori. Sorry to bother you. I'll see my own attorney about this tomorrow."

Blowing angrily into his moustache, Qwilleran strode through the main hall and glared out the front window, where autumn leaves smothered sidewalks, lawns, pavement, and the median. Then, smashing his fist in the palm of his hand, he returned to the library and phoned Osmond Hasselrich of Hasselrich Bennett & Barter. Only someone with the nerve of a veteran journalist would call the senior partner at home during the dinner hour, and only someone with Qwilleran's bankroll could get away with it. The elderly lawyer listened courteously as Qwilleran made his request concisely and firmly. "I want an appointment for tomorrow afternoon, Mr. Hasselrich, and I want to consult you personally. It's a matter of the utmost secrecy."

FOUR

WHILE WAITING FOR his Wednesday afternoon appointment with Mr. Hasselrich, Qwilleran tuned in the WPKX weather report several times, hoping for an update—hoping to hear that dire atmospheric developments in the Yukon Territory or Hudson Bay would close in on Moose County, depositing eighteen inches of snow and closing the schools. No such luck! The meteorologist, who called himself Wetherby Goode, had a hearty, jovial manner that could make floods and tornadoes sound like fun, and on this occasion he was actually singing:

"Blow, blow, blow the leaves/ Gently in the street./ Merrily, merrily, merrily, merrily,/ Fall is such a treat! ... Yes, folks, the mayor—who is running for

re-election—has promised leaf pickup before Halloween. The vacuum truck will be operating east of
Main Street on Friday and west of Main Street on
Saturday. So lock up your cats and small dogs,
folks!"

By the time Qwilleran walked downtown to the office of Hasselrich Bennett & Barter, the whine of leaf
blowers paralyzed the eardrums like a hundred-piece
symphony orchestra playing only one chord.

At the law office he sipped coffee politely from Mr.
Hasselrich's heirloom porcelain cups, inquired politely
about Mrs. H's health, and listened politely to the elderly attorney's discourse on the forthcoming snow—
all this before getting down to business. When
Qwilleran finally stated his case, Mr. Hasselrich re-
acted favorably. As chief counsel for the Klingenschoen Foundation, he had become accustomed to
unusual proposals from the Klingenschoen heir, and
although he seldom tried to dissuade Qwilleran, his
fleshy eyelids frequently flickered and his sagging
jowls quivered. Today the august head nodded without a flicker or a quiver.

"I believe it can be accomplished without arousing
suspicion," he said.

"With complete anonymity, of course," Qwilleran
specified.

"Of course. And with all deliberate haste."

Qwilleran walked home with a long stride.

That evening, when he took Polly Duncan out to
dinner, she asked casually, "What did you do today?"

"Walked downtown . . . Made a few phone calls . . .
Ran through my script . . . Brushed the cats." He
avoided mentioning his meeting with Hasselrich.

They were dining at Tipsy's, a log cabin restaurant

in North Kennebeck, Polly with her glass of sherry and Qwilleran with his glass of Squunk water. "Guess what's happening on Christmas Eve!" he said. "Arch and Mildred are tying the knot."

"I'm so happy for them," she said fervently, and Qwilleran detected a note of relief. He had always suspected that she considered Mildred a potential rival.

"Arch suggested we might make it a double wedding," he said with a sly sideways glance.

"I hope you disabused him of that notion, dear."

He gave their order: "Broiled whitefish for the lady, and I'll have the king-size steak, medium rare." Then he remarked, "Did you read the obituary in today's paper?"

"Yes. I wonder where they found those interesting pictures."

"Did you know Mrs. Gage very well?"

"I believe no one knew her very well," said Polly. "She served on my library board for a few years, but she was rather aloof. The other members considered her a snob. At other times she could be quite gracious. She always wore hats with wide brims—never tilted, always perfectly level. Some women found that intimidating."

Qwilleran said, "I detect a lingering floral perfume in one of the upstairs bedrooms at the house."

"It's violet. She always wore the same scent—to the extent that no one else in town would dare to wear it. I don't want to sound petty. After all, she was good enough to rent the carriage house to me when I was desperate for a place to live."

"That was no big deal," Qwilleran said. "No doubt she wanted someone around to watch the main house while she was in Florida."

"You're always so cynical, Qwill."

"Were you surprised that she'd take her own life?"

Polly considered the question at length before replying. "No. She was completely unpredictable. What was your impression when you interviewed her, Qwill?"

"She came on strong as a charming and witty little woman, full of vitality, but that may have been an act for the benefit of the press."

"What happens now?"

"Junior is in Florida, winding up her affairs and trying to get home before snow flies."

"I hope the weather is good for the trick-or-treaters. Are you all ready for Halloween?"

"Ready? What am I supposed to do?"

"Turn on your porch light and have plenty of treats to hand out. Something wholesome, like apples, would be the sensible thing to give, but they prefer candy or money. They used to be grateful for a few pennies, but now they expect quarters."

"Quarters! Greedy brats! How many kids come around?"

"Only a few from the boulevard, but carloads come from other neighborhoods. You should prepare for at least a hundred."

Qwilleran grunted his disapproval. "Well, they'll get apples from me—and like it!" He was quiet when the steak was served; Tipsy's specialized in an old-fashioned cut of meat that required chewing. Eventually he said, "We put the show on the road tomorrow. Mooseland High is our first booking, unless we're fortunate enough to have an earthquake."

"You don't sound very enthusiastic, dear. Do they have a good auditorium?"

"They have a gym. They're building a platform for us. Hixie made the arrangements. I've practiced packing the gear, and I can set up in nine minutes flat and strike the set in seven."

The afternoon at Mooseland High School was better than he expected, in one way; in another, it was worse. In preparation for the show he packed the lights, telescoping tripods, cables, props, and sound equipment in three carrying cases and checked off everything on a list: script, mike, telephone, extension cords, double plugs, handkerchief for the announcer to mop his sweating brow, and so forth. In college theatre there had been a backstage crew to handle all such details; now he was functioning as stage manager, stagehand, and propman as well as featured actor. It was not easy, but he enjoyed a challenge.

Everything on the checklist was accounted for, with one exception: Hixie's cuecard. He unpacked the three cases, thinking it might have slipped in accidentally, but it was not there. He remembered gluing the cuesheet on a card in the newspaper office; could he have left it there? He phoned Riker.

"You took it when we went to lunch," Riker said. "I saw it in your hand."

"Go and see if it's still in the car," Qwilleran said urgently. "And hurry! We have a show in half an hour! I'll hold." While holding he appraised the calamitous situation. How could Hixie operate the sound system and lighting without her cuecard? There were six cues for music, eight for voices, five for lights—all numbered to correlate with digits on the stereo counter. With more experience she might be able to wing it, but this was only their second performance.

Riker's search of the car was fruitless. Without even a thank you Qwilleran banged down the receiver and returned to the ballroom, where he paced the floor and looked wildly about the four walls.

The Siamese watched his frantic gyrations calmly, sitting on their briskets and wearing expressions of supreme innocence.

Their very pose was suspect. *"Did you devils steal the card?"* he shouted at them.

The thunder of his voice frightened them into flight.

Now he knew! It was the glue! He had used rubber cement, and Koko had a passion for adhesives.

In desperation Qwilleran figured it would take twenty minutes to drive to the school, nine minutes to set up; that left eleven minutes to find the cuecard in a fifteen-room house with fifty closets, all of which looked like dumpsters. Impossible!

Take it easy, he told himself; sit down and think; if I were a cat, where would I . . . ?

He dashed upstairs to the kitchen. It was their bailiwick, and the six-foot table was a private baldachin sheltering their dinner plate, water dish, and Koko's closet treasures. Among them was the cuecard with two perforations in one corner.

Muttering words the Siamese had never heard, Qwilleran raced back downstairs and repacked the equipment while keeping one eye on his watch. He was cutting it close. He had to drive to the school, find the right entrance, unload the suitcases, carry them to the gym, set up the stage, test the speakers, focus the lights, change clothes, and get into character as a twentieth-century radio announcer in a nineteenth-century situation. Hixie would be waiting for him, worried sick and unable to do anything until he arrived with the equipment.

He exceeded the speed limit on Sandpit Road and parked at the front entrance where a yellow curb prohibited parking. As he was opening the trunk of the car, a short, stocky man in a baggy business suit came running from the building, followed by a big, burly student in a varsity jacket.

"Mr. Qwilleran! Mr. Qwilleran!" the man called out. "We thought you'd forgotten us! I'm Mr. Broadnax, the principal. This is Mervyn, our star linebacker. He'll carry your suitcases. It's a long walk to the gym."

The three of them hustled into the building and walked rapidly down one long corridor after another, and all the while the principal was saying, "Will it take you long to set up? Mervyn will help. Just tell him what to do . . . The classes change in eight minutes. Everyone's looking forward to this. Lyle Compton raved about it . . . Don't give up! We're almost there. The custodian built a special platform. Is there anything you need? Is there anything I can do?"

Qwilleran thought, Yes, shut up and let me figure out how to set up in eight minutes.

"Is Miss Rice going to be here today?" the principal asked.

"Is she *going to be here?* She's half the show! Hasn't she arrived? I can't go on without her!" Qwilleran's forehead started to perspire profusely. What could have happened to her? Why hadn't she phoned? He'd give her ten minutes. Then he'd have to cancel. It would be embarrassing.

They finally arrived at the gym—Mr. Broadnax chattering and waving his arms, Mervyn lugging the three suitcases, Qwilleran mopping his brow. The custodian had constructed a platform—rough wood, three feet high, plywood surface supported by two-by-fours and reached by a short flight of wooden steps at the rear. On it were two small folding tables and two folding chairs.

"Now, is everything all right?" asked Mr. Broadnax. "Are the tables big enough? Would you like larger ones from the library? Mervyn will bring them in . . . Mervyn, go to the library—"

"No! No! These are fine," Qwilleran said absently. He was worrying about other things.

"Shall we help you unpack? Where do you want the tripods? Do you need a mike? We have a good PA system . . . Mervyn, get Mr.—"

"No! No! I don't need a mike." He pointed to a door behind the stage. "Where does that lead? I need a door for entrances and exits."

"That's a tackroom for gym equipment. It's locked, but I'll get the key . . . Mervyn, go to the office and bring me the key to the tackroom. Hep!"

Mervyn plunged out of the gym like a linebacker blitzing a quarterback. Meanwhile, Qwilleran mounted the shaky steps to position the furniture and speakers. The floor of the stage, he discovered, bounced like a trampoline. Walking gingerly, he placed the speakers at the front corners of the stage, beamed the two spotlights on the announcer's table, and situated the engineer's table at one side so that Hixie—if she ever arrived—would have more stability underfoot. Where, he asked himself, could she possibly be? Glancing frequently at his watch, he tested the two speakers, tested the two lights (one white, one red), and tested his own voice.

Just as Mervyn returned with the key to the tackroom, a bell rang, and there was instant tumult in the hall.

"May we stall a few minutes?" Qwilleran asked the principal. "I don't know what's happened to my partner. I'm seriously concerned."

The uproar in the hall grew louder, like the roar of a rampaging river when the dam has broken. The double doors burst open, and a flood of noisy students surged into the gym. The two men went into a huddle behind the stage.

"I can't do the show alone. We'll be obliged to cancel," Qwilleran said.

"Could you just give the students a talk about the fire and answer questions?"

"It wouldn't work."

"Maybe a talk on journalism as a career choice."

"I'm sorry, but we'll have to cancel, Mr. Broadnax."

At that moment a side door was flung open, and a distraught Hixie rushed on the scene. "Qwill, you'll never believe what happened!"

"I don't want to know," he snapped. "Everything's been tested. Get up there and take over. Walk carefully. The floor bounces." He ducked into the tackroom, leaving the door ajar in order to hear his cues.

The principal was saying, "These people from the newspaper have come out here to present an exciting show for you, and I want you to give them your complete and courteous attention. There will be no talking during the program and no moving around!"

Great! Qwilleran thought; they hate us already, and they're going to be bored out of their skulls; I should have brought a guitar.

Mr. Broadnax went on. "The show is about a radio broadcast during a great forest fire in 1869, when your great-great-great-grandparents were alive. It's all make-believe, because radio hadn't been invented in those days. I want you to sit quietly and pretend you're the studio audience."

The students became miraculously quiet. A moment later they erupted in cheers and whistles as Hixie, a young and attractive woman, mounted the platform and went to the engineer's station.

"Students!" came the sharp voice of the principal, and they were silenced as if by some secret weapon.

After a few bars of "Anitra's Dance," Qwilleran emerged from the tackroom, climbed the shaky steps, and walked across the stage with knees bent to minimize the bounce. "We interrupt this program to bring you a bulletin . . ."

Perhaps it was the size and magnificence of his moustache or the knowledge that this was the richest man in the northeast central United States. Or perhaps Qwilleran did indeed have a compelling stage presence. Whatever it was, the young people in the bleachers were spellbound, and they were entranced by the other voices coming from the speakers, especially that of the old farmer. Fleeing the flames in a horse-drawn wagon, he had brought his family to safety in a lakeport town, where he was being interviewed by telephone.

"Tell me, sir," said the announcer, "is the fire consuming everything in its path?"

"No," said a parched and reedy voice, "it's like the fire was playin' leapfrog, jumpin' right over one farm and burnin' the next one down to the ground. I don't know what the Lord is tryin' to tell us! We picked up one ol' feller wanderin' around, blind as a bat. Didn't even know where he was! His clothes, they was all burned off. He was stark naked and black as a piece o' coal. We sure had a wagonload when we come into town. We was lucky. They was all alive. Some wagons came into town full o' corpses."

There were gasps and whimpers in the audience as flames were reported to be sweeping across the countryside and consuming whole villages. Suddenly red light filled the stage, and the announcer jumped to his feet.

"Pickax is in flames!" he yelled. Knocking over his chair, he ran gasping and choking from the stage. In his panic he bounced the plywood floor, and both speakers fell over, facedown, while one leg of the folding table collapsed, sliding the telephone and mike to the floor.

"Oh, God!" Qwilleran muttered as he dashed into the tackroom and slammed the door. How would Hixie set up the stage again? Would the audience consider it slapstick comedy? There was an excited uproar in the bleachers, rising above the crashing Tchaikovsky fire music. By opening the door an inch, Qwilleran thought, he could get an idea how Hixie was coping, but the door refused to open. He was locked in!

"Oh, no!" He pounded on the panels with both fists, but the crescendo of the music and the student pandemonium drowned out his appeal for help. His face was already flushed by the emotion of the scene, and now he could hardly breathe in the airless, sweaty closet. He found a dumbbell and hammered on the door; no one heard. Soon the music would signal him to make his entrance, and if he failed to respond on cue, the tape would run out of music, and the disembodied

voice of the Irish innkeeper would come from no-
where, answering questions that were not being
asked—unless Hixie had the sense to stop the tape.
But how would she know he was locked in?

The music ended, and Hixie realized something was
wrong; she pressed the button. The hubbub in the audience subsided. In the momentary silence, Qwilleran
pounded on the door frantically with the dumbbell,
bringing Mr. Broadnax with the key. It was an over-
heated but poised radio announcer who mounted the
flimsy steps—to deafening applause.

As the voice of the Irish innkeeper came from the
speakers, the students were shocked to hear him say,
"There's plenty o' sad tales they're tellin'. One poor
man tried to rescue his two children—both of them
half suffocated—but he couldn't carry both of the little
ones because his right arm was burned off. Burned
clean off, mind you! He had to *choose between them,*
poor man!"

When it was over, the performers took cautious
bows to vociferous applause. Then the audience piled
out of the gym, and Hixie said, "They loved it when
everything fell over. They thought it was part of the
show."

"Best program we've ever had!" the principal told
them as they packed their gear. "Even the troublemakers liked it, especially the part where the man's
arm was burned off . . . Now, what can we do for you?
Mervyn will carry your suitcases. Would you like a
cold drink in our cafeteria?"

Qwilleran and Hixie were both glad to get out of the
building. "Okay, chum, what happened to you?" he
asked peevishly.

"You'll never believe this," she said. "I had lunch at

Linguini's, and the parking lot was full, so I parked in the weeds behind the restaurant. When I came out, it was getting chilly, so I put on the coat that was on the backseat. As soon as I pulled onto the open highway, I felt something crawling inside my sleeve. I screamed, ran the car off the road, and jumped out. At the same time a mouse ran out of my coat."

"But that doesn't explain why you were so late," he objected with a lack of sympathy.

"I had to wait for a farmer to come with a tractor and pull me out of the ditch."

"Well ... if you say so," Qwilleran said dubiously. "But I'll tell you one thing: I'll never set foot on another platform unless I've personally tested it."

"And I'll never park in the weeds behind Linguini's again! *Je le jure!*"

Upon returning home from Mooseland High School, Qwilleran's first move was to phone Gary Pratt at the Black Bear Café. "Gary," he said, "I'd like to run up there tomorrow afternoon and see where we're going to present our show for the Outdoor Club. I don't want any surprises Monday night."

"Sure thing. What time tomorrow?"

"How about two o'clock?"

"I'll be here," said the barkeeper. "There's somebody I want you to meet, too—a nice little girl who comes in quite often."

"How little?"

"Well, I mean, she's in her twenties, but a heck of a lot smaller than your other farm girls around here. She has a problem you might be able to help her with."

"If it's a financial problem, tell her to check with

the Klingenschoen Foundation," Qwilleran said. "I don't get involved with anything like that. I'm lucky to be able to balance my checkbook."

"It's nothing like that," Gary said. "The thing of it is, it's a family problem, and it sounds kind of fishy to me. I thought you might give her some advice."

Qwilleran said he would listen to her story. He had little interest in a young farm girl's family problems, however. What really piqued his curiosity was the suicide of a woman with no apparent motive. He was glad when Junior phoned him on Friday morning.

"Turn on the coffeemaker," the young editor ordered. "I'll be right there with some doughnuts from Lois's. I have some things to report."

Lois's doughnuts were freshly fried every morning, with no icing, no jelly, no chopped nuts—just old-fashioned fried cakes with a touch of nutmeg. The two men sat at the kitchen table, hugging coffee mugs and dipping into the doughnut bag.

Qwilleran said, "I've figured out why nineteenth-century tycoons built big houses and had fourteen kids. Eight of them were girls and considered a total loss. Two of the sons died in infancy; another was killed while stopping a runaway horse; one was deported Down Below to avoid local scandal; one became a journalist, which was even worse—halfway between a cattle rustler and snake oil salesman. They were lucky to have one son left to run the family business."

"That's just about what happened in the Gage family," Junior said. "Grandpa was the last male heir."

"When did you get back from Florida?"

"Around midnight. Almost missed the last shuttle out of Minneapolis."

"Did you get everything wrapped up?"

"To tell the truth," Junior said, "there wasn't that much to do. Grandma had sold her car; the furniture went with the house; we gave her clothes to charity; and the only jewelry she had was seashells and white beads. She'd unloaded her good jewelry, antiques, and real estate early on, to simplify the probate of her will, she said. The only property she couldn't dump was Lois's broken-down building. If anyone bought it, the city would make them put in a new john, widen the front door, fix the roof, and bring the electricity up to code. Don Exbridge was interested in buying the building, but he'd want to tear it down, and the public would be outraged."

Qwilleran agreed. "There'd be rioting in the streets and class-action lawsuits."

"You know, Qwill," said Junior, "I don't care about getting a big inheritance from Grandma Gage, but it would be nice if she established an education trust for her great-grandchildren. Jack has two kids; Pug has three; and Jody and I have one and seven-eighths, as of today."

"How is Jody feeling?"

"She's fine. We're starting the countdown. It's going to be a girl."

Qwilleran said, "Didn't you tell me that your grandmother put all three of you through college?"

"Yeah, my dad was broke. She despised him, so paying our tuition was a kind of put-down, not an act of generosity. At least, that's what my mother told me."

"More coffee, Junior?"

"Half a cup, and then I've got to get to the office. Golly, it's good to be home! There were two things that sort of shocked me at the Park of Pink Sunsets. One was that the management will buy Grandma's mobile home back again—for one-fourth of what she paid them for it! Wilmot advised me to accept the offer and cut my losses."

"What was the other shocker?"

"Grandma had developed a passion for the greyhound races! Can you picture that sedate little old lady stepping up to the pari-mutuel window and putting two on number five in the sixth?"

"Who told you this?"

"Her neighbor, the one who found the body."

"Did you talk much with her?"

"She wanted to gab, but I didn't have time. I just wanted to get home to my family and my job."

Qwilleran patted his moustache thoughtfully. "I've been thinking, Junior, that I could write an interesting profile of Euphonia Gage. There are plenty of people around here who knew her and would like to reminisce. I could also phone her neighbor at the mobile home park. What's her name?"

"Robinson. Celia Robinson."

"Will she be willing to talk?"

"She'll talk your ear off! Brace yourself for a large phone bill."

"Don't be naive! I'll charge it to the newspaper."

Before leaving, Junior said, "Qwill, I've decided why Grandma did what she did. She believed in reincarnation, you know, so maybe she was bored with shuffleboard and was ready to get on with another life. Is that too far out?"

A strange sound came from under the kitchen table. "What's that?" Junior asked in surprise.

"That's Koko," Qwilleran explained. "He and Yum Yum are both under the table waiting for doughnut crumbs."

FIVE

WHEN JUNIOR MENTIONED his reincarnation theory as a motive for Euphonia's suicide, the chattering under the kitchen table had a negative, even hostile sound.

"You didn't care for the idea," Qwilleran said to Koko after Junior had left for the office. "Neither did I. I don't know what it is, but there's something we don't know about the lady."

Three doughnuts and two cups of coffee had only whetted Qwilleran's appetite, and he walked to Lois's for buckwheat pancakes with Canadian bacon, maple syrup, and double butter. Lois herself was waiting on tables, and when she brought his order, he thought the pancakes looked unusual. He tasted them cautiously.

"Lois," he called out, "what's wrong with these pancakes?"

She stared briefly at the plate before snatching it away. "You got Mrs. Toodle's oat bran pancakes!" She took the plate to another table and returned with the right one. "Do these look better? She put margarine and honey on 'em, but she hadn't started to eat."

That's the way it was in that restaurant—informal. Lois was a hard-working woman who owned her own business, labored long hours, enjoyed every aspect of her job, and jollied or insulted the customers with impunity. She had been feeding downtown Pickax for thirty years, and her devoted clientele regularly took up collections to finance building repairs, since the "stingy old woman" who owned the place would do nothing about maintenance. Twice Qwilleran had dropped a twenty-dollar bill into the pickle jar.

"So you lost one of your good customers!" he said to Lois when he paid his check.

"Who?"

"Euphonia Gage."

"That old witch? You gotta be kidding! She was too hoity-toity to come in here," Lois said with lofty disdain. "She sent her housekeeper to collect the rent. When her husband was alive, he came in himself, and I fixed him a thick roast beef sandwich with horseradish. Nice man! If I was short of cash, he didn't mind coming back the next day."

"For another sandwich?" Qwilleran inquired.

"You men!" Lois snapped with a grimace that was half rebuke and half fondness.

Walking home, Qwilleran began to formulate his profile of Junior's grandmother. He would call it "The Several Hats of Mrs. Gage." She was dancer, snob, health nut, and "purplist," a word he had coined. She was generous, stingy, elegant, aloof, witty, unpredictable, gracious, and hoity-toity.

Later, he was sitting at his desk, making notes for the profile, when Koko trudged past the library door with something in his mouth. The plodding gait, lowered head, and horizontal tail suggested serious business. Kao K'o Kung was not a mouser—he left that occupation to Yum Yum—but his behavior was suspiciously predatory, and Qwilleran followed him stealthily. When within tackling distance, he grabbed Koko around the middle and commanded, "Drop that filthy thing!"

Koko, who never took orders gladly, squirmed and clamped his jaws on the prey, shaking his head to prevent the forcible opening of his mouth. Realizing it was no mouse, Qwilleran coaxed in a gentler voice, "Let go, Koko. Good boy! Good boy!" And he massaged the furry throat until Koko was induced to lick his nose and lose his grip.

"What next!" Qwilleran said aloud, snatching the trophy. It was a partial denture—left and right molars connected by a silver bridge—and it was destined for the collection site under the kitchen table.

The objects that Yum Yum charmingly pilfered from pockets and wastebaskets were toys, to be hidden behind seat cushions for future reference. Koko was the serious treasure hunter, however. Qwilleran thought of his excavations as an archaeological dig for fragments that might be pieced together to reconstruct a social history of the Gage dynasty. In fact, he had started a written inventory. Now he confiscated the denture and carried it to the library, while Koko followed in high dudgeon, scolding and jumping at his hand.

"It's only an old set of false teeth," Qwilleran remonstrated as he dropped it into the desk drawer. "Why don't you dig up a Cartier watch?" He added "partial denture" to the other recent acquisitions on the inventory: leather bookmark, recipe for clam chowder, purple satin bedroom slipper, man's argyle sock, 1951 steeplechase ticket, wine label (Bernkasteler Doktor und Graben Hochfeinst '59).

On Friday afternoon Qwilleran drove to the Black Bear Café, wearing his new multicolor sweater. Although his prime purpose was to inspect the staging area for "The Big Burning," he was also slated to meet a young farm woman who needed advice, and the sweater made him look ten years younger—or so he had been told.

Gary's bar and grill operation was located in the Hotel Booze in the town of Brrr, so named because it was the coldest spot in the county. The hotel had been a major landmark since the nineteenth century, when sailors, miners, and lumberjacks used to kill each other in the saloon on Saturday nights, after which the survivors each paid a quarter to sleep on the floor of the rooms upstairs. It was a boxy building perched on a hilltop overlooking the harbor, and ships in the lake were guided to port by the rooftop sign: BOOZE . . . ROOMS . . . FOOD.

When Gary Pratt took over the Hotel Booze from his ailing father, the bar was a popular eatery, but the upper floors violated every building regulation in the book. Yet, the banks refused to lend money to bring it up to code, possibly because of Gary's shaggy black beard and wild head of hair, or because he had been a troublesome student in high school. Qwilleran had a hunch about Gary's potential, however, and the Klingenschoen Foundation obliged with a low-interest economic development loan. With the addition of elevators, indoor plumbing, and beds in the sleeping rooms, the Hotel Booze became the flagship of Brrr's burgeoning tourist trade, and Gary became president of the chamber of commerce. Wisely he maintained the seedy atmosphere that appealed to sportsmen. The mirror over the backbar still had the radiating cracks where a bottle had been flung by a drunken patron during the 1913 mine strike.

When Qwilleran arrived on that Friday afternoon he slid cautiously onto a wobbly barstool, and Gary, behind the carved black walnut bar, asked, "Squunk water on the rocks?"

"Not this time. I'll take coffee if you have it. How's business?"

"It'll pick up when the hunting season opens. I hope we get some snow. The hunters like a little snow for tracking."

"They say we're in for a lot of it this winter." It was one of the trite remarks Qwilleran had learned to make; local etiquette called for three minutes of weatherspeak before any purposeful conversation.

"I like snow," said Gary. "I've been dog-sledding the last couple of winters."

"Sounds like an interesting sport," Qwilleran said, although the idea of being transported by dogpower had no appeal for him.

"You should try it! Come out with me some Sunday!"

"That's an idea," was Qwilleran's carefully ambiguous response.

"Say, I've been meaning to ask you about the different characters in your show. It must have been hard to change your voice like that. I sure couldn't do it."

"I've always had a fairly good ear for different kinds of speech," Qwilleran said with a humble shrug. "The big problem was recording the voices. When I played them back, the tape was punctuated with the yowling of cats. So I locked them out of the room and tried again. This time the mike picked up a trash impactor and the sheriff's helicopter. I finally recorded at three o'clock in the morning and hoped no one in my neighborhood would require an ambulance."

"Well, it sure was impressive. Where did you get all your information? Or did you make some of it up?"

"Every statement is documented," Qwilleran said. "Do you know anything about the Gage family? One of them was an amateur historian."

"All I know is that this woman who just died—her husband used to hang around the bar when my father was running it. Dad said he was quite a boozer. Liked to swap stories with the hunters and fishermen. Never put on airs. Just one of the guys."

"Did you ever meet him?"

"No, he died before I took over—struck by lightning. He was horseback riding when a storm broke, and he made the mistake of sheltering under a tree. Killed instantly!"

"What about the horse?" Qwilleran asked.

"Funny, nobody ever mentioned the horse . . . Another cup of coffee?"

"No, thanks. Let's go and see where we're going to present our show."

"Okay. Just a sec." Gary picked up the bar telephone and called a number. "Nancy, he's here," he said in a low voice. "Okay, Qwill, let's go. The meeting room's across the lobby." He led the way to a large room that was barren except for a low platform and helter-skelter rows of folding chairs. "Here it is! What do you need? We can get you anything you want."

Qwilleran stepped up on the platform and found it solid. "We need a couple of small tables, preferably noncollapsible, and a couple of plain chairs . . . I see you have plenty of electric outlets . . . What's behind that door?"

"Just a hall leading to the restrooms and the emergency exit."

"Good! I'll use it for entrances and exits. Hixie says there'll be families attending, so I suggest seating the kids in the front rows. They'll have better sight lines and be less fidgety, I hope . . . And now I'll take that second cup of coffee."

Back in the bar Gary said, "Hey, there's Nancy, the girl I want you to meet."

Seated on one of the tilt-top barstools was a young woman in jeans, farm jacket, and field boots. She was slightly built, and her delicate features were half hidden by a cascade of dark, wavy hair. In dress and stature she might have been a seventh grader on the way home from school, but her large brown eyes were those of a grown woman with problems. She turned her eyes beseechingly on Qwilleran's moustache.

"Nancy, this is Mr. Q," Gary said. "Nancy's a good customer of ours. Burgers, not beer, eh, Nancy?"

She nodded shyly, clutching her bottle of cola.

"How do you do," Qwilleran said with a degree of reserve.

"Nice to meet you. I've seen your column in the paper."

"Good!" he said coolly. Had she read it? Did she like it? Or had she just *seen it?*

Gary served Qwilleran a fresh cup of coffee. "Well, I'll leave you two guys to talk." He ambled to the other end of the bar to visit with a couple of boaters.

The awkward silence that followed was broken by Qwilleran's uninspired question. "Are you a member of the Outdoor Club?"

"Yes," she said. "I'm going to see your show Monday night."

He huffed into his moustache. Had she heard good things about it? Was she looking forward to it? Or was she simply going to *see it?* Again it was his turn to serve in this slow-motion game of Ping-Pong. "Do you think we'll have snow next week?"

"I think so," she said. "The dogs are getting excited."

"Dogs? Do you have dogs?"

"Siberian huskies."

"Is that so?" he remarked with a glimmer of interest. "How many do you have?"

"Twenty-seven. I breed sled dogs."

"Are you a musher?"

"I do a little racing," she said, blushing self-consciously.

"Gary tells me it's becoming quite a popular sport. Do you breed dogs as a hobby or a vocation?"

"Both, I guess. I work part-time at the animal clinic in Brrr. I'm a dog-handler."

"Do you live in Brrr?"

"Just outside. In Brrr Township."

How long, Qwilleran wondered, can this painful di-

alogue continue? He was determined not to inquire
about her problem. If she had a problem, let her state
it! They both wriggled on the ancient barstools that
clicked noisily. He tried to catch Gary's eye, but the
barkeeper was arguing heatedly with the boaters
about the new breakwall.

"Nancy, I'm afraid I don't know your last name,"
Qwilleran said.

"Fincher," she said simply.

"How do you spell it?" He knew how to spell it, but
it was an attempt to fill the silence.

"F-i-n-c-h-e-r."

Fortunately Gary glanced in their direction, and
Qwilleran pointed to his empty cup and Nancy's half-
empty bottle.

Gary approached with his bearish, lumbering gait.
"Did you tell him about your problem?" he asked
Nancy.

"No," she said, looking away.

Gary poured coffee and produced another bottle of
cola. "The thing of it is, Qwill, her dad disappeared."
Then he went back to the boaters.

Qwilleran looked inquiringly at the embarrassed
daughter. "When did that happen?"

"I haven't been able to find him since Sunday." She
looked genuinely worried.

"Do you live in the same house?"

"No, he lives on his farm. I have a mobile home."

"What kind of farm?"

"Potatoes."

"Where did you see him on Sunday?"

"I went over to cook Sunday dinner for him, the
way I always do. Then he watched football on TV, and
I went home to my dogs."

"And when did you first realize he was missing?"

"Wednesday." There was a long, exasperating pause. Qwilleran waited for her to go on. "The mail carrier stopped and told me that Pop's mailbox was filling up, and his dog was barking in the house, and there was no truck in the yard. So I drove over there, and Corky was so starved, he almost took my arm off. He'd wrecked the house, looking for something to eat. And the place smelled terrible!"

"Did you notify the police?"

Nancy looked at her clenched hands. They were small hands, but they looked strong. "Well, I talked to a deputy I know, and he said Pop was most likely off on a binge somewhere."

"Is your father a heavy drinker?"

"Well . . . he's been drinking more since Mom died."

"Did you do anything further?"

"Well, I cleaned up the mess and took Corky home with me, and on the way I stopped at the Crossroads Tavern. That's where Pop goes to have a beer with the other farmers and chew the rag. They said he hadn't been around since Saturday night. They figured he was working in the fields."

"Has your father ever done this before?"

"Never!" Her eyes flashed for the first time. "He'd never do such a thing at harvest. The weather's been wet, and if he doesn't dig his potatoes before the first heavy frost, the whole crop will be ruined. It's not like him at all! He's a very good farmer, and he's got a lot invested in his crop."

"And this deputy you mentioned—does he know your father?"

"Yes," she said, shrinking into her burly jacket.

"What's his name?"

"Dan Fincher."

"Related to you?"

She turned away as she said, "We were married for a while."

"I see," said Qwilleran. "What's your father's name?"

"Gil Inchpot."

He nodded. "The Inchpot name goes back a long way in the farming community. The farm museum in West Middle Hummock has quite a few things from early Inchpot homesteads."

"I've never been there," Nancy said. "I never cared much for history."

"What kind of truck does your father drive?"

"Ford pickup. Blue."

"Do you know the license number?"

"No," she said, pathetically enough to arouse Qwilleran's sympathy.

"Let me think about this matter," he said, pushing a cocktail napkin and a ballpoint pen toward her. "Write down your address and telephone number, also the address of your father's farm."

"Thank you," she said simply, turning her expressive brown eyes toward him.

He thought, Beware of young women with beseeching brown eyes, especially when they look twelve years old. "If you learn anything further, ask Gary how to get in touch with me."

"Thank you," she said again. "Now I have to go back to work. I just ran over from the clinic."

She left, lugging a shoulder bag half her size. Qwilleran watched her go, smoothing his moustache like the villain in an old melodrama, but the gesture meant something else. It meant that he sensed an element of intrigue in this country tale. The reaction started with a tingle on his upper lip—in the roots of his moustache—and he had learned to respect the sensation.

Gary returned with the coffee server.

"Please! Not again! It's good coffee, but I'm driving."

"Nice little girl, isn't she?" the barkeeper remarked.

"I don't visualize her racing with a pack of sled dogs. She looks too delicate."

"But she's light, like a jockey, and that makes a good racer. What do you think of her story?"

"It bears a closer look."

"Yeah, that ex-husband of hers is a jerk! Imagine brushing her off like that!"

"If she wants to talk to me, you dial the number for her, Gary."

"Sure, I understand. I'll bet you're pestered by all kinds of people."

Qwilleran threw a ten dollar bill across the bar. "Keep the change for a down payment on some new barstools. And I'll see you Monday night."

From the Hotel Booze he drove directly to the police station in downtown Pickax, where his friend Andrew Brodie was chief.

Brodie waved him away. "If you're looking for free coffee, you're too late. The pot's dry."

"False deduction," Qwilleran said. "My prime objective is to see if you're doing your work, issuing lots of parking tickets, and arresting leaf burners. Did you blow your leaves into the street, Andy? The vacuum truck will be on your side of town tomorrow."

The chief shot him a veiled look. "The wife takes care of that."

"Oh, ho! Now I understand why you're always advocating matrimony! I knew there was some ulterior reasoning."

Brodie scowled. "What's on your mind, besides leaves?"

"Do you know a guy named Gil Inchpot?"

"Potato farmer. Brrr Township."

"Right. His daughter's worried about him. He's disappeared. His truck's gone. He abandoned his dog. And he decamped when the potatoes were ready to harvest."

"That's the sheriff's turf," Brodie pointed out. "Did she report it to the sheriff's department?"

"She talked to a deputy named Dan Fincher."

"That guy's a lunkhead! I used to work for the sheriff, and I have firsthand evidence."

"Well, the lunkhead laughed it off, said Inchpot was off on a binge somewhere."

"The daughter should notify the state police. They cover three counties. Do you know the license number of the missing vehicle?"

"No, but it's a blue Ford pickup, and I have Inchpot's address, in case you want to run a check on it—with that expensive computer the taxpayers bought for you."

"Seeing as how it's you," Brodie said, "I'll run down the number and turn it over to the state police post."

"That's decent of you, Andy. If you ever want to run for mayor, I'll campaign for you."

The chief scowled again. "It would do me good to give Dan Fincher a swift kick in the pants, that's all."

SIX

WHEN QWILLERAN RETURNED home after his discussion with the police chief, Goodwinter Boulevard was transformed. All the leaves had been blown from the front lawns and sidewalks into the gutters, in preparation for the vacuum truck on Saturday. He found a lawn service vehicle parked behind the house, and three industrious young men with backpack blowers were coaxing the backyard leaves into heaps.

"Did Junior Goodwinter hire you?" Qwilleran asked one of them, feeling guilty that he had failed to take care of it himself. "Send the bill to me, but first, answer one question: What happens to these huge piles of leaves?"

"We'll be back tomorrow to finish up. We've run out

of leaf bags," said the boss of the crew. "It's been a
busy day. Everybody's in a rush to get rid of the leaves
before snow flies."

"What happens if a big wind comes up tonight and
blows these piles all over the yard?"

"We get another day's work, and you get another
bill," the lawnman said with a guffaw.

As the backpackers went on their merry way,
Qwilleran walked about the yard through rustling
leaves—a joyous activity he remembered from boy-
hood. Suddenly, through the corner of his eye, he saw
something crawling through the shrubs that bordered
the property. He was prepared to yell "Scat!" when he
realized it was the attorney's son. He called out
sternly, "Is there something you want, young man?"

Timmie Wilmot scrambled to his feet. "Is Oh Jay
over here?"

"I don't know anyone of that name."

"He's our cat. A great big orange one with bad
breath."

"Then he'd better not hang around here," Qwilleran
said in a threatening voice.

"I'm afraid he'll go out in the street and get sucked
up in the leaf sucker." The boy was looking anxiously
about Qwilleran's yard. "There he is!" He ran across
the grass to a pile of leaves that effectively camou-
flaged a marmalade cat. Grabbing the surprised animal around the middle, he staggered back across the
yard, clutching the bundle of fur to his chest, the orange tail dangling between his knees and the orange
legs pointing stiffly in four directions. The pair
reached the row of shrubs on the lot line and crawled
through the brush to safety.

Indoors, the Siamese were concerned chiefly with

Qwilleran's recent association with a dog-handler who also raised Siberian huskies. Their noses, like Geiger counters detecting radiation, passed over every square inch of Qwilleran's clothing, their whiskers registering positive.

He arranged some roast beef and boned chub from Toodle's Deli on a plate and placed it under the kitchen table. Then, turning on the kitchen radio for the weather report, he heard the following announcement instead:

"The hobgoblins will be out tomorrow night, which is official Beggars' Night in Pickax. A resolution passed by the city council limits trick-or-treating to one-and-a-half hours, between six o'clock and seven-thirty. Children should stay in their own neighborhoods unless accompanied by an adult. In all cases, two or more children should go together. The police department makes the following recommendations in the interest of safety:

"Stay on the sidewalk; don't run into the street. Don't go into houses if invited. Avoid wearing long costumes that could cause tripping. Don't eat treats until they have been inspected by a parent or other responsible person. Discard unwrapped cookies and candies immediately. Happy Halloween!"

Qwilleran turned to the cats, who were washing up. "Did you hear that? It would be more fun to stay home and do homework."

Saturday morning, after he had heard the announcement for the third time, he went back to Toodle's Market and bought a bushel of apples. When he arrived home, his phone was ringing, and Koko was announcing the fact by racing back and forth and jumping on and off the desk.

"Okay, okay!" Qwilleran yelled at him. "I can hear it, and I know where it is!"

Junior's voice said, "Where've you been so early? Did you stay out all night? I've been trying to reach you."

"I was buying apples for trick-or-treat."

"Apples! Are you nuts? They'll throw 'em at you! They'll soap your windows!"

"We'll see about that," Qwilleran said grimly. "What's on your mind? Are you at the office?"

"I'm going in later, but first: How would you like to take a little ride?"

"Where?"

"To the Hilltop Cemetery. Grandma was buried there yesterday—privately."

"How come?"

"Her last wishes, on file in Wilmot's office, specified no funeral, no mourners, no flowers, and no bagpipes."

"That will break Andy Brodie's heart," Qwilleran said. The police chief prided himself on his piping at weddings and funerals.

"It was Grandma's revenge on the police for all the traffic tickets she got, not that she ever paid them."

"Then why are you going to the cemetery this morning?"

"Somehow," said her grandson, "it isn't decent to let her be buried with only the Dingleberry brothers and a backhoe operator in attendance. Want to come along? I'll pick you up."

"I'll bring a couple of apples," Qwilleran offered.

The Hilltop Cemetery dated back to pioneer days when the Gages, Goodwinters, Fugtrees, Trevelyans, and other settlers were buried across the crest of a ridge. Their tombstones could be seen silhouetted against the sky as one approached.

On the way to the cemetery Junior said, "Pickax lost to Lockmaster again last night, fourteen to zip."

"We should give up football and stick to growing potatoes," Qwilleran remarked.

"How's everything at the house?"

"Koko just came out of a closet with a man's spat. I haven't seen one of those since the last Fred Astaire movie. He was dragging it conscientiously to the collection site in the kitchen, staggering and stumbling. His aim in life is to empty the closets, ounce by ounce."

"They'll have to be cleaned out sooner or later."

"Watch it!" Qwilleran snapped. Junior had a friendly way of facing his passenger squarely as he spoke, and they narrowly missed hitting a deer bounding out of a cornfield. "Keep your eyes on the road, Junior, or we'll be residents of Hilltop ourselves." They were passing through farm country, and he asked Junior if he knew a potato farmer named Gil Inchpot.

"Not personally, but his daughter was my date for the senior prom in high school. She was the only girl short enough for me."

"You're no longer short, Junior. You're what they call vertically challenged."

"Gee, thanks! That makes me feel nine feet tall."

They parked the car and walked up the hill to a granite obelisk chiseled with the name Gage. Small headstones surrounded it, and there was one rectangle of freshly turned earth, not yet sodded or marked.

"There she is," said her grandson. "I was supposed to ship her books to Florida, but I had too many other things on my mind—my job, and the baby coming. I promise, though, she's going to get a memorial service exactly how she wanted it."

"Has her will been read?"

"Not until my brother and sister get here. Jack has to come from L.A., and Pug lives in Montana. Grandma wrote a new will after moving to Florida. It was in the manager's safe at the mobile home park, all tied up with red ribbon and sealed with red wax. It will be interesting to know what changes she made."

"You told me once that you were her sole heir."

"That's what she said at the time, but I think she was just cajoling me into doing something for her. A world-class conniver, that's what she was!"

"When Pug and Jack arrive," Qwilleran suggested, "I'd like to take all of you to dinner at the Old Stone Mill."

"Gee! That would be great!"

"Would you like an apple?"

The two men stood munching in silence for a while, Junior staring at the grave and Qwilleran gazing around the horizon. "Pleasant view," he remarked.

"Pallbearers always hated burials up here. No access road. They have to carry the casket up that steep path . . . Wish I had a flower to throw on the grave before we leave."

"We could bury our apple cores. They'd sprout and produce apple blossoms every spring."

"Hey! Let's do it!" Junior exclaimed.

They scooped out some soil and buried the cores reverently, then drove back to town without saying much until Qwilleran ventured, "You never told me anything about your grandfather."

"To tell the truth, my grandparents are closer in death than they ever were in life," Junior said. "She was into arts and health fads; he was into sports and booze. The Gage shipyard had folded, and he spent his time manipulating the family fortune, not always legally. Grandpa spent two years in federal prison for financial fraud. That was in the 1920s."

"If they were so mismatched, why did they marry? Does anyone know?"

"Well, the way my mother told me the story, Euphonia's forebears were pioneer doctors by the name of Roff. They'd deliver a baby for a bushel of apples or set a broken bone for a couple of chickens, so the family never had any real money. Somehow Euphonia got pressured into marrying the Gage heir. The Roffs, being from Boston, had a certain 'class' that Grandpa lacked, so it seemed like a good deal all around, but it didn't work."

"Was your mother their only child?"

"Yeah. She called herself a Honeymoon Special."

Qwilleran asked to be dropped off at the variety store, where he bought a blue light bulb and a Halloween mask. Then he spent an hour with his recording machine taping weird noises. The Siamese watched with bemused tolerance as their human companion uttered screeches, anguished moans, and hideous laughs into the microphone.

The performance was interrupted by the telephone, when Gary Pratt called. "Nancy's here. She wants to tell you something. Okay?"

"Put her on."

In a breathless, little-girl voice Nancy said, "The state police found Pop's truck!"

"That was fast. Where was it?"

"At the airport."

"In the parking structure?"

"No. In the open lot."

He nodded with understanding. There was a charge for parking indoors, and most locals preferred to park free in the cow pasture. "Is there any clue as to his destination?"

"No . . ." She hesitated before continuing in a faltering way. "He never . . . he doesn't like to travel, Mr. Qwilleran. He's hardly been . . . out of Moose County . . . except for Vietnam."

"Still, some unexpected business transaction may have come up—suddenly. What did the police say?"

"They told me to report a missing person, and they'll check the passenger list for flights."

"Let me know what they find out," Qwilleran said. He was beginning to feel genuinely sorry for her, and in an effort to divert her from her worries he said, "You know, Nancy, I'd like to write a column on dog-sledding. Are you willing to be interviewed?"

"Oh, yes!" she said. "The mushers would love the publicity."

"How about tomorrow afternoon?"

"Well, I want to go to Pop's house after church to clean out the refrigerator, but I could be home by two."

"By the way, what's the situation in the potato fields?"

"No severe frost yet. I'm praying he comes back before the crop's ruined."

"Could you hire someone to do the harvesting in an emergency?"

"I don't know who it would be. They're all busy with their own work."

"It won't hurt to ask around, Nancy. And I'll see you tomorrow afternoon."

The hour of hobgoblins approached. Qwilleran tried on his death's-head mask and prepared a sheet to shroud his head and body. The tape player was set up near the entrance, and at six o'clock he turned on the blue porch lamp that cast an eerie light on the gray stonework. He was ready for them.

The first squealing, chattering trio to come up the front walk included a miniature Darth Vader, a pirate, and a bride in a wedding dress made from old curtains. They were carrying shopping bags. Before they could ring the bell, the front door opened slowly, and unnatural sounds emanated from the gloomy interior. "Ooooooooooh! Oooooooooooo!" Then there was a horrifying screech. As the pop-eyed youngsters stared, a shrouded skeleton emerged from the shadows, and a clawlike hand was extended, clutching an apple. The three screamed and scrambled down the steps.

Later groups were scared stiff but not stiff enough to run away without their treats, so the supply of apples diminished slightly. Many beggars avoided the house entirely. They trooped down the side drive, however, to the brightly lighted carriage house where Polly was distributing candy.

The last intrepid pair to brave the haunted house were a cowboy with large eyeglasses and a moustache glued on his upper lip, accompanied by a tiny ballerina with a white net tutu and sequined bra over her gray warmup suit. The cowboy pressed the doorbell, and Qwilleran pressed the button on the player: "Ooooooooooh! Oooooooooooh!" The spooky wail was followed by a screech and a cackling laugh as a ghostly figure appeared.

"I know you!" said the cowboy. "You told us about those people burning up."

In a sepulchral drone Qwilleran said, "I . . . am the . . . scrofulous skeleton . . . of Skaneateles!"

The boy explained to his small companion, "He can talk so you don't know who he is. He's that man with the big moustache."

"What . . . do . . . you want?" the apparition intoned.

"Trick or treat!"

The clawlike hand dropped apples into the out-stretched sacks, and Timmie Wilmot turned to his sister. "Apples!" he said. "Cheapo!"

At seven-thirty Qwilleran was glad to turn off the blue light and shed his mask and sheet.

Soon Polly phoned. "Did you have many beggars?"

"Enough," he said. "I have some apples left over, in case you feel like making eight or nine pies. How about going out to dinner?"

"Thanks, but I couldn't possibly! I'm exhausted after running up and down stairs to answer the doorbell. Why don't you come to brunch tomorrow? Mushroom omelettes and cheese popovers."

"I'll be there! With apples. What time?"

"I suggest twelve noon, and don't forget to turn your clocks back. This is the end of Daylight Saving Time."

Before resetting his two watches, three clock radios, and digital coffeemaker, Qwilleran added several new acquisitions to the collection in the desk drawer: swizzle stick, stale cigar, brown shoelace, woman's black lace garter, handkerchief embroidered "Cynara," and box of corn plasters.

On Sunday morning it was back to Standard Time for the rest of the nation but not for Koko and Yum Yum, who pounced on Qwilleran's chest at seven A.M., demanding their eight o'clock breakfast. He shooed them from the bedroom and slammed the door, but they yowled and jiggled the doorknob until he fed them in self-defense. He himself subsisted on coffee and apples until it was time to walk back to the carriage house. He used his own key and was met at the top of the stairs by a husky Siamese who fixed him with a challenging eye.

"Back off!" Qwilleran said. "I was invited to brunch . . . Polly, this cat is much too heavy."

"I know, dear," she said regretfully, "but Bootsie always seems to be hungry. I don't know how Koko stays so svelte. When he stretches, he's a yard long."

"I suspect he has a few extra vertebrae. He walks around corners like a train going around a curve; the locomotive is heading east while the caboose is still traveling north . . . Do I smell coffee?"

"Help yourself, Qwill. I'm about to start the omelettes."

When he tasted the first succulent mouthful, he asked in awe, "How did you learn to make omelettes like these?"

"I prepared one every day for a month until I mastered the technique. That was several years ago, before we were all worried about cholesterol."

"I'm not worried about cholesterol," he retorted. "I think it's a lot of bunk."

"Famous last words, dear."

He helped himself to another popover. "Junior's siblings are coming to town for the formalities, and I'm taking them to dinner. I hope you'll join us."

"By all means. I remember Pug when she used to come into the library for books on horses; she married a rancher. Jack went into advertising; he was always a very clever boy."

"Did you know that Mrs. Gage owned Lois's building?"

"Of course. The Gage family has had it for generations."

"Did you ever meet Euphonia's husband?"

"No, our paths never crossed."

"They say he and his wife didn't get along."

With a slight stiffening of the spine Polly said, "I'm not in a position to say, although they never appeared in public together."

"He and Lois seemed to hit it off pretty well."

"Qwill, dear, for someone who deplores gossip, you seem to be wallowing in it today."

"For purely vocational reasons," he explained. "I'm planning an in-depth profile of Euphonia."

Polly nodded knowingly, being familiar with his ambitious writing projects that never materialized.

He went on. "No one has come up with an acceptable motive for her suicide. Junior thinks it has to do with her belief in reincarnation, but I don't buy that explanation."

"Nor I . . . May I fill your cup, Qwill?"

"It's superlative today. What did you do to it?" he asked.

"Just a touch of cinnamon."

They sipped in contented silence, as close friends can do, Qwilleran wondering whether to tell her about Koko's latest salvage operations. Besides the purple hair ribbon and purple bedroom slipper, there had been an empty vial of violet perfume, an English lavender sachet, and a lipstick tube labeled "Grape Delish." Koko had chosen these mementoes out of an estimated 1.5 million pieces of junk. Why? Could he sense Euphonia's innate energy in purpleness? Or was he trying to communicate some catly message?

"What are you reading these days?" Polly asked.

"For myself, a biography of Sir Wilfred Grenfell, but the cats and I are going through *Robinson Crusoe.* That was Koko's choice. The opening sentence has 105 words—a maze of principal and subordinate clauses. It's interesting to compare with the staccato effect of simple declarative clauses in *Tale of Two Cities,* which opens with 120."

Polly smiled and nodded and asked if he would like to hear a Mozart concerto for flute, oboe, and viola. Qwilleran had always preferred a hundred-piece symphony orchestra or thousand-voice choir, but he was learning to appreciate chamber music. All in all, it was a cozy Sunday afternoon until he excused himself, saying he had to interview a breeder of Siberian huskies.

He avoided mentioning that the breeder was a woman—a young woman—a slender young woman with appealing brown eyes and a mass of dark, wavy hair and a little-girl voice.

Half an hour later, when he arrived at the address in Brrr Township, he knew he was in the right place. A twenty-seven-dog chorus could be heard behind the mobile home. The excited huskies were chained to a line-up of individual posts in front of individual shelters. Nancy's truck was not in the yard, and when he knocked on the door there was no answer, except from Corky within. He strode about the yard for a while, saying "Good dogs!" to the frenzied animals, but it only increased the clamor. He was preparing to leave when a pickup with a boxy superstructure steered recklessly into the yard, and Nancy jumped out.

"Sorry I'm late," she said excitedly. "The police came to Pop's house while I was there. They checked the airline, and he never bought a ticket!"

Or, Qwilleran thought, he bought a ticket without giving his right name.

"I don't understand it!" she went on. "Why would he leave his truck there? I was worried about the potatoes, but now I'm worried that something has happened to Pop!"

Sympathetically Qwilleran asked, "Was he having trouble of any kind? Financial problems? Enemies he was trying to avoid?"

"I don't know . . . I don't see how . . . He was well liked by the other farmers—always helping them out. When I lived at home, I remember how stranded motorists would come to the house to use the phone. They were out of gas, or their car had broken down. Pop had his own gas pump, and he'd give them a gallon or stick his head under the hood of their car and fix what was wrong. He could fix anything mechanical and was proud of it . . . So now I'm worrying that he was helping someone out and they took advantage of him. You never know who's driving on these country roads nowadays. It used to be so safe! Everyone was honest. But now . . . someone could come along and stun my dogs and make off with the whole pack. They stole a big black walnut tree from a farm near here." The dogs were still barking until she silenced them with a command.

"How old is your father?" Qwilleran asked.

"Fifty-seven."

"When did your mother die?"

"She passed away three—no, four years ago. Pop changed a lot after that."

"Could there be anything new in his lifestyle that you don't know about?"

"You mean . . . like women? Or drugs?" She hesitated.

A reassuring manner was his stock in trade. "You can tell me, Nancy. I may be able to help."

"Well . . . he used to be very tight-fisted, but lately he's spending a lot of money."

"Extravagance can be a way of coping with grief. How is he spending the money?" Qwilleran asked.

"On farm improvements. Nothing wrong with that, I suppose, but"—she turned frightened eyes to him—*"where is he getting it?"*

SEVEN

QWILLERAN AND THE dog-handler were standing in the farmyard. "Well, you don't want to listen to my troubles all day," Nancy said with a gulp. "Do you want to go and see the dogs?"

"First, let's sit down and talk for a while. I've seen them, and I've heard them," he said dryly.

"You should hear them before a race! They love to hit the trail, and they go wild when they're waiting for the starting flag."

They entered a small mobile home where they were greeted by a large, friendly, all-American, farm-type, cork-colored mongrel whose wagging tail was wreaking havoc in the tight quarters.

"Good boy!" Qwilleran said while being lashed by the amiable tail.

"This is Pop's dog," Nancy said. "Where would you like to sit?" She brushed debris from a couple of chair seats and hastily picked up litter from the floor.

"Is it okay if I tape this interview?" He placed a small recorder on a nearby table, and a swipe of the tail knocked it off.

"I'd chain him outdoors, but he'd drive the other dogs crazy," she said apologetically. "Corky! Go in the other room!" She pointed, and obediently he walked six feet away and stretched out with his chin on his paw.

"You have a way with dogs," Qwilleran complimented her. "How did you get into this specialty of yours?"

"Well, I spent a couple of years in Alaska, and when I came home I bought a sled and a pair of huskies—Siberians. They're smaller than Alaskans but stronger and faster." Her small, wavering voice became stronger as she warmed up to her subject.

"Then you're the one who started the sport here?"

"It was easy. When somebody tries dog-sledding on a beautiful winter day, they're hooked! I'll take you for a ride after we get some snow."

"How do you accommodate passengers?"

"You ride in the basket, and I ride the runners."

"Hmmm," he murmured, thinking he'd feel foolish sitting in a basket pulled by a pack of dogs. "Are all sled dogs as frisky as yours?"

"If they're good racers. A high attitude is what they should have. Mine are born to be racers, not pets, but I love them like family."

"What else makes a good racer?"

"Hard muscles in the right places. A good gait. And they have to like working in a team."

"Training them must be a science," Qwilleran said.

"I don't know about that, but it takes a lot of patience."

"I believe it. How many dogs make a team?"

"I've seen as many as twenty in Alaska. I usually run eight."

"How do you drive them?"

"With your voice. They learn to take orders. Would you like a cola, Mr. Qwilleran?"

He said yes, although it ranked with tea at the bottom of his beverage list.

Nancy went on with enthusiasm as she opened a can. The shy, inarticulate, almost pathetic young woman became self-possessed and authoritative when talking about her vocation. "Each dog has a partner. They're paired according to the length of their stride and their personality. They become buddies. It's nice to see."

"Isn't it a great deal of work?"

"Yes, but I love feeding them, brushing them, socializing, cleaning up after them. Do you have dogs?"

"I have cats. Two Siamese. When do the race meets start?"

"After Christmas. We're training already. You should see us tearing around the back roads with the dogs pulling a wheeled cart! They know snow is on the way. They're getting so excited!" She showed a picture of a dog team pelting down a snowy trail; out of a total of thirty-two canine feet, only four seemed to be touching the ground.

"I believe they're flying!" Qwilleran said in amazement.

His willingness to be amazed, his sympathetic manner, and his attitude of genuine interest were the techniques of a good interviewer, and Nancy was relaxing and responding warmly. He could read her body language. Take it easy, he told himself; she's vulnerable. In businesslike fashion he asked, "Did you attend veterinary school?"

"I wanted to, but I got married instead—without telling my parents."

"How did they react?"

She looked at the tape recorder, and he turned it off.

"Well . . . Pop was furious . . . and Mom got cancer. I had to be nurse for her and housekeeper for Pop." Shrugging and wetting her lips, she said, "Dan didn't want a part-time wife."

"And that led to your divorce?"

She nodded. "When Mom died, I went to Alaska to get away from everything, but dog-sledding brought me back."

"And your father—how did he react to your return?"

"Oh, he was getting along fine. He had a housekeeper three days a week and a new truck and a harvester with stereo in the cab and half a million dollars' worth of drain tile. He was a lot nicer to me than before, and he gave me a piece of land for my mobile home and kennels . . . I don't know why I'm telling you all this. I guess it's because you're so understanding."

"I've had troubles of my own," he said. "One question occurred to me: Is your father a gambler?"

"Just in the football pool at the tavern. He never even buys a lottery ticket . . . Would you like another

cola?" Corky had just rejoined the group, and a swish
of his tail had swept Qwilleran's beverage off the table.

"No, thanks. Let's go out and see what a sled looks
like."

The seven-foot sled, like a basket on runners, was
in a small pole barn, where it shared space with a
snowplow, snow blower, and other maintenance equipment.

"It's made of birch and oak," Nancy said. "This is
the handrail. That's the brake board down there. It's
held together with screws and glue and rawhide lac-
ing. I varnish it before each sledding season."

"A work of art," Qwilleran declared. "Now let's
meet your family."

The dogs anticipated their coming. Puppies in a
fenced yard were racing and wrestling and jumping
for joy. The adults raised a high-decibel clamor that
Nancy quieted with a secret word. They were lean,
handsome, high-waisted, long-legged animals in assorted colors and markings, with slanted blue eyes
that gave them a sweet expression.

"These two are the lead dogs, Terry and Jerry.
They're the captains, very brainy. Spunky and Chris
are the wheel dogs, right in front of the sled."

Both Qwilleran and Nancy turned as a police vehicle pulled into the yard. It was a sheriff's car, and an
officer in a wide-brimmed hat stepped out.

She shouted, "Hi, Dan! This is Mr. Qwilleran from
the newspaper."

Qwilleran, recognizing the deputy's reticent and almost sullen attitude, said, "I believe we've met. You
rescued me after a blizzard a couple of years ago."

The deputy nodded.

"Mr. Qwilleran is going to write up my dog team, Dan."

"But we'll hold the story until after snow flies. I'll work on it and call if I have any more questions . . . Beautiful animals. Interesting sport. Good interview." He moved toward his car.

"You don't have to leave," she protested.

"I have to go home and feed the cats," he explained, making an excuse that was always accepted.

Nancy accompanied him to his car. "Gary says you're living in Mrs. Gage's big house."

"That's right. I'm renting it from Junior Goodwinter, her grandson." He noticed a flicker in her eyes, which he attributed to memories of the high school prom, but it was something else.

"I've been in that house many times," she said. "It's huge!"

"Did you know Mrs. Gage?"

"Did I! My mother was her housekeeper for years and years. Every year Mom took me there for Christmas cookies and hot chocolate, and Mrs. Gage always gave me a present."

"That was gracious of her," Qwilleran said. "What did you think of her?"

"Well, she didn't fuss over me, but she was . . . nice."

Now he had one more adjective to describe the enigmatic Euphonia Gage, and another reason to call Florida and quiz her talkative neighbor.

"Do you like apples?" he asked Nancy before leaving. He handed her a brown paper bag.

Back at the mansion he submitted to the Siamese Sniff Test. After an afternoon with Corky and twenty-seven Siberian huskies, he rated minus-zero. Their investigation was cut short by a ringing telephone.

"Hey, Qwill!" said an excited Junior Goodwinter. "Can you stand some good news?"

"It's a boy," Qwilleran guessed.

"No, nothing like that; Jody's still here, getting antsy. But somebody wants to buy the Gage mansion! I just got a long distance phone call!

"Congratulations! Who's making the offer?"

"A realtor in Chicago."

"Is it a good offer?"

"Very good! What do you suppose it means? The house wasn't even listed for sale. And why should they pick mine when there are seven for-sale signs on the street? I'll bet Grandma Gage tipped someone off before she died."

"Don't ask questions," Qwilleran advised. "Take the money and run."

"I'm going to tell them it's rented until spring, so don't worry about having to move out, Qwill."

"I appreciate that. And let's not tell Polly until the deal's closed. She'll be upset about losing the carriage house."

"Okay, I won't. Golly! This is the best news I've had since I-don't-know-when."

"Good things come in threes," Qwilleran said. "Maybe Jody will have twins. By the way, was there a woman in the Gage family by the name of Cynara?"

"I don't think so. How do you spell it?"

"Like the poem: C-y-n-a-r-a."

"Nope. Doesn't ring a bell."

At a suitable hour—late enough for the fifty-percent discount but not too late for a Pink Sunset resident—

Qwilleran placed a call to Florida, and Koko leaped to the desk in anticipation. "Arrange your optic fibers," Qwilleran advised him. "This may be enlightening." The cat's whiskers and eyebrows curved forward.

When a woman's cheery voice answered, he asked in a rich and ingratiating tone, "May I speak with Celia Robinson?"

There was a trill of laughter. "I know it's you, Clayton. You can't fool your old grandmother. Does your mother know you're calling?"

"I'm afraid I'm not Clayton. I'm a colleague of Junior Goodwinter, Mrs. Gage's grandson. I'm calling from Pickax. My name is Jim Qwilleran."

She hooted with delight tinged with embarrassment. "Oh, I thought you were my prankish grandson, changing his voice. He's a great one for playing practical jokes. What did you say your name was?"

"Jim Qwilleran. Junior gave me your number."

"Yes, he was here for a few days. He's a nice boy. And I know all about you. Mrs. Gage showed me the articles you write for the paper. What's the name of the paper?"

"The Moose County Something."

"I knew it was a funny name, but I couldn't remember. And I loved your picture! You have a wonderful moustache. You remind me of someone on TV."

"Thank you," he said graciously, although he preferred compliments on his writing. Clearing his throat he began, "The editor has assigned me to write a profile of Euphonia Gage, and I'd like to talk with someone who knew her in Florida. Were you well acquainted with her?"

"Oh, yes, we were next-door neighbors, and I sort of looked after her."

"In what way? I'm going to tape this if you don't mind."

"Well, I checked up on her every day, and I'd always drive her where she wanted to go. She didn't like driving in the bumper-to-bumper traffic we have around here. She was eighty-eight, you know. I'm only sixty-eight."

"Your voice sounds much younger, Mrs. Robinson."

"Do you think so?" she said happily. "That's because I sing."

"In nightclubs?" he asked slyly.

Mrs. Robinson laughed merrily. "No, just around the house, but I used to sing in a church choir before I moved down here. Would you like to hear me sing something?"

Qwilleran thought, I have a live one here! "I was hoping you'd suggest it," he said. He expected to hear "Amazing Grace." Instead she sang the entire verse and chorus of "Mrs. Robinson" in a clear, untrained voice. Listening, he tried to visualize her; it was his custom to picture strangers in his mind's eye. He imagined her to be buxom and rosy-cheeked, with partly gray hair and seashell earrings. "Brava!" he shouted when she had finished. "I've never heard it sung better."

"Thank you. It's Clayton's favorite," she said. "You have a nice voice, too . . . Now, what was I telling you about Mrs. Gage? She didn't like to be called by her first name, and I don't blame her. It sounded like some kind of old-fashioned phonograph."

"You said you did the driving. Did she still have her yellow sport coupe?"

"No, she sold that, and we took my navy blue se-

dan. She called it an old lady's car. I thought she was
being funny, but she was serious."

"And where would you two ladies drive?"

"Mostly to the mall—for lunch and to buy a few
things. She liked to eat at a health food place."

"Would you say she was happy at the Park of Pink
Sunsets?"

"I think so. She went on day trips in the activity
bus, and she liked to give talks at the clubhouse."

"What kind of talks?"

Mrs. Robinson had to think a moment. "Mmmm . . .
diet and exercise, music, art, the right way to
breathe . . ."

"Were these lectures well attended?"

"Well, to tell the truth, they weren't as popular as
the old movies on Thursday nights, but a lot of people
went because they didn't have anything better to do.
Also they had tea and cookies after the talk. Mrs.
Gage paid for the refreshments."

Qwilleran said, "I met Mrs. Gage only once and
that was for a short time. What was she like?"

"Oh, she was very interesting—not like the ones
that are forever talking about their ailments and the
grandchildren they never see. The park discourages
young visitors. You have to get a five-dollar permit before you can have a visitor under sixteen years of age,
and then it's only for forty-eight hours. Clayton likes
to spend the whole Christmas week with me, because
he doesn't like his stepmother. She's too serious, but
his granny laughs a lot. Maybe you've noticed," she
added with a giggle.

"How old is Clayton?"

"Just turned thirteen. He's a very bright boy with a
crazy sense of humor. We have a ball! Last Christmas

he figured out how to beat the system. When I picked him up at the airport, he was wearing a false beard! The sight of it just broke me up! He said I should introduce him to my neighbors as Dr. Clayton Robinson of Johns Hopkins. I went along with the gag. It's lucky that none of our neighbors have very good eyesight."

"Did he have his skateboard?" Qwilleran asked.

"Yow!" said Koko in a voice loud and clear.

"Do I hear a baby crying?" Mrs. Robinson asked.

"That's Koko, my Siamese cat. He's auditing this call."

"I used to have cats, and I'd love to have one now, but pets aren't allowed in the park. No cats, no dogs, not even birds!"

"How about goldfish?"

"Oh, that's funny! That's really funny!" she said. "I'm going to ask for a permit to have goldfish, and see what they say. They have no sense of humor. Last Christmas Clayton brought me a recording of a dog singing 'Jingle Bells.' Maybe you've heard it. 'Woof woof woof . . . woof woof woof!' "

"Yow!" Koko put in.

"Was Mrs. Gage amused?" Qwilleran asked.

"Not exactly. And the management of the park threw a fit!"

"Who are these people who issue five-dollar permits and throw fits?"

"Betty and Claude. He owns the park, and she's the manager. I don't think they're married, but they're always together. Don't get me wrong; they're really very nice if you play by the rules. Then there is Pete, the assistant, who takes over when they're out of town.

He's handy with tools and electricity and all that. He fixed my radio for nothing."

"How did Mrs. Gage react to all the restrictions?"

"Well, you see, she was quite friendly with Betty and Claude, and she got special treatment, sort of. They took her to the dog races a lot. She enjoyed their company. She liked younger people."

"Including Dr. Clayton Robinson?"

His grandmother responded to the mild quip with peals of laughter. "Clayton would love to meet you, Mr. . . ."

"Qwilleran. Did he get away with the beard trick?"

"Oh, we didn't hang around the park too much. We went to the beach and movies and video arcades and antique shops. Clayton collects old photos of funny-looking people and calls them his ancestors. Like, one is an old lady in bonnet and shawl; he says it's his great-grandfather in drag. Isn't that a hoot?"

"Your grandson has a great future, Mrs. Robinson."

"Call me Celia. Everybody does."

"Talking with you has been a pleasure, Celia. You've given me a graphic picture of Mrs. Gage's last home. Just one serious question: Does anyone have an idea why she took her life?"

"Well . . . we're not supposed to talk about it."

"Why not?"

"Well, this isn't the first suicide we've had, and Claude is afraid it'll reflect on the park. But Mr. Crocus and I have whispered about it, and we can't figure it out."

"Who is Mr. Crocus?" Qwilleran asked with renewed interest.

"He's a nice old gentleman. He plays the violin. He had a crush on Mrs. Gage and followed her around like a puppy. He misses her a lot. I hope he doesn't pine away and die. There's a big turnover here, you know, but there's always someone waiting to move in. They've already sold Mrs. Gage's house to a widower from Iowa."

"Considering all the restrictions, why is the park so desirable?"

"Mostly it's the security. You can call the office twenty-four hours a day, if you have an emergency. There's limousine service to medical clinics, although you pay for it. They recommend doctors and lawyers and tax experts, which is nice because we're all from other states. I'm from Illinois. Also, there are things going on at the clubhouse, and there's the activity bus. Would you like to see some snapshots of Mrs. Gage on one of our sightseeing trips? Maybe you could use them with your article."

Qwilleran said it was an excellent suggestion and asked her to mail them to him at the newspaper office.

"What was the name of it, did you say?"

"The Moose County Something."

"I love that! It's really funny!" she said with a chuckle. "I'll write it down."

"And do you mind if I call you again, Celia?"

"Gosh, no! It's fun being interviewed."

"Perhaps you'd like to see the obituary that ran in Wednesday's paper. I'll send two copies—one for Mr. Crusoe."

"Crocus," she corrected him. "Yes, he'd appreciate that a lot, Mr. Qwilleran."

"For your information, I'm usually called Qwill."

"Oh! Like in quill pen!"

"Except that it's spelled with a Qw."

"Yow!" said Koko.

"I'd better say goodnight and hang up, Celia. Koko wants to use the phone."

The last sound he heard from the receiver was a torrent of laughter. He turned to Koko. "That was Mrs. Robinson at the Park of Pink Sunsets."

The cat was fascinated by telephones. The ringing of the bell, the sound of a human voice coming from the instrument, and the mere fact that Qwilleran was conversing with an inanimate object seemed to stimulate his feline sensibilities. And he showed particular interest in the Florida grandmother with lively risibility. Qwilleran wondered why. He thought, Does he know something I don't? Koko's blue eyes were wearing their expression of profound wisdom.

"Treat!" Qwilleran announced, and there was the thud of galloping paws en route to the kitchen.

EIGHT

ON MONDAY MORNING Qwilleran was weighing the advantages of staying in bed versus the disadvantages of listening to a feline reveille outside his door. The decision was made for him when the telephone rang in the library. He hoisted himself out of bed, put his slippers on the wrong feet, and padded down the hall.

"Hey, Qwill!" came the familiar voice of Junior Goodwinter. "I need help! Tomorrow's election day, and we're gonna do a run-down on the candidates in today's paper. Would you handle one for us? It's an emergency. Everyone's pitching in, even the maintenance guy."

"Now's a helluva time to think of it," said Qwilleran in the grumpy mood that preceded his first cup of coffee. He looked at his watch and computed the length of time before the noon deadline.

"Don't blame me! Arch came barging in half an hour ago with the idea, and he's the boss."

"What's he been doing for the last two weeks, besides courting Mildred?"

"Listen, Qwill, all you have to do is question your candidate on the list of issues, but not on the phone. Personal contact."

Qwilleran growled something inaudible. There were three candidates for the mayoralty, seven for two vacancies on the city council, and six for one post on the county board. "Okay," he said, "of the sixteen incumbents, outsiders, nobodies, and perennial losers, which one is assigned to me?"

"George Breze."

"I might have known you'd give me an airhead."

"Stop at the office first to get a list of the issues. Deadline is twelve noon, so you'd better get hopping."

Fifteen minutes later, Qwilleran—unbreakfasted, unshaved, and only casually combed—reported to the newspaper office. Junior handed him a list. "Just tape the interview. We'll transcribe it."

"By the way," Qwilleran said, "I phoned Celia Robinson in Florida last night."

"Tell me about it later," the editor said as both phones on his desk started to ring.

George Breze was a one-man conglomerate who operated his sprawling empire from a shack on Sandpit Road, surrounded by rental trucks, mini-storage buildings, a do-it-yourself car wash, and junk cars waiting to be cannibalized. Usually there was merchandise for sale under a canvas canopy, such as pumpkins in October, Christmas trees in December, and sacks of sheep manure in the spring. His parking lot was always full on Saturday nights. Teens were admonished not to stop there on the way home from school.

Breze was one of two candidates opposing the incumbent mayor, the well-liked Gregory Blythe. On the way to interview him, Qwilleran stopped for breakfast at the Dimsdale Diner, where the number of pickups in the parking lot assured him that the coffee hour was in full swig. Inside the decrepit diner the usual bunch of men in feed caps gathered around a big table, smoking and shouting and laughing. They made room for Qwilleran after he had picked up two doughnuts and a mug of coffee at the counter.

"What's the latest weather report?" he asked.

"Heavy frost tonight," said a sheep rancher.

"Light snow later in the week," said a farm equipment dealer.

"The Big Snow is on the way," a trucker predicted.

"Who's our next mayor?" Qwilleran then asked.

"Blythe'll get in again. No contest," someone said. "He drinks a little, but who doesn't?"

"Do you see George Breze as a threat?"

The coffee drinkers erupted in vituperation, and the county agricultural agent said, "He's exactly what we need, a mayor with wide experience: loan shark, ticket fixer, ex-bootlegger, part-time bookie, tealeaf reader . . ."

The last triggered an explosion of laughter, and the group broke up.

Qwilleran caught the ear of the ag agent. "Do you know Gil Inchpot?"

"Sure do. He shipped out a week ago without harvesting his crop or fulfilling his contracts. He must've cracked up."

"Is there any chance of hiring fieldhands to dig his potatoes? The K Foundation has funds for economic emergencies."

"Don't know how you could swing it," said the agent, removing his cap to scratch his head. "Everybody's short of help, and they're racing to get their own crops in before frost."

"Inchpot always helped other people in a pinch," Qwilleran argued.

"That he did; I'll give him credit. Gimme time to think about it, Qwill, and pray it doesn't freeze tonight."

With this scant encouragement Qwilleran drove to the Breze campaign headquarters on Sandpit Road and found the candidate seated behind a scarred wooden desk in a ramshackle hut. He was wearing a blue nylon jacket and red feed cap.

"Come in! Come in! Sit down!" Breze shouted heartily, dusting off a chair with a rag he kept under his desk. "Glad you called before comin' so I could cancel my other appointments." He spoke in a loud, brisk voice. "Cuppa coffee?"

"No, thanks. I never drink when I'm working."

"What can I do you for?"

"Just answer a few questions, Mr. Breze." Qwilleran placed his tape recorder on the desk. "Why are you running for office?"

"I was born and brought up here. The town's been good to me. I owe it to the people," he answered promptly.

"Do you believe you'll be elected?"

"Absolutely! Everybody knows me and likes me. I went to school with 'em."

"What do you plan to accomplish if elected mayor?"

"I want to help the people with their problems and keep the streets clean. Clean streets are important."

"Would you favor light or heavy industry for economic development in Pickax?"

"Light or heavy, it don't matter. The important thing is to make jobs for the people and keep the streets clean."

"What do you think about the current controversy over sewers?"

"It'll straighten out. It always does," Breze said with a wave of the hand.

"There's talk about township annexation. Where do you stand on that issue?"

"I don't know about that. I don't think it's important. Jobs—that's what matters."

"Do you support the proposal to install parking meters in downtown Pickax?"

"Is that something new? I haven't heard about it. Free parking is best for the people."

"What do you think of the education system in Pickax?"

"Well, I went to school here, and I turned out all right." The candidate laughed lustily.

"Do you think the police department is doing a good job?"

"Absolutely! They're a good bunch of boys."

"In your opinion, what is the most important issue facing the city council?"

"That's hard to say. Myself, I'm gonna fight for clean streets."

Qwilleran thanked Breze for his cogent opinions

and delivered the tape to the paper. "Here's my interview with the Great Populist," he told Junior.

"Sorry to brush you off this morning," said the editor. "What did you want to tell me about Celia Robinson?"

"Only that I talked with her for half an hour and didn't get a single clue to your grandmother's motive."

"I know you like to get to the bottom of things, Qwill, but frankly, I've got too many other things on my mind. Jack and Pug are flying in tomorrow. The reading of the will is Wednesday in Wilmot's office. The memorial service is Thursday night. And every time the phone rings, I think it's Jody, ready to go to the hospital."

"Then I won't bother you," Qwilleran said, "but count on dinner Wednesday night, and let me know if there's anything I can do. I could drive Jody to the hospital if you're in a bind."

After stopping for lunch, he went home and parked under the porte cochere. Even before he approached the side door, he could hear the commotion indoors, and he knew he was in trouble. Two indignant Siamese were yowling in unison, pacing the floor and switching their tails in spasms of reproach.

"Oh, no!" he groaned, slapping his forehead in guilt. "I forgot your breakfast! A thousand apologies! Junior threw me a curve." He quickly emptied cans of boned chicken and solid-pack tuna on their plate. "Consider this a brunch. All you can eat!"

That was his second mistake. All the food went down, but half of it came up.

Qwilleran spent the afternoon preparing for his third performance of "The Big Burning," and when he drove to the Hotel Booze at seven o'clock, the parking lot was jammed. The Outdoor Club was in the café, enjoying boozeburgers, when he set up the stage in the meeting room. There were extra chairs, he noted, the front row being a mere six feet from the platform.

"Largest crowd they've ever had!" Hixie Rice exulted as she tested the sound and lights, "and I've got bookings for three more shows!"

A rumble of voices in the lobby announced the approaching audience, and Qwilleran ducked through the exit door, while Hixie shook hands with the officers of the club and seated the youngsters in the front rows.

With his ear to the door he heard the first notes of "Anitra's Dance" and counted thirty seconds before making an entrance and mounting the stage. "We interrupt this program to bring you a bulletin on the forest fires that are rapidly approaching Moose County . . ."

In the first three rows eyes and mouths were wide open. A small girl in the front row, whose feet could not reach the floor, was swinging them back and forth continuously. Her legs, in white leggings, were like a beacon in the dark room. When the old farmer's voice came from the speakers, the legs swung faster. The old farmer was saying:

"I come in from my farm west o' here, and I seen some terrible things! Hitched the hosses to the wagon and got my fambly here safe but never thought we'd make it! We come through fire rainin' down out of the sky like hailstones! Smoke everywhere! Couldn't see the road, hardly. Hay in the wagon caught fire, and we had to throw it out and rattle along on the bare boards. We picked up one lad not more'n eight year old, carryin' a baby—all that were left of his fambly. His shoes, they was burned clean off his feet!"

The white legs never stopped swinging, back and forth like a pendulum: left, right, left, right. Qwilleran, aware of the movement through the corner of his eye, found himself being mesmerized. He had to fight to maintain his concentration on the announcer's script:

"Here in Pickax it's dark as midnight. Winds have suddenly risen to hurricane fury. Great blasts of heat and cinders are smothering the city. We can hear screams of frightened horses, then a splintering crash as a great tree is uprooted or the wind wrenches the roof from a house. Wagons are being lifted like toys and blown away! . . . There's a red glare in the sky! . . . *Pickax is in flames!*"

The red light flicked on. Coughing and choking, the announcer rushed from the studio.

In the hallway beyond the exit door Qwilleran leaned against the wall, recovering from the scene he had just played. A moment later, Hixie joined him. "They love it!" she said. "Especially the part about the boy with his shoes burned off. The kids identify."

"Did you see that one swinging her legs in the front row?" Qwilleran asked irritably.

"She was spellbound!"

"Well, those white legs were putting a spell on me! I was afraid I'd topple off my chair."

"Did you hear the girl crying when you told about the little baby? She created quite a disturbance."

"I don't care if the whole audience cries!" Qwilleran snapped. "Get those white legs out of the front row!"

When he made his entrance for Scene Two, an instant hush fell upon the room. Surreptitiously he glanced at the front row; the white legs had gone.

"After a sleepless night, Pickax can see daylight. The smoke is lifting, but the acrid smell of burning is everywhere, and the scene is one of desolation in every direction. Only this brick courthouse is left standing, a haven for hundreds of refugees. Fortunately a sudden wind from the lake turned back the flames, and Mooseville and Brrr have been saved."

Qwilleran had not seen the last of the white legs, however. Halfway through Scene Two he was interviewing the Irish innkeeper by phone: "Sir, what news do you hear from Sawdust City?"

A thick Irish brogue came from the speakers: "It's gone! All gone! Every stick of it, they're tellin'. And there's plenty of sad tales this mornin'. One poor chap from Sawdust City walked into town carryin' the remains of his wife and little boy in a pail—a ten-quart pail! Wouldja believe it, now?"

At that tense moment, Qwilleran's peripheral vision picked up a pair of white legs walking toward the stage. What the devil is she doing? he thought.

The girl climbed onto the stage, crossed to the exit door at the rear, and went to the restroom.

The radio announcer went on. "Many tales of heroism and fortitude have been reported. In West Kirk thirteen persons went down a well and stood in three feet of water for five hours. In Dimsdale a mother saved her three children by burying them in a plowed field until the danger had passed . . ."

The white legs returned, taking a shortcut across the stage. It didn't faze the audience. At the end of the show they applauded wildly, and the president of the Outdoor Club made Qwilleran and Hixie honorary members. Then she fielded questions while he packed the gear, surrounded by the under-ten crowd. They were fascinated by the tape player, lights, cables, and other equipment being folded into compact carrying cases.

"I liked it when you talked on the telephone," one said.

"How do you know all that stuff?" another asked.

"Why didn't everybody get in a bus and drive to Mooseville or Brrr to be saved?"

"How could he get his wife and little boy in a pail?"

"I liked the red light."

One three-year-old girl stood silently sucking her thumb and staring at Qwilleran's moustache.

"Did you like the show?" he asked her.

She nodded soberly before taking the thumb from her mouth. "What was it about?" she asked earnestly.

He was relieved when Nancy Fincher came to the stage. "Mr. Qwilleran, it was wonderful! I never liked history before, but you made it so real, I cried."

"Thank you," he said. "As soon as I put these cases in my car, may I invite you for a drink in the café?"

"Let me carry one," she said, grabbing the largest of the three. Delicate though she seemed, she handled the heavy case like a trifle.

When they were established on the wobbly barstools, he asked, "Will you have something to eat? I'm always famished after the show. 'The Big Burning' burns up a lot of energy."

"Just a cola for me," she said. "I had supper here, and half of my burger is in a doggie bag in my truck."

Qwilleran ordered a boozeburger with fries. "You mentioned that potatoes are a complicated crop to raise," he said to Nancy. "I always thought they'd be a cinch."

Nancy shook her head soberly. "That's what everybody thinks. But first you have to know what kind to plant—for the conditions you're working with and the market you're selling to. Different markets want large or small, whiteskins or redskins, bakers or boilers or fryers."

"You seem to know a lot about the subject."

"I grew up with potatoes."

"Don't stop. Tell me more." He was concentrating on the burger, which was enormously thick.

"Well, first you have to have the right kind of soil, and it has to be well drained. Then you have to know the right time to plant and the right kind of fertilizer. Then you worry about crop diseases and weeds and insects and rain. You need enough rain but not too much. And then you have to gamble on the right time to harvest."

"I have a new respect for potato farmers . . . and potatoes," he said.

A soft look suffused Nancy's face. "When Mom was alive, we used to dig down with our fingers and take out the small new tubers very carefully, so as not to interfere with the others. Then we'd have creamed new potatoes with new peas."

Gary Pratt shuffled up to them. "Are you folks ready for another drink or anything?"

"Not for me," she said. "I have to stop and check Pop's mailbox and then go home and take care of my dogs. I've been working at the clinic all day."

The two men watched her go, lugging her oversized shoulderbag.

"Quite a gal," Gary said. "She has that tiny little

voice, and you think she doesn't have much on the ball, but the thing of it is, she's a terrific racer, and she really knows dogs. I tried to date her when she came back from Alaska, but her old man didn't like my haircut. So what? I didn't like the dirt under his fingernails. Anyway, Nancy still had a thing for Dan Fincher. Women think he's the strong, silent type, but I think he's a klutz."

"Interesting if true," said Qwilleran, making light of the gossip. "What's the latest on the weather?"

"Heavy frost tonight. Snow on the way."

On the trip back to Pickax Qwilleran drove through farming country, where the bright headlights of tractors in the fields meant that farmers were working around the clock to beat the frost. He felt a twinge of remorse. If he had acted sooner, the Klingenschoen clout might have saved Gil Inchpot's crop.

He was carrying a sample of boozeburger for the Siamese. "After my faux pas this morning," he told them, "I owe you one." Later, the three of them were in the library, reading *Robinson Crusoe,* when the sharp ring of the telephone made all of them jump.

Qwilleran guessed it would be Junior, announcing that Jody had given birth; or it would be Polly, inquiring about the show in Brrr; or it would be Arch Riker, saying that Breze was suing the paper because the other candidates sounded better than he did.

"Hello?" he said, ready for anything.

"Mr. Qwilleran," said a breathless voice, "Gary gave me your number. I hope you don't mind."

"That's all right."

"I discovered something when I got to Pop's house, and I notified the police, but I wanted to tell you because you've been so kind and so interested."

"What was it, Nancy?"

"When I got to the farm, I cut my hand on the mailbox pretty bad, so I went indoors for some antiseptic and a bandage. And in a medicine cabinet I saw Pop's dentures in a glass of water. He would never leave home without his dentures!"

Qwilleran combed his moustache with his fingertips as he thought of the partial denture in the desk drawer. He glanced at the Siamese. Yum Yum was pedicuring her left hind foot; Koko was sitting there looking wise.

NINE

THERE WAS HEAVY frost in Moose County that night.
The tumble-down hamlet of Wildcat, the quaint resort
town of Mooseville, the affluent estates of West Middle Hummock, the condominiums in Indian Village,
the vacation homes in Purple Point, the stone canyons
of downtown Pickax, the mansions of Goodwinter
Boulevard, the abandoned mineshafts, the airport ...
all looked mystically hoary in the first morning light.
Qwilleran felt moody as he drank his morning coffee.
There was the usual letdown after the excitement and
challenge of doing a show, plus a gnawing regret
about the Inchpot crop. Hundreds of acres of potatoes
had been lost—after being scientifically planted, fer-
tilized, weeded, sprayed, and prayed over. And now,

after hearing Nancy's grim news about the dentures, Qwilleran felt real concern about Gil Inchpot himself.

He was somewhat gladdened, therefore, when Lori Bamba called to ask if her husband could deliver some letters and checks for signing. Nick Bamba was an engineer at the state prison; he shared Qwilleran's interest in crime and the mystery that often surrounds it. Whenever Qwilleran mentioned his suspicions and hunches to his friends, Polly remonstrated and Riker taunted him, but Nick always took him seriously.

He was a young man with alert black eyes that observed everything. "Someone ran a truck over your curb," he said upon arrival.

"Those blasted leaf blowers! They're a slap-happy crew!" Qwilleran complained. "Did you vote this morning?"

"I was first in line. There was a good turnout in Mooseville because of the millage issue. The voters don't get excited about the candidates; one's no better than another. But propose increased millage, and they're all at the polls to vote no. Why don't you run for county office, Qwill? You could make waves."

"I'd rather see Koko's name on the ballot . . . Will you have coffee or hot cider?"

"I'll try the cider." Nick handed over a folder of correspondence. "Lori says you're getting a lot of fan mail since your 'Big Burning' preview. The Mooseville Chamber of Commerce wants to book the show after the holidays."

"I trust the members are all over eight years old," Qwilleran said testily.

They carried their cider mugs into the library, and

Nick remarked, "I see you've got an elevator. Does it work?"

"Definitely. We used it at the preview of our show. Adam Dingleberry was here in his wheelchair."

At that point Koko walked into the library with deliberate step and rose on his hind legs to rattle the closet doorknob.

"What's old slyboots got on his mind?" Nick asked.

"This is the only closet in the house that's locked, and it drives him bughouse," Qwilleran said. "All the closets are filled with junk, and Koko spends his spare time digging for buried treasure."

"Has he found any gold coins or diamond rings?"

"Not as yet. Mostly stale cigars and old shoelaces."

"Want me to pick the lock for you? I'll bring my tools next time I'm in town."

"Sure. I'm curious about this closet myself."

"I suppose you heard on the radio about the missing potato farmer, Gil Inchpot. Police are investigating his disappearance ten days ago."

"I heard something about it," Qwilleran mentioned.

"He's quite a successful farmer, you know. I never met the guy, but his daughter was married to a deputy sheriff I know, Dan Fincher. It didn't last long; her father broke it up."

"Why? Do you know?"

Nick shrugged. "Dan isn't very big on particulars. I know that Gil Inchpot is well liked at the Crossroads Tavern and at the farm co-op, but Dan says he's a bully at home."

Qwilleran reached for Nick's cider mug. "Fill 'er up?"

"No, thanks. I've got errands to do—prison business."

"Do you like apples at your house? I've got some you can take home to the kids."

Nick left, carrying a brown paper bag, and after Qwilleran had signed his letters and checks, he took another sackful to the newspaper office.

"I'll trade these for a cup of coffee," he told Junior. "How's everything going?"

"Jack and Pug have arrived. They're staying at the New Pickax Hotel. Jody doesn't feel like having company."

"That's wise. Will she come to dinner tomorrow night? Polly is joining us."

"Why don't you make the reservation for six?" said the expectant father, "and we'll see how she feels."

"When is the will being read?"

"Ten-thirty tomorrow morning. Keep your fingers crossed."

While the will was being read in Pender Wilmot's office, Qwilleran was at home, eating an apple and estimating the extent of Euphonia Gage's estate. No doubt she had cashed in heavily when she liquidated her jewels, real estate, fine paintings, and family heirlooms. No doubt her late husband, being financially savvy and not entirely honest, had left her some blue-chip securities. Her recent economies, such as living in a mobile home and wearing seashell jewelry, were no more peculiar than his own preference for driving a used car and pumping his own gas. And, nearing the end of her life, she may have been moved by a nobly generous impulse to provide handsomely for her six great-grandchildren and the one yet unborn.

That evening, his guests were late in arriving at the Old Stone Mill. He and Polly sat waiting and talking about the election results. As everyone expected, Gregory Blythe had been re-elected. He was an investment counselor, a good administrator, and a former high school principal with Goodwinter blood on his mother's side. The public had forgotten the scandal that ousted him from the education system in Pickax, and he was always sober when he conducted city council meetings.

After half an hour Polly asked, "What do you suppose has happened to them? Junior is always so punctual. Perhaps he's taken Jody to the hospital."

"I'll phone their house," Qwilleran said.

To his surprise, Jody answered. "He left about half an hour ago to pick up Pug and Jack," she said. "I decided not to go. I hope you don't mind." She sounded depressed.

"Do you feel all right, Jody?"

"Oh, yes, I'm all right, considering . . ."

When the hostess conducted the tardy guests to the table, Qwilleran rose to greet three unhappy faces: Pug as distraught as a Montana rancher who has had to shoot her favorite horse; Jack as glum as a California advertising executive who has lost his major client; Junior as indignant as an editor who is being sued for libel.

Introductions were made, chairs were pulled out, napkins were unfolded, and Polly tried to make polite conversation: "Are you comfortable at the hotel? . . . How do you like Montana? . . . Have you adjusted to sunny California?" Her efforts failed to elevate the mood.

"What would you like to drink?" Qwilleran asked. "Champagne? A cocktail? Pug, what is your choice?"

"Bourbon and water," she said, pouting.

"Scotch margarita," said Jack grimly.

"Rye on the rocks," said Junior, fidgeting in his chair.

While they were waiting to be served, Qwilleran talked about the weather for five minutes: the weather last month, the outlook for the rest of this month, the prediction for next month . . . all of this to fill the void until the drinks arrived. Then he raised his glass. "Would anyone like to propose a toast?"

"To bad news!" Junior blurted.

"To a royal rip-off!" said Jack.

"Oh, dear," Polly murmured.

"Sorry to hear that," Qwilleran said.

Scowling, Jack said, "Pug and I flew thousands of miles just to be told that she left us a hundred dollars apiece! I'm damned mad! She was a spiteful old woman!"

"Surprising!" Qwilleran turned to Junior for corroboration.

"Same here," said the younger brother, "only I didn't have to cross the continent to get the shaft."

"I had the impression," Qwilleran remarked, "that your grandmother was a generous person."

"Sure," said Pug. "She put us all through college, but there were strings attached. We didn't know it gave her the privilege to direct our lives, dictate our careers, choose our hobbies, approve our marriages! She was furious when Jack went to the coast and I married a rancher. For a wedding present she sent us a wooden nutcracker."

Polly asked, "Can anyone explain the reason for her attitude?"

"If you're looking for excuses, I can't think of any."

Junior said, "Here's a typical example of her

thoughtlessness. Her ancestors were pioneer doctors here, and she inherited a beautiful black walnut box of surgical knives and saws and other instruments, all pre–Civil War. Why didn't she give them to the Museum of Local History, where they'd mean something? Instead she sold them with everything else."

"She was a selfish egocentric, that's all," said Jack.

"How about your grandfather?" Qwilleran asked. "What was he like?"

"Kind of jolly, although he wasn't around much."

"Our paternal grandmother was different," said Pug. "She wasn't rich, but she was warm and cuddly and loving."

"And she made the best fudge!" Jack added.

There was a nostalgic silence at the table until Qwilleran cleared his throat preparatory to introducing a sensitive subject. "If you're all left out of the will, who are the beneficiaries?"

The three young people looked at each other, and Junior said bitterly, "The Park of Pink Sunsets! They get everything—to build, equip, and maintain a health spa for the residents. She revised her will after she got to Florida."

Polly said, "It's not unusual for the elderly to forget family and friends and leave everything to strangers they meet in their final days. That's why wills are so often contested."

"Well, if it's any consolation," Qwilleran said in an effort to brighten the occasion, "Junior owns the contents of the locked closet in the library, which may be full of Grandpa Gage's gold coins and Grandma Gage's jewelry."

No one was amused, and Junior replied, "There's

nothing in that closet but her private papers, and I'm instructed to burn them."

Then Jack said, "If anyone thinks we're sticking around for the memorial service tomorrow night, they can stuff it! We've changed our flight reservations."

"That hotel," Pug said, "is the worst I've ever experienced! I can't wait to get out of this tank town!"

Qwilleran said, "I think we should all have another drink and order dinner." He signaled for service.

"I second the motion," Junior said. "Enough gnashing of teeth! Let's enjoy our food, at least . . . How are your cats, Qwill?" To his sister and brother he explained, "Qwill has a couple of Siamese."

Polly said, "Qwill, dear, tell them about Koko and the cleaning closet."

He hesitated, trying to recollect the incident in all of its absurdity. "Well, you see, where I live in the summer, there's a closet for Mrs. Fulgrove's prodigious collection of waxes, polishes, detergents, spray bottles, and squirt cans."

"Is that woman still cleaning houses?" Pug asked. "I thought she'd be dead by now."

"She's still cleaning and still complaining about cathairs. I always leave the house to avoid her harangues. One day I came home after the dear lady had left and found the male cat missing! But the female was huddled in front of the cleaning closet, staring at the door handle. I yanked open the door, and out billowed a white cloud. It filled almost the whole closet, obliterating shelves, cans, and bottles. And above it all was Koko, sitting on the top shelf, looking nonchalant. Mrs. Fulgrove had accidentally shut him in the closet, and he had accidentally activated the can of foam carpet cleaner."

"Or purposely," Junior added.

"I reported the story in my column, and the manufacturer sent me enough foam cleaner to do all the rugs in Moose County."

After that interlude, everyone was somewhat relaxed though not really happy, and Qwilleran was relieved when the meal came to an end. As the party was leaving, Junior handed him an envelope.

"Forgot to give you this, Qwill. It came to the office today, addressed to you."

It was a pink envelope with a Florida postmark and the official logo of the Park of Pink Sunsets. He slid it into his pocket.

On the way home to Goodwinter Boulevard, Qwilleran said to Polly, "Well, the mood at our table was not very favorable for the consumption of food. I apologize for involving you."

"It could hardly be called your fault, Qwill. How were you to know? The entire situation is regrettable."

"I don't suppose you want to attend the memorial service tomorrow night."

"I wouldn't miss it!" Polly's tone was more bitter than sweet.

Qwilleran dropped her off at her carriage house, saying he would pick her up the next evening. He was in a hurry to open the letter from Florida.

Sitting at his desk he slit the pink envelope—a chunky one with double postage—and out fell some snapshots as well as a note. Celia had remembered how to spell his name; that was in her favor.

Dear Mr. Qwilleran,
    I enjoyed talking to you on the phone. Here are

the snaps of Mrs. Gage with some other people from the park. We were on a bus trip. I'm the giddy-looking one in Mickey Mouse ears. That's Mr. Crocus with Mrs. Gage and a stone lion. Hope you can use some of these with the article you're writing.

Yours very truly,
Celia Robinson

Spreading the snapshots on the desk, Qwilleran found the diminutive Euphonia neatly dressed in a lavender pantsuit and wide-brimmed hat, while her companions sported T-shirts with the Pink Sunset logo splashed across the front. Also conservatively dressed in tropical whites was an old man with a shock of white hair; he and the stone lion could have passed for brothers.

The Siamese, always interested in something new, were on the desktop, sitting comfortably on their briskets and idly observing. Then, apparently without provocation, Koko rose to his feet with a guttural monosyllable and sniffed the pictures. There was something about the glossy surface of photographs that always attracted him. Studiously he passed his nose over every one of the Florida pictures and flicked his tongue at a couple of them.

"No!" Qwilleran said sharply, worrying about the chemicals used in processing.

"Yow!" Koko retorted in a scolding tone of his own and then left the room. Yum Yum trailed after him without so much as a backward look at the man whose lap she so frequently commandeered.

An uneasy feeling crept across Qwilleran's upper lip, and he patted his moustache as he examined the snapshots the cat had licked. Sandpaper tongue and potent saliva had left rough spots on the surface. In both of them Euphonia looked happy and pert, posed with a yellow sports car in one shot and with the Pink Sunset tour bus in the other. More important than the damage, however, was the realization that two of her companions looked vaguely familiar. He had no idea who they were or where he had met them or under what circumstances.

TEN

Thursday was bright and clear, although Wetherby Goode reminded his listeners that November was the month of the Big Snow, a threat that annually hung over the heads of Moose County residents like a Damoclean icicle.

Qwilleran said to Koko, "Would you like to take a walk? This may be your last chance before snow flies. I'll get the leash."

Yum Yum, whose vocabulary included the word "leash," immediately disappeared, but Koko purred and rolled on his side while the harness was being buckled around his middle. Then, on the back porch, he checked out the spots where the nefarious Oh Jay had left his scent. Next, he led the way down the back steps to a paved area where the last few leaves of autumn were waiting to be pawed, batted, chased, and chewed. While Koko was enjoying these simple pleasures, Qwilleran became aware of a familiar figure scrambling through the shrubs on the lot line.

"If you're looking for Oh Jay," he said to the attorney's son, "he's not here."

It appeared, however, that this was a social call. "It's gonna snow," Timmie said.

"So they say," Qwilleran replied, making no attempt to continue the conversation.

The boy looked critically at Koko. "Why is he so skinny?"

"He's not skinny. He's a Siamese."

"Oh." This was followed by a pause, then: "I can stand on my head."

"Good for you!"

There was another long pause as Timmie spread his arms wide and balanced on one leg. Finally he said, "You should marry the lady that lives in the back. Then you could live in one house, and she wouldn't have to take out the trash."

"Why don't you go and stand on your head?" Qwilleran asked.

"We're gonna move."

"What?"

"We're gonna move away from here."

"I sincerely hope you're planning to take Oh Jay with you."

"I'm gonna go to a new school and ride the school bus and have fun with the kids."

"Why do you want to leave a nice neighborhood like this?"

"My dad says some dumb fool bought the house."

"Excuse me," Qwilleran said. "I have to make a phone call." He hurried up the back steps, pulling a reluctant cat.

Ringing Junior at the office he said, "Have you heard the news? Another house on the boulevard has been sold. Pender Wilmot's. That makes two of them, side by side. What do you make of that?"

"Who bought it?" Junior demanded with suspicion. "Was it the realtor in Chicago?"

"My six-year-old informant wasn't specific."

"I hope this doesn't turn out to be anything detrimental to the neighborhood, like one of those cults or a front for something illegal."

"You don't need to worry about anything like that— not in Pickax," Qwilleran assured him, "but I admit it piques the curiosity . . . Well, get back to work. I'll see you tonight at the memorial service. Do you know why it's being held at the theatre instead of the Old Stone Church?"

"That's the way she wanted it, and Grandma never did anything in the ordinary way."

The K Theatre, converted from the former Klingen-schoen mansion, shared the Park Circle with the public library, courthouse, and two churches. Shortly before eight o'clock on Thursday evening, more than a hundred residents of Moose County converged on the theatre, their expressions ranging from respectful to avidly curious. In dress they were less sweatery than usual, denoting the solemnity of the occasion.

When Qwilleran and Polly arrived in the lobby, they were greeted by two young members of the Theatre Club, who smiled guardedly and handed them programs. He said to Polly, "According to Junior, Eupho-

nia planned this service down to the last detail, and I
suspect the ushers were instructed to smile with
sweetness and respect and not too much sadness."

After a glance at the program Polly said, "This is
not a memorial service! It's a concert!"

In Memoriam

EUPHONIA ROFF GAGE

Piano prelude: Six Gnossiennes ....*Satie*
  1. *Adagio*..*Albinoni*
  2. *Sonnet XXX*.............................*Shakespeare*
  3. *Pavane pour une Infante Défunte* .....*Ravel*
  4. *Renouncement* ....*Meynell*
  5. *En Sourdine (Verlaine)* ....*Fauré*
  6. *Pas de Deux*.............................*anonymous*
  7. *Duet for Flutes* ....*Telemann*
  8. *Non sum qualis eram bonae*
      sub regno Cynarae.......................*Dowson*
  9. *Adagio from Symphonie*
      Concertante.......................................*Spohr*
 10. *Maestoso from*
      Symphony No. 3 ....*Saint-Saëns*

Polly said in a voice unusually sharp, "Don't you
think it's a trifle too precious? Number Five is a
French art song. Number Eight . . . only Euphonia
would use the Latin title for 'Cynara.' It's her last
gasp of cultural snobbery. And what do you think of
Number Three?"

"Try saying it fast three times," he said with a lack
of reverence.

Polly threw him a disapproving glance. "You're being flip. I'm wondering if the reference to a dead princess means that she considered herself royalty."

Carol Lanspeak, a trustee of the theatre, hurried up to them. "I think you're in for some surprises tonight. Junior asked me to handle the staging because their baby is due momentarily. Larry's doing the readings, and we rehearsed the entire program to get the timing right. Euphonia left instructions for the stage set, lighting, programs, everything! Such a perfectionist!"

Qwilleran reached into his pocket for an envelope of snapshots. "One of her Florida neighbors sent these. You might like to see how she looked toward the end."

"Why, she looks wonderful!" Carol exclaimed after examining them. "Wouldn't you know she'd choose to go out while she was looking wonderful?"

"Do you recognize anyone else in the pictures?"

"No, I don't . . . Should I?"

"I thought some of them might be from Moose County. Snowbirds tend to flock together."

Carol and Polly conferred and agreed that they were all strangers. "But here comes Homer. Ask him," Carol suggested.

The aged Homer Tibbitt was entering with his brisk but awkward gait, accompanied by his attentive new wife. During his career as a teacher and principal he had shepherded several generations through the school system and claimed to know everyone in two counties.

He changed glasses to study the snapshots. "Sorry. I can't identify a soul except Euphonia."

"Let me see them," said Mrs. Tibbitt.

"You don't know anyone here," he said with impatience. "You never even met Euphonia . . . Rhoda's from Lockmaster," he explained to the others, as if she were from the Third World.

"Homer likes to put on his irascible-old-man act," his wife said sweetly.

"I believe it's time to go upstairs," Carol suggested. "Take the elevator, Homer."

Two matching stairways led to the auditorium entrance on the upper level, from which the amphitheatre seating sloped down to a dark stage. A pianist in the orchestra pit was playing the moody, mysterious prelude specified by the deceased.

"Who's that at the piano?" Qwilleran asked Polly.

"The new music director for the schools. I believe she taught in Lockmaster."

He admired anyone who could play the piano and found the pianist strikingly attractive. When the prelude ended, she moved to a seat in front of them, and her perfume made a strong statement. Polly wafted it away with her program.

A hush fell on the audience as the house lights slowly dimmed. There were a few dramatic seconds of total darkness before two glimmers of light appeared. One spotlighted a bouquet of purple and white flowers on a pedestal, stage right. The other, stage center, illuminated a thronelike chair on the seat of which was a wide-brimmed straw hat with a band of purple velvet. Flung across the high chairback was a filmy scarf in shades of lavender.

Qwilleran and Polly exchanged glances. He could read her mind: The pedestal! The throne! The royal purple!

The theatre had an excellent sound system, and from hidden speakers came the haunting music of Albinoni, the wistful yearning of the solo violin underscored by the heartbeat of the cello. The audience listened and stared, as if Euphonia herself might glide onto the stage. Other instruments joined in, and the volume swelled, then faded, leaving only the last searching notes of the violin.

The spotlights disappeared, and a beam of light focused on a lectern at stage left, where Larry Lanspeak stood waiting. His rich voice gripped the audience:

*"When to the sessions of sweet silent thought
I summon up remembrance of things past . . ."*

Qwilleran glanced questioningly at Polly, who was frowning as if unable to connect the woman she had known with the poem she was hearing. He wondered about it himself and listened for clues to Euphonia's past and possibly a clue to her suicide motive.

*"Then can I drown an eye, unused to flow,
For precious friends hid in death's dateless night,
And weep afresh love's long since cancelled woe."*

Again the spotlights flooded the throne and flowers as Ravel's slow dance painted its melancholy picture. Then came the poem *"I must not think of thee,"* followed by the French song "In Secret." Qwilleran deduced that Euphonia was mourning a lost lover, and it was not Grandpa Gage. The anonymous poem confirmed his theory:

*"Two white butterflies
Kissing in mid-air,
Then darting apart*

To flutter like lost petals,
Drifting together again
For a quivering moment in the sun,
Yet wandering away
In a white flurry of indecision,
Meeting once more
On the upsweep of a breeze,
Dancing a delirious pas de deux
Before parting forever,
One following the wind,
The other trembling with folded wings
On this cold rock."

After the "Duet for Flutes" Qwilleran's suspicions were reinforced by the poem *"I have been faithful to thee, Cynara, in my fashion."* He could hear sniffling in the audience, and even Polly was dabbing her eyes, a reaction that made him uncomfortable; he knew she was remembering her own past.

The program was building to its conclusion. A screen had been lowered at the rear of the stage, and when the "Adagio" for flute and harp began its flights of melody, the image of a dancer appeared, moving languidly across the screen, arching her back, fluttering her scarfs, twirling, twisting, sinking to her knees with bowed head, rising with head thrown back and arms flung wide. It was a joyous celebration. The dancer's white hair was twisted into a ballerina's topknot and tied with purple ribbon.

There had been gasps at first, but when the video ended, there was silence—and utter darkness. Then the stage burst into brilliant light as the crashing chords of the Organ Symphony stunned the audience. The majestic music rocked the auditorium in triumph—until one final prolonged chord stopped dead, leaving a desolate emptiness in the hall.

"Whew!" Qwilleran said as the house lights were turned up. Among the audience a gradual murmur arose as groups began to wander to the exit. In the lobby friends were meeting, asking questions, fumbling for appropriate comments.

Arch Riker said, "That was quite a blast-off!"

Carol Lanspeak informed everyone that the flower arrangement—dahlias, glads, lavender asters, orchids, and bella donna lilies—had been flown in from Chicago.

Susan Exbridge, the antique dealer, explained that the carved highback chair had been in the foyer of the Gage mansion and she had bought it from Euphonia for $2,000.

Lisa Compton wondered how Euphonia's knees could continue to function so well at eighty-eight.

Qwilleran and Polly were speaking with the Comptons when the pianist joined their group, and Lyle Compton introduced her as June Halliburton, the new music director from Lockmaster. "Now if they'll only send us their football coach," he said, "we'll be in good shape."

Her red hair was cut shorter and curlier than the accepted style in Moose County, and her perfume was a scent not sold at Lanspeak's Department Store. With playful hazel eyes fixed on Qwilleran's moustache, she said, "I enjoyed your historical show at Mooseland High School. How did you make your choice of music for the interludes?"

"Just some cassettes I happened to have in my meager collection," he replied.

"They worked beautifully! If I wanted to nitpick,

though, I could object that 'Anitra's Dance' had not been written in 1869 when your imaginary radio station played it."

"Don't tell anyone," he said. "They'll never guess. Actually I doubt whether anyone has even noticed the music."

"I noticed it," said Polly crisply. "I thought the 'Francesca da Rimini' excerpts were perfect for the fire scene. I could visualize flames raging, winds howling, and buildings crashing."

Lyle said, "June is going to implement Hilary VanBrooks's theories about music education. You ought to write something about that in your column, Qwill."

"Okay, we'll talk," he said to her. "Where is your office located?"

"Why don't you come to my apartment in Indian Village where I have all my music?" she suggested engagingly.

Polly flushed, and Qwilleran could feel the heat waves coming from her direction. He said, "What we really need is to sit down at a desk and discuss the VanBrooks Method."

Lisa plunged in diplomatically. "Before I forget, Qwill, would you be willing to do 'The Big Burning' for the Senior Care Facility?"

"Sounds okay to me," he said gratefully. "When would you want it?"

"Before Thanksgiving."

"Call Hixie Rice to book it."

On the way out of the theatre he and Polly were intercepted by Junior Goodwinter. "What did you think of Grandma's send-off?"

"Thought-provoking, to say the least," Qwilleran replied.

"Want to hear something interesting? The attorney is questioning Grandma's will! He's talking about mental instability and undue influence."

"Does he plan to sue?"

"I don't know yet. It'll depend on the value of the estate, but it's a distinct possibility. She must have been worth millions around the time she liquidated everything."

On the way home Qwilleran and Polly were silent, for their own reasons. When she invited him to her apartment for dessert and coffee, he declined, saying he had work to do. It was the first time he had ever turned down such an invitation, and she regarded him with mild anxiety. She may have guessed he was about to call another woman.

ELEVEN

WHEN QWILLERAN RETURNED from Euphonia's memorial extravaganza, he found the Siamese on the library sofa, curled into a round pillow of fur. One raised a sleepy head; the other twitched an ear irritably. "Excuse me for disturbing you," he said as he turned on the desk lamp. "I need to make a phone call."

They exchanged a few perfunctory licks, disengaged their entwined extremities, struggled to their feet, yawned widely, and stretched vertically and horizontally before leaving the room with purposeful step. He knew where they were going: to the kitchen to lap a tongueful of water and gaze hopefully at their empty plate.

He gave them a few crunchy morsels and prepared coffee for himself before placing his call to Florida. When a woman's voice answered, he said, "This is Dr. Clayton Robinson calling from Johns Hopkins." He changed his voice to sound like a thirteen-year-old changing his voice to sound like an M.D.

"Clayton!" she cried. "Does your mother know you're calling long distance? Hang up before you get in trouble!"

"April Fool!" he said hastily. "This is Jim Qwilleran phoning from Pickax. I hope I'm not calling you too late."

"Oh, what a relief!" said Clayton's grandmother, laughing at her gullibility. "No, it's not too late for me. The rest of the park thinks nine o'clock is midnight, but I stay up till all hours, reading and eating chocolate-covered cherries."

"What do you read?"

"Mostly crime and undercover stuff. I buy second-hand paperbacks at half price and then send them to Clayton. We like the same kind of books pretty much, although I could never get interested in science fiction."

"How's the weather down there?"

"Lovely! Have you had snow yet?"

"No, but they say the Big One is on the way. I want to thank you, Celia, for sending the snapshots. I took them to Mrs. Gage's memorial program tonight, and her friends remarked how well she looked. Shall I send you a copy of the program?"

"Oh, yes, please! And would it be too much trouble to send one for Mr. Crocus?"

"Not at all. Perhaps he'd also like one of her books as a keepsake. There's one here on correct breathing."

"He'd be overjoyed! That's very kind of you. He misses her a lot. I think there was something cooking between those two."

"Is Mr. Crocus the man with a magnificent head of white hair?"

"That's him. He plays the violin."

"You have some interesting-looking people in the park. Who's the couple standing with Mrs. Gage in front of a gigantic flowering shrub? They're wearing Pink Sunset T-shirts."

"They're new in the park—from Minnesota, I think. The bush is a hibiscus. Beautiful, isn't it? I never saw one so large."

"And who's the attractive woman at the wheel of the yellow convertible?"

"That's Betty, our manager. Isn't she glamorous? She sells cosmetics on the side. They're too expensive for me, but Mrs. Gage bought the works, and she really did look terrific."

Qwilleran said, "The car looks like the one she bought in Pickax before she left."

"That's right. She sold it to Betty—or maybe gave it to her. They were very chummy, like mother and daughter."

"Yow!" said Koko, who had ambled back into the library.

"I hear your cat."

"I like the picture of you in Mickey Mouse ears, Celia. Not everyone can wear them with so much panache."

She responded with a trill of pleasure. "I don't know what that means exactly, but it sounds good."

Qwilleran said, "I'm looking at a shot of your activity bus with the pink sunset painted on the side.

There's a middle-aged man with his arm around Mrs. Gage, and they're both looking unusually happy."

"That's Claude, the owner of the park. He was very fond of her. He feels terrible about what she did. Everybody does."

"The Sunsetters impress me as one big happy family," he observed.

"Oh, sure. As long as you don't break the rules, everything's hunky-dory, but don't put pink plastic flamingoes on your lawn or all heck will break loose!"

"This Claude and Betty—are they the ones who used to take Mrs. Gage to the dog track?"

"Yes. She wanted me to drive her there, but the crowds are humongous, you know, and not only that but I don't believe in gambling. I couldn't afford to take chances, for one thing. And then it hurts me to see those beautiful dogs being used that way. I've heard that they're killed after racing a few years."

Koko had been moving closer to the phone and was now breathing heavily into the mouthpiece. Qwilleran pushed him away. "Did Mrs. Gage enjoy gambling or just the excitement of the races?"

"Well, she seemed to get an awful big kick out of winning. Of course, people never tell you when they lose."

"Very true," he agreed. "By the way, she was a very wealthy woman. Did she give that impression?"

"She didn't talk big, but she was kind of high-toned, and her mobile home was a double-wide. I guessed she had plenty stashed away."

"Had she changed in any way since moving into the park? Was her mind still keen?"

"Oh, she was very sharp! She always knew what she wanted to do—and how to do it—and she did it!

She sometimes said 'teapot' when she meant 'lamp shade,' but we all do that around here. I'm beginning to say 'left' when I mean 'right.' Clayton says it's something in the water in Florida," she said with a giggle.

Qwilleran cleared his throat, signifying an important question: "Were you aware that she drew up a new will after moving to the park?"

"Well, she never talked about anything like that—not to me, anyway—but I told her about this fellow—this lawyer—who does work for the Sunsetters for very reasonable fees. He did my will for only twenty-five dollars, and it was all tied up with red ribbon and red wax. Very professional! Of course, it was a simple will; I'm leaving everything to Clayton—not that I have much to leave."

"Yow!" said Koko.

"I hear my master's voice," Qwilleran said. "Good night, Celia. Thank you again for the snapshots, and give my regards to the thirteen-year-old doctor."

Her merry laughter was still pealing when he hung up. He arranged the snapshots in rows and studied them. Koko was purring loudly, and Qwilleran let him pass his nose over the glossy surfaces. Once again the long pink tongue flicked at two of the prints—the same two that had attracted him before. Qwilleran smoothed his moustache in deep thought; the cat never licked, sniffed, or scratched anything without a reason.

It snowed that night. There was a breathless stillness in the atmosphere as large, wet flakes fell gently, clinging to tree branches, evergreen shrubs, porch railings, and the lintels of hundreds of windows.

Pickax, known as the City of Stone, was transformed
into the City of Marshmallow Creme.

It was a good day to stay indoors and putter,
Qwilleran decided after breakfasting on strong coffee
and warmed-up rolls. He rummaged through the collection of Gage memorabilia that was accumulating in
the desk drawer. The relics defined Grandpa Gage as
a bon vivant, who smoked cigars, drank wine, collected women's garters, and liked the feel of money.
There was a piece of Confederate money, and there
were two large dollar bills of the kind issued before
1929. A pearl-handled buttonhook dated back to the
days of high-button shoes. There was an old ivory
pawn from a chess set that may have belonged to Euphonia's studious father-in-law. Koko's excavations
were not entirely scientific; they included a small, dry
wishbone and a racy postcard from Paris.

By afternoon the snow had stopped falling, and
Qwilleran was tempted to drive out into the countryside and enjoy the fresh snow scene. He would take
his camera. He would also check the church in Brrr
where Hixie had scheduled the next performance of
"The Big Burning." Phoning the number listed for the
Brrr Community Church, he was assured that someone would meet him there. He dressed in heavy
jacket, boots, and wool cap and was saying goodbye to
the Siamese when Koko staged one of his eloquent
demonstrations, jumping at the handle of the back
door and muttering under his breath.

"Okay, this is your last ride of the season,"
Qwilleran told him. He started the car and ran the
heater for a few minutes before carrying the cat coop
out and placing it on the backseat.

The Moose County landscape—with its flat farmland, abandoned mine sites, and rows of utility poles—could be bleak in November, but today it was a picture in black and white. The plows were operating on the major highways, sending plumes of snow ten feet high. Even the town of Brrr, with its undistinguished architecture, looked like an enchanted village.

The church was a modest frame building with a cupola; it might have been a one-room schoolhouse except for the arched windows. As soon as Qwilleran pulled up to the curb, the front door opened and a woman came out to greet him, bundled up in a parka with the hood tied securely under her chin.

"Mr. Qwilleran, I'm Donna Sims. I was watching for you. Come in out of the cold, but don't expect to get warm. The furnace is out of order."

Qwilleran threw a blanket over the cat coop and followed the woman into the building. The vestibule was a small one, with a few steps leading up to the place of worship and a few steps leading down to a spick-and-span basement. Its concrete floor was freshly painted brick red, and its concrete block walls were painted white.

Ms. Sims apologized for the frigid temperature. "We're waiting for the furnace man. Emergencies like this are usually handled by a member of our congregation, but no one knows where he is. Maybe you heard about the potato farmer that disappeared. We're very much upset about it. He was such a wonderful help. When we decided to build a basement under this hundred-year-old church, he told us how to jack it up and do the job. He had all kinds of skills . . . So now we're waiting for a heating man from Mooseville."

"Don't apologize," Qwilleran said. "I'll cut this visit short because I have a cat in the car. What is that door?"

"That's the furnace room."

"Good! I'll use it for entrances and exits. Do you have anything in the way of a platform?"

"Not a regular platform, but one of our members manufactures industrial palettes—you know, those square wooden things—and we can borrow as many as necessary and stack them up. I think they're four by four feet."

"Are they sturdy? Are they solid?"

"Oh, yes, they're built to hold thousands of pounds."

"Eight of them should be enough, stacked two high in an eight-by-eight-foot square. How about electric outlets?"

"Two over here, and two over there. These tables are what we use for pot-luck suppers, but they fold up, and we can arrange the chairs in rows. Is there anything else you need?"

"A small table and chair on the platform and another table and chair for my engineer, down on the floor." He handed her a typewritten card. "This is how we like to be introduced. Will your pastor be doing the honors?"

"I'm the pastor," she said.

The chill of the basement had been worse than the cold snap outdoors, but the car interior was still comfortable. Qwilleran turned up the heat and said to Koko, "If it's all right with you, we'll go for a little ride along the shore, and see if the cabin's buttoned up for the winter." He had inherited a log cabin along with the rest of the Klingenschoen estate.

They headed along the lakeshore, where boarded-up cottages and beached boats huddled under a light blanket of snow. Then came a wooded stretch posted with red signs prohibiting hunting. At one point a large letter K was mounted on a post at the entrance to a narrow driveway, and this is where Qwilleran turned in. It was hardly more than an old wagon trail, meandering through the woods, up and down over brush-covered sand dunes. At the crest of one slight hill Koko created a disturbance in the backseat, throwing himself around in the carrier and yowling.

"Hold it, boy! We're just having a quick look," said Qwilleran, thinking the cat recognized the place where they had spent two summers. He stopped the car, however, and released the door of the coop.

Quivering with excitement, Koko darted to the rear window on the driver's side and pawed the glass.

"It's cold out there! You can't get out! You'd freeze your little tail off."

In a frenzy Koko dashed about the interior of the car as Qwilleran ducked and protested. "Hey! Cool it!" he said, but then he looked out the driver's window. Twisted trunks of wild cherry trees were silhouetted against the snow, and between them were animal tracks leading into the woods. Qwilleran jumped out, slammed the door, and followed the tracks.

A few yards into the woods there was a slight hollow, and what he found there sent him running back to the car, stumbling through the brush, slipping on wet snow. Without stopping to put Koko in the carrier, he backed down the winding trail to the highway. At the nearest gas station, on the outskirts of Mooseville, he called the sheriff.

TWELVE

AT ELEVEN P.M. the WPKX newscast carried this item: "Acting on an anonymous tip, police today found the body of a Brrr Township man in the Klingenschoen woods east of Mooseville. Gil Inchpot, fifty-two, a potato farmer, had been missing since October 24. Because of the condition of the body, decomposed and mutilated by wild animals, the medical examiner was unable to determine the cause of death. State forensic experts have been notified, according to the sheriff's department."

In phoning the tip to the police, Qwilleran had identified himself as a hunter trespassing on posted property and declining to give his name. He had altered his voice to sound like one of the locals who went "huntn" both in and out of "huntn" season. As the Klingenschoen heir and a well-known philanthropist, he had to fight to keep a low profile. Qwilleran preferred to be a newswriter, not a newsmaker.

As soon as he heard the broadcast, he called Gary Pratt at the Black Bear Café. "Have you heard the news?"

"Yeah, it's tough on Nancy," said the barkeeper. "She had to identify the body, and about all that was left was clothing. They didn't say anything about homicide on the air, but the thing of it is: If he'd been out hunting varmint and tripped on something in the woods, he'd be wearing a jacket and boots, wouldn't he? And what about a gun? He was wearing a plaid shirt and house slippers."

And no dentures, Qwilleran thought. "Is there anything we can do to help Nancy?"

"I don't know what it would be. She's a tough little lady, and I think she can take care of herself all right. When she talked to me on the phone, she didn't break down or anything like that—just said that her dogs need her and she can't afford to crack up."

As soon as the conversation ended, Arch Riker called. "Qwill, have you heard what happened? They found a body on your property."

Then Polly called. Next it was Junior with the same information. Qwilleran stopped answering the phone and went to bed. Twice he heard a distant ringing, followed by a much appreciated silence. In the morning he found the receiver off the phone. The cats, who slept on the library sofa, had been equally annoyed by the ringing phone and had taken matters into their own paws.

Qwilleran wrote Nancy a note of sympathy and

mailed it at the same time he shipped a box of
chocolate-covered cherries to Celia Robinson. Then, on
Monday he attended Gil Inchpot's funeral at the Brrr
Community Church, taking care to dress warmly. The
furnace had been repaired, however, and the building
was stiflingly hot. Gary Pratt was sitting alone in a
rear pew, where an occasional blast of frigid air from
the front door was a welcome relief. Qwilleran slipped
in beside him.

Gary whispered, "Nancy's sitting down front with
her ex. They'll be together again before long, I'm willing to bet."

Two days later, Qwilleran was back at the same
church for the third time—to present "The Big Burning of 1869." It was snowing again, and he picked up
Hixie Rice at the newspaper for the drive to Brrr.
Large, wet snowflakes landed on the windshield.

"They're so beautiful, it's a shame to run the windshield wipers," she said.

"Beautiful, maybe, but this is the kind of snow that
wrecks the power lines. I don't know what to expect at
the church tonight. The first time I went there, the
building was too cold; the second time, it was so hot
we couldn't breathe."

Hixie was too happy to care about the temperature.
She said, "Can you stand some good news? Arch is
making me a vice president, in charge of advertising
and promotion!"

"Congratulations! You deserve it."

"I have you to thank, Qwill, for steering me up to
Pickax in the first place. You know, it's a funny thing.
When I first met you Down Below, all I wanted was to
find a husband. Now all I want is to be a vice president with a private office and a cute male secretary.

I'll be sharing Wilfred with Arch. Wilfred isn't my idea of cute, but he's conscientious and reliable and computer-literate."

"You can't have everything," he philosophized. "But tell me something, Hixie: With your increased responsibilities, are you sure you want to go on pressing buttons and flipping switches for this show?"

"Are you kidding? I adore show biz!"

When they arrived at the church, he dropped her at the curb, telling her to check the stage while he unloaded the gear. By the time he opened the trunk, and set the suitcases on the sidewalk, Hixie came running out of the building.

"The furnace has conked out again! It's like a walk-in freezer! The audience is already there, and they're sitting in heavy jackets and wool hats and gloves. There's a little kerosene stove, but it doesn't do any good."

"The show must go on," he replied stoically. "If the audience can stand it, so can we. You keep your coat on, and I'll have the forest fire to keep me warm. It's surprising how much heat can be generated by concentrating on a role."

This was sheer bravado on Qwilleran's part. In portraying the studio announcer he was supposed to be working in 110-degree heat, and the act called for a short-sleeved summer shirt.

Hixie suggested, "Couldn't you cheat for once and wear a jacket?"

"And destroy the illusion? Better to contract pneumonia than to compromise one's art," he replied facetiously and a trifle grimly.

"Well, I'll visit you in the hospital," she said cheerfully.

There was a full house for the show, with everyone muffled to the eyebrows. Qwilleran stood in the furnace room, shivering as he waited for his entrance cue.

During the first act he steeled his jaw to keep his teeth from chattering as he said, "Railroad tracks are warped by the intense heat . . . Great blasts of hot air and cinders are smothering the city." The church basement was fogged by the frosty breath of the audience, while he went through the motions of mopping a sweating brow.

In the second act his frozen fingers fumbled with the script as he said, "The temperature is 110 degrees in the studio, and the window glass is still too hot to touch." It was not surprising that he completed the forty-five-minute script in forty minutes.

After the final words the audience clapped and cheered and stamped their feet. He suspected they were only trying to warm their extremities, but he bowed graciously and held out his hand to Hixie, who joined him on the stage. As they took their bows, Qwilleran could think only of a warm jacket and hot coffee, wishing fervently that the audience would sit on their hands. And then—during the fourth round of applause—the lights went out! Without warning the basement was plunged into the blackest darkness.

"Power's off!" the pastor's voice called out. "Everybody, stay right where you are. Don't try to move around until we can light some candles."

A man's voice said, "I've got a flashlight!" Its beams danced crazily around the walls and ceiling, and at that moment there was a cry, followed by the thud of a falling body and groans of pain. A dozen voices shrieked in alarm.

The flashlight beamed on the platform, where Qwilleran stood in a frozen state of puzzlement; Hixie was no longer beside him. She was writhing on the floor.

"Dr. Herbert! Dr. Herbert!" someone shouted.

"Here I am. Hand me that flashlight," said a man's gruff voice. Two battery-operated lanterns and some candles made small puddles of light as he kneeled at Hixie's side.

The audience babbled in shock. "What happened? . . . Did she fall off the stage? . . . It's lucky that Doc's here."

Qwilleran leaned over the doctor's shoulder. "How is she?"

"She can be moved. I'll drive her to the hospital." He jangled his keys. "Will someone bring my car around?"

While the others milled about anxiously, two men linked arms to form a chair lift and carry Hixie up the stairs.

"Hang in there," Qwilleran told her, squeezing her hand.

"*C'est la* rotten *vie,*" the new vice president said weakly.

He found his way to the furnace room for his flannel shirt and sweater and was packing the suitcases when Nancy Fincher walked up to the platform. "I'm very sorry about the accident," she said solemnly, "but Dr. Herbert will take good care of her. I feel bad about you, too. Your face looked frostbitten while you were talking, and at the end your lips were almost blue."

"I think I'll live," he said, "but I worry about my

colleague. Let's go to the Black Bear for a hot drink. We can call the hospital from there."

They rode to the hotel in Qwilleran's car and found the café lighted by candles. Gary poured steaming cider heated on a small campstove and inquired, "What will Hixie's accident do to your show?"

Nancy spoke up, with more vigor than usual. "I could help out until she gets better. This is the second time I've seen the show, and I could learn the ropes if you'd tell me what to do."

"But what are your hours at the clinic? We have three shows scheduled back to back, and they're all matinees," Qwilleran pointed out.

"I could change my shift."

"The newspaper will reimburse you for your time, of course."

"They don't need to," she said. "I'd just like to do it. To tell the truth, Mr. Qwilleran, something like this would do me a lot of good. It'll take my mind off what's happened, you know."

He nodded sympathetically. "This is a painful time for you."

"Just having someone to talk to helps a lot. It was such a terrible thing!"

"Do you know if the police are getting anywhere with the investigation?"

"I don't know. They come to the house and ask questions but never tell me anything."

Qwilleran said gently, "You mentioned that your father had changed considerably after your mother died."

"Well, he was drinking more than before, and he stopped going to church on Sunday, although he still helped them when they needed repairs. And I told you about the way he was spending money on field equipment and drain tile. He said it was Mom's insurance, but she didn't have that kind of coverage. Another time he said he'd borrowed money from the bank, but everybody knows they aren't lending much to farmers these days."

"Did you tell the police about his spending spree?"

"No, I didn't," she said guiltily. "Do you think I should have?"

"They know it anyway. In a community like this it's no secret when someone starts making lavish expenditures." He looked at his watch. "We can call the hospital now." He used the bar telephone and reported to Nancy, "She's been transferred to the Pickax hospital. No information on her condition is available."

Qwilleran drove Nancy back to the church, where her truck was parked. "Our next booking is Saturday afternoon in downtown Pickax. We should have a rehearsal."

"Yes, I want to," she said eagerly. "I could stop by your house tomorrow when I drive to town for supplies."

Brrr was still blacked out when he drove away from the church, but Pickax had power. The old-fashioned street lamps on Goodwinter Boulevard glowed through a veil of gently falling snow. Hurrying into the house, he telephoned the Pickax hospital and learned that the patient had been admitted and was resting comfortably. No further information was available.

He immediately phoned Arch Riker at home in Indian Village. Without preliminaries he announced, "Your new vice president is in the hospital, and your star columnist is a candidate for an oxygen tent."

"What happened to her, for God's sake?"

"The power failed where we were giving our show, and she fell off the stage, probably because she was frozen stiff. The furnace was out of order. Fortunately there was a doctor in the house. He had her moved to Pickax. I don't know the nature or extent of the injury. The robot on the telephone isn't giving out any information."

"Our night desk will find out," Riker said. "I hate to sound crass, Qwill, but what will this do to our show schedule?"

"I have a substitute lined up. I told her you'd reimburse her, so be prepared to sign some checks, and don't be parsimonious."

"Who is it? Anyone I know?"

"Nancy Fincher, daughter of the potato farmer whose body was found last week."

Riker said, "I'll bet he was growing something besides potatoes."

"I don't know about that," Qwilleran said, "but it appears that he broke up his daughter's marriage to a deputy sheriff. How about that for a suggestive situation?"

"Don't waste your time sleuthing, Qwill. You always get off the track when you're playing detective."

Qwilleran ignored the advice. "And what were you doing tonight? Romancing Mildred?"

"We had dinner at Tipsy's and talked about her apartment in town and my condo here in the Village and her cottage at the beach. The apartment's gotta go, but we may build an addition to the cottage."

"Don't!" Qwilleran warned, speaking from experience.

"By the way, the Lanspeaks want us to have the

wedding at their place on Purple Point, Christmas Eve."

"Excuse me a moment, Arch." He was sitting with his arms on the desk, and Koko was digging in the crook of his elbow. "What's your problem?" he asked the cat. "You're wearing out my sweater sleeve!"

Both cats liked to knead before settling down to sleep, but Koko was working industriously. At the sharp rebuke he jumped off the desk and went to the locked closet, where he rattled the door handle.

Turning back to the phone Qwilleran explained, "Koko wants me to pick the lock on the library closet."

"I wish you took orders from your editor-in-chief the way you take orders from that cat! Hang up! I'll call the night desk about Hixie's accident."

The next morning Qwilleran phoned the hospital and learned that the patient was receiving treatment; no further information was available. It was noon when he finally reached the patient herself.

"Hixie! How are you? We're all worried about you! What's the diagnosis?"

With her usual debonair flourish she replied, "Broken foot! But I've met this perfectly wonderful Dr. Herbert! He drove me to the Brrr hospital and stayed while they X-rayed and put on a soft cast. Then he drove me down here, where they have an orthopedic surgeon. Dr. Herbert is adorable, Qwill! He cares! He has a cabin cruiser! And he's not married!"

"You sound cheerful," Qwilleran said, "but how are you from the ankle down?"

"C'est si bon! And the food! I'm sitting here with a delectable bowl of seafood chowder on my lunch tray.

They have a gourmet dietician who's *fantastique!* I expect a split of champagne on my dinner tray."

"Okay, I'll drop in to see you this afternoon. Now get back to your chowder while it's hot."

"Hot? I never said it was *hot!* This is a hospital, *mon ami!*"

When Qwilleran visited her a few hours later, he found her in a private room with soft pink walls, sitting in an arm chair with her foot elevated and encased in a bright pink cast.

"Chic, *n'est-ce pas?*" she said. "Casts now come in five decorator colors, and I thought the hot pink would coordinate with the walls."

"Never mind the color scheme. What did the surgeon say?"

"I have a displaced fracture of the metacarpus. Doesn't that sound exotic?"

"Do you have any pain?"

"Watch your language, Qwill. Four-letter words aren't allowed in the hospital. We don't feel *pain;* we don't *hurt;* we only experience discomfort. Fortunately I have a high discomfort threshold."

"How long will you be in a cast?"

"Six weeks, but when Dr. Herbert found out I live alone in a second-floor walk-up in Indian Village, he insisted that I stay with his mother in Pickax for a while. In a couple of weeks I can go into the office with a walker."

"I'll drive you," Qwilleran offered.

"But what about the show? Who'll be your engineer? Perhaps Arch will let you have Wilfred."

"I have someone prettier than Wilfred. Don't worry about it, Hixie. Meanwhile, is there anything you need?"

"No, thanks. Just keep your fingers crossed that I get out of the hospital before the Big Snow."

Qwilleran started to leave but remembered the snapshots in his pocket. "Did you ever meet Euphonia Gage?"

"No, but I saw her around town—in her eighties and walking like a young girl!"

"I have pictures of her taken in Florida, and some of her friends look familiar. You may recognize them."

"*Donnez-moi.* I'm good at remembering faces." Hixie studied the photos carefully. "I think I've seen a couple of these people before. Is it important?"

"It may be. I don't know," he admitted.

"Okay, leave them with me, and if I get a noodle, I'll call you."

From the hospital Qwilleran went to the Senior Care Facility to arrange the staging for the Sunday afternoon show. Lisa Compton, in charge of patient activities, showed him the all-purpose room with its rows of long tables.

"They take their meals here," she said, "but we remove the tables for a program like yours. We put the hearing-impaired in the front row and the mumblers in the back."

"What's behind that door?"

"The kitchen."

"Good! I can have a piece of pie between the acts." Everything, in fact, checked out: platform, electric outlets, two tables, two chairs.

"Cup of coffee?" Lisa asked.

"Thanks, but I've got to go home and rehearse a new partner for the show. Hixie has broken her foot."

"Oh, the poor dear! That can be so painful."

"She doesn't seem to have any discomfort," he said.

"But this is only the beginning. When the shock wears off, the nerve ends start to ache. Ask me! I've been there!"

"Let's not tell Hixie," he said. "I'll see you Sunday afternoon, Lisa."

When he arrived on Goodwinter Boulevard, Nancy's pickup—with its box top and eight barred windows—was already parked in the side drive. He ushered her directly downstairs to the ballroom, where the stage was set for rehearsal.

"I remember this room when I was a little girl," she said. "Mrs. Gage had dozens of little gold chairs around the walls. I loved those little chairs and always wished she'd give me one for Christmas instead of a book. I wonder what happened to them."

"Who knows?" he remarked, in a hurry to get down to business. He explained the code on the cuecard and the operation of the equipment. Then they rehearsed the timing and ended with a complete run-through.

"Perfect," Qwilleran said.

He packed the gear in preparation for the forthcoming performance and thanked his new engineer for coming to rehearse, but she showed no signs of leaving. "All of this is so exciting for me," she said. "And it's funny, Mr. Qwilleran—when I first met you I was tongue-tied because you were so important and so rich and everything, and I thought your moustache was—well—frightening, but now I feel very comfortable with you."

"Good," he said with an offhand inflection.

"It's because you *listen*. Most men don't listen to women when they talk—not really."

"I'm a journalist. Listening is what we do." His defenses were up. As a millionaire bachelor he had learned to dodge. Briskly he said, "Shall we wind up this session with a quick glass of cider in the library?"

She dropped with familiar ease into the scooped-out library sofa, displacing the Siamese, who walked stiffly from the room, and Qwilleran feared she was feeling too comfortable. Now that she had his therapeutic ear to talk into, she talked—and talked—about living in Alaska, potato farming, breeding dogs, working for a vet. Dinnertime approached, and he had had no real food since breakfast. Under other circumstances he might have invited such a guest out to dinner, but if the Klingenschoen heir were seen dining with a young woman half his age—the daughter of a murdered man whose body had been found on Klingenschoen property—the Pickax gossips would put two and two together and get the national debt.

The Siamese were still absent and unnaturally quiet, even though it was past their feeding time. Suddenly eight thundering paws galloped past the library door toward the entrance.

"What was that?" she asked.

"The cats are trying to remind me it's their dinnertime," he replied, looking at his watch.

"You should hear my dogs at feeding time! Go ahead and feed them if you want to." Nancy was obviously too comfortable to move.

The pelting paws rushed past again, like a herd of wild horses as they charged toward the kitchen. Next there was a frenzy of scuffling, thwacking, and snarling that brought Qwilleran and his guest to the scene in time for a shattering of glass.

"The coffee jar!" he shouted. Coffee beans and broken glass were everywhere, and the Siamese were on top of the refrigerator, looking down on the devastation with bemused detachment.

"I'll help you clean up," Nancy offered. "Don't cut yourself."

"No! No! Thanks, but . . . let me cope with this. I'll see you Saturday afternoon. You'll have to excuse me now."

As she drove away he swept up the mess, wondering whether they simply wanted their dinner or were trying to get rid of the dog-handler. They always knew how to get what they wanted, and sometimes they merely wanted to be helpful.

While he was scrambling around the kitchen floor on his hands and knees, Hixie phoned and said excitedly, "I'm checking out of the hospital and moving in with Dr. Herbert's mother! He says she was born in Paris. I can brush up on my French!"

"Glad you're getting out before the Big Snow," he said.

"Shall I mail these Florida snapshots back to you?"

"If it isn't too much trouble. Did anyone look familiar?"

"Well," said Hixie, "there's a man with upswept eyebrows—a middle-aged man. And there's a young woman in a yellow convertible—"

"They're the ones," he interrupted. "Who are they?"

"I'm not sure, but . . . do you remember the gate-crashers at the preview of our show? The woman was wearing an obvious wig."

"Thanks, Hixie. That's all I need to know. Enjoy your stay with Madame Herbert."

Qwilleran returned to the kitchen to finish cleaning up. The Siamese were still on the refrigerator. "What were Betty and Claude doing in Pickax?" he asked them. "And why did they attend the preview?"

THIRTEEN

QWILLERAN WAS INCLINED to discount the tales of the Big Snow. For six winters he had heard about this local bugaboo, which was never as nasty as predicted. Yet, every year the residents of Moose County prepared for war: digging in, mobilizing snowplows and blowers, enlisting snowfighters, deploying troops of volunteers, disseminating propaganda, and stockpiling supplies. Every day a virtual convoy of trucks brought necessities from Down Below: food, drink, videos, batteries, and kerosene.

Everyone had some urgent task to finish or goal to achieve before the white bomb dropped: Hixie to get out of the hospital, Jody to get into the hospital and have her baby, Lori to finish Qwilleran's correspondence, and Nick to deliver it. Qwilleran's only important business was to do three shows: for a women's group on Saturday, for the Senior Care Facility on Sunday, and for a school on Monday.

Friday morning he was drinking coffee and conversing idly with the Siamese when, suddenly, Koko heard something! The cats were always hearing something. It might be a faucet dripping, or a truck on Main Street shifting gears, or a dog barking half a mile away. This time Koko stretched his neck, swiveled his noble head, and slanted his ears toward the foyer. Qwilleran investigated. There was a moving van across the street, backing into Amanda Goodwinter's driveway. She was Junior's elder relative, a cantankerous businesswoman, and a perennial member of the city council.

Qwilleran hurried into boots and parka and climbed over the piles of snow that the sidewalk blowers had thrown into the street and the city plows had thrown back onto the sidewalk. A truck from the Bid-a-Bit Auction House had lowered its ramp, and Amanda herself was on the porch, directing the operation. She looked dowdier than ever in her army surplus jacket, Daniel Boone hat, and unfastened galoshes.

"Amanda! What's going on here?" Qwilleran hailed her as he plunged through the drifts.

"I'm getting out before the Big Snow! I'm selling everything! I'm moving to Indian Village!"

"But what will you do with your house?"

"It's sold! Good riddance! I always hated it!"

"Who bought it?"

"Some real estate vulture from Down Below!"

He joined her on the porch and teased her by saying, "You'll be sorry! Pickax is attracting investors. Land values will go up."

"Nothing'll go up on this godforsaken street until the property owners get off their hind ends and permit re-zoning . . . Stop! Stop!" she screamed at the movers, who were struggling with a hundred-year-old black walnut breakfront, twelve feet wide. "You're scratching the finish! Take the drawers out! Watch the glass doors!"

At the same moment a second moving van pulled up to the Wilmot house. Qwilleran shrugged, pulled up the hood of his parka, and trudged the length of the boulevard, counting for-sale signs. There were only four left, out of a recent seven. He enjoyed walking in snow and took the opportunity to hike downtown to the church where he would present "The Big Burning" the following afternoon.

The fellowship hall in the church basement was a large room paneled in pickled pine, with a highly waxed vinyl floor and a good solid platform. The custodian told Qwilleran he could use the men's restroom for exits and entrances. Seventy-five women were expected for lunch at noon, and they'd be ready for the show at one o'clock. Everything appeared to be well organized, and Qwilleran was impressed by the facilities.

As he arrived home, Nick Bamba was pulling into the driveway. "Come on in, Nick, and have a hot drink," he said hospitably.

"Not this time," Nick declined. "I have a dozen errands to do before the Big Snow." He handed over a folder. "Here's your correspondence from Lori, and I've brought my tool kit. I'll pick the lock in the library. Are you all ready for the Big Snow?"

"Polly has been nagging me about that," Qwilleran said, "but my vast experience convinces me that it's never as big as the kerosene dealers would have us believe."

"How long have you been here? Five years? The seventh year is always the really big one. Trust me!" Nick tackled the closet lock in professional fashion while dispensing advice. "You need a camp stove and kerosene heater in case of a long power outage . . . canned food, not frozen, in case you're snowbound . . . five-gallon jugs of water in case a water main busts . . . fresh batteries for your radio and flashlights."

"What do they do at the prison?" Qwilleran asked.

"We have generators. So does the hospital. Remember not to use your elevator after it starts to snow hard; you could be trapped in a blackout." Nick opened the closet door, collected his tools, and accepted Qwilleran's thanks, and on the way out he said, "If you're not concerned about yourself, Qwill, think about your cats."

Koko lost no time in entering the closet. It was filled with files in boxes and drawers, and a small safe stood open and empty. When Qwilleran left to go shopping for canned food, the cat was sitting in the safe like a potentate in a palanquin.

Throughout the weekend a storm watch was in effect, but Suitcase Productions presented all three scheduled shows to capacity audiences. By Monday afternoon Wetherby Goode announced a storm alert and said he was prepared for the worst; he had a sleeping bag in the studio as well as a package of fig newtons.

Monday evening Koko and Yum Yum began to behave abnormally, dashing about and butting furniture. They showed no interest in food or *Robinson*

Crusoe. Eventually Qwilleran shut himself in his bedroom to escape the fracas, but he could still hear bursts of madcap activity. He himself slept fitfully.

Shortly after daybreak a peaceful calm settled on the house. Peering out the window, he witnessed a rare sight: the entire sky was the vivid color of polished copper. A weather bulletin on WPKX made note of the phenomenon and warned that it was the lull before the storm. Duck hunters and commercial fishermen were advised to stay on shore and resist the temptation to make one more haul before the end of the season.

By mid-morning large flakes of snow began to fall. Shortly after, the wind rose, and soon fifty-mile-an-hour gusts were creating blizzard conditions.

At noon the WPKX newscast announced: "A storm of unprecedented violence is blasting the county. Visibility is zero. Serious drifting is making roads impassable. All establishments are closed with the exception of emergency services. Even so, fire fighters, police, and medical personnel attempting to respond to calls are blinded by the whirling snow and are completely disoriented. State police have issued these directives: Stay indoors. Conserve water, food, and fuel. Observe safety precautions in using kerosene heaters and wood-burning stoves. In case of power failure, use flashlights or oil lanterns; avoid candles. Be prepared to switch radios to battery operation. And stay tuned for further advisories."

On Goodwinter Boulevard it was snowing in four directions: down, up, sideways and in circles. Strangely, the Siamese, having accomplished their advance warning, settled down to sleep peacefully.

At three o'clock WPKX reported: "Two duck hunters

from Lockmaster left shore in a rented boat west of
Mooseville early this morning and have not been seen
since that time. Their boat was found bottom-up,
blown high on the shore near Brrr . . . Distress calls
from commercial fishing boats are being received, but
the sheriff's helicopter is grounded in the blizzard,
and rescue crews are unable to launch their boats in
the mountainous waves. Thirty-five-foot waves are reported on the lake."

Then the power failed, and when Qwilleran tried to
call Polly, the telephone was dead. The blizzard continued relentlessly, hour after hour, and he experienced the unnerving isolation of a house blanketed
with snow. Without mechanical noises and without
the sound of street traffic, the unnatural stillness left
a muffled void that only amplified the howling of the
wind, and a cold darkness settled on the rooms as
snow drifted against the windows.

The blizzard lasted sixteen hours, during which
Qwilleran found he could neither read nor write nor
sleep. Then the wind subsided. The Big Snow was
over, but it would take almost a week for the county
to struggle back to normal. Broadcasting was limited
to weather updates and police news on the half hour:

"The worst storm in the history of Moose County
was the result of a freak atmospheric condition. Three
low-pressure fronts—one coming from Alaska, one
from the Rocky Mountains, and one from the Gulf of
Mexico—met and clashed over this area. Winds of sev-
enty miles an hour were recorded as thirty-two inches
of snow fell in sixteen hours. Drifts of fifteen to thirty
feet have buried buildings and walled up city streets
and country roads, paralyzing the county."

For the next two days Qwilleran lived life without

power, telephone, mail delivery, daily newspapers, or sociable pets. Koko and Yum Yum appeared to be in hibernation on the library sofa. His own intentions to catch up on his reading and write a month's supply of copy for the newspaper were reduced to a state of jittery boredom. Even when snowplows started rumbling and whooshing about the city streets, cars were still impounded in their garages and residents were imprisoned in their houses. The health department warned against overexertion in digging out.

On the morning of the fourth day Qwilleran was in the library, eating a stale doughnut and drinking instant coffee prepared with not-quite-boiling water, when the shrill and unexpected bell of the telephone startled him and catapulted the Siamese from their sofa. It was Polly's exultant voice: "Plug in your refrigerator!"

"How are you, Polly? I worried about you," he said.

"Bootsie and I weathered the storm, but I lacked the energy to do anything. I had planned to wash the kitchen walls, clean closets, and make Christmas gifts. How are you faring?"

"Strangely, I'm getting tired of canned soup and stale doughnuts."

"We'll be prisoners for a few days more," she predicted, "but fortunately we're in touch with the outside world."

Qwilleran immediately called the outside world, but all lines were busy. The gregarious, garrulous populace of Pickax seemed to be making up for lost time.

WPKX went on the air with more storm news, good and bad:

"The first baby born during the Big Snow is a seven-pound girl, Leslie Ann. The parents are Mr. and

Mrs. Junior Goodwinter. Mother and child are snow-bound at the Pickax hospital.

"In rural areas many persons are reported missing. It is presumed that they lost their way in the blizzard and have frozen to death. Homes have burned to the ground because help could not reach them. Much livestock is thought to be frozen in fields and barns. Bodies are still washing ashore from wrecked boats."

The sound of Polly's voice and the rumbling of the refrigerator restored Qwilleran's spark of life. He did some laundry, washed the accumulation of soup bowls in the kitchen sink, and eventually reached Junior to offer congratulations.

"Yeah, I got her to the hospital just before the storm broke and then had to rush home to take care of our little boy. I still haven't seen the baby," Junior said. "But hey, Qwill, let me tell you about the call I got from Down Below just before the phones went dead. It was some guy who deals in architectural fragments. He wanted to buy the light fixtures and fireplaces in Grandma's house!"

"You mean he wanted to strip this place?" Qwilleran asked in indignation.

"I told him to get lost. Boy, he had a lot of nerve! How do you suppose he found out what we've got?"

"I could make an educated guess. How valuable are the fixtures?"

"Susan Exbridge could tell you exactly. I only know that the chandeliers on the main floor are real silver, and the ones in the ballroom are solid brass and copper, imported from France before World War I . . . Anyway, I thought you'd be shocked, the way I was."

After five o'clock Qwilleran phoned Celia Robinson. "Good evening," he said in the ingratiating tone that had melted female defenses for years. "This is Jim Qwilleran."

"Oh! Thank you so much for the chocolate cherries!" she gushed. "They're my absolute favorite! But you didn't have to do it."

"It was my pleasure."

"I've been watching the weather on TV. Was it very bad up where you are?"

"Very bad. We've been snowbound for four days, with no meltdown in sight. Meanwhile, Celia, I'm working on my profile of Mrs. Gage and need to ask a few more questions. Do you mind?"

"You know I'm glad to help, Mr. Qwilleran—and not just because you sent me those lovely chocolates."

"All right. Going back to the morning when you found her body, what did you do?"

"I called the office, and they called the authorities. They came right away."

Casually he asked, "And how did Betty and Claude react?"

"Oh, they weren't here. They were out of town, and Pete was in charge. He's the assistant—very nice, very helpful."

"Did he appear shocked?"

"Well, not really. We've had quite a few deaths, you know, which you can understand in a place like this. Actually we have quite a turnover."

"Do Betty and Claude go out of town very often?"

"Well, they're from up north, and they go to see their families once in a while."

"Where up north?" he asked as if mildly curious.

"It could be Wisconsin. They talk about the Green Bay Packers and the Milwaukee Brewers. But I'm not sure. Want me to find out?"

"No, it's not important. But tell me: Did Mrs. Gage ever mention her mansion in Pickax? It was in her husband's family for generations."

"I know," said Celia. "She showed a video of it in the clubhouse—not that she wanted to show off, I'm sure, but we visited some historic homes down here, and she thought we'd like to see a hundred-year-old house up north. She had some wonderful things."

"Did Mr. Crusoe see the video?"

"Crocus," she corrected. "Yes, and he still talks about it. He comes over to my yard and wants to talk about her. Today he told me something confidential. I'm not supposed to mention it in the park until it's official, but I can tell you. You probably know already that she left a lot of money to the park to build a health club."

"How did he know about it?"

"She told him. They were very good friends, I guess. They liked the same things. We all thought it would be nice if they got married. That's why it's so sad."

"Yes," Qwilleran murmured, then asked, "Do you suppose Mr. Crocus would care to be interviewed for this profile?"

"I don't know. He's kind of shy, but I could ask him. Would you like me to break the ice, sort of?"

"Would you be good enough to do that?" he requested. "Your cooperation is much appreciated. And may I call you again soon?"

"You know you don't have to ask, Mr. Qwilleran. It's lots of fun answering your questions."

After the call he dropped into a lounge chair to think, and Yum Yum walked daintily into the library. "Hello, princess," he said. "Where have you been?"

Taking that as an invitation, she leaped lightly to his knee, turned around three times, and found a place to settle down.

He adjusted her weight slightly without discommoding her and asked, "What happened to your confrère?"

The muted answer came from the closet—a series of soft thumps that aroused Qwilleran's curiosity. He excused himself and went to investigate. Koko was batting a small object this way and that, apparently having fun. It was a small maroon velvet box.

Qwilleran intercepted it and immediately called Junior again. "Guess what Koko has just dredged up in one of the closets! A jeweler's box containing a man's gold ring, probably your grandfather's! It's the only valuable item he's found."

"What kind of ring?"

"A signet, with an intricate design on the crown. I'll turn it over to you as soon as they dig us out."

"Which can't be too soon for me," Junior said. "I'm getting cabin fever."

"I've been talking to Celia Robinson again. Did you know your grandmother had a video of the house when it was still furnished?"

"Sure. She had me film the interior before she broke it up. After she died, I found the tape among her effects and brought it home for the historical museum."

"Well, for your information, she showed the film at the Park of Pink Sunsets, so we can assume that the park management knew about the lavish appointments. Now I'm wondering if they came to see for themselves—with an ulterior motive. Listen to this, Junior: Betty and Claude were in this house when we previewed 'The Big Burning.' They wandered around the rooms with the rest of the crowd."

"How do you know?"

"I saw them. Hixie saw them. We both wondered who they were. Since then, we've identified them from snapshots that Celia sent us. Now you know and I know that nobody—*nobody*—ever stops in Pickax on the way to somewhere else. They come here for a purpose or not at all, and Betty and Claude don't strike me as being duck hunters. They must have known about the preview—and the exact date. Could your grandmother have told them? Did she know about it?"

"Jody wrote to her once a week and probably mentioned it," Junior said. "Grandma would be interested because the script was based on her father-in-law's memoirs, and she had a crush on him."

Qwilleran said, "Frankly, I've had doubts about the Pink Sunset operation ever since you told me they profiteer on the repurchase of mobile homes. Are they also in partnership with the guy who wanted to buy the light fixtures? We may have uncovered a story that's bigger than a profile of your eccentric grandmother."

"Wow! When it breaks," Junior said, "let's keep it exclusive with the *Moose County Something!*"

FOURTEEN

GRADUALLY MOOSE COUNTY struggled out from under the snow, as armies of volunteers swarmed over the neighborhoods, tunneling through to buried buildings. The snowdrifts never diminished, only shifted from one location to another, with one more inch of snow falling every day. WPKX now aired the lighter side of the news:

"Sig Olsen, a farmer near Sawdust City, had his chicken coop wrecked by the storm, and a loose board sailed through his kitchen window. He didn't know it until morning, when he got up and found his whole flock roosting around the wood-burning stove."

Qwilleran finally reached Hixie by phone. "Your line's constantly busy," he complained.

"I'm working on logistics for the Christmas parade," she explained. "The *Something* is cosponsoring it with Lanspeak's Department Store."

"Are you comfortable where you're staying?"

"Mais oui! Madame Herbert is a *joli coeur!* Did you do the three shows I scheduled before the Big Snow? I thought the one at the Senior Care Facility might be amusing."

"Hilarious!" Qwilleran said dryly. "I played for fifty wheelchairs and two gurneys. They were attentive, but the assorted bodily noises in the audience were a new experience. After the show the attendants passed out bananas, and I circulated among the old-timers to hear their comments. They all handed me their banana peels."

"You're so adaptable, Qwill! *Je t'adore!*" she said.

He huffed into his moustache. "What are you planning for Thanksgiving?"

"Dr. Herbert is coming down from Brrr with some friends, and Madame is doing stuffed quail with apricot coulis. What about you?"

"Polly is roasting a turkey, and Arch and Mildred will join us."

When he hung up, both cats reported to the library, having heard the word "turkey."

"Sorry. False alarm," he said.

Koko, returning to work after the storm, was no longer collecting emery boards, teabags, pieces of saltwater taffy, and other domestic trivia. He was excavating the library closet and leaving a paper trail of postcards, newspaper clippings, envelopes with foreign stamps, and such. One was a yellowed clipping from the *Pickax Picayune,* the antiquated predecessor of the *Moose County Something.* It was a column headed "Marriages," and one of the listings attracted Qwilleran's attention:

LENA FOOTE, DAUGHTER OF
MR. AND MRS. ARNOLD FOOTE OF LOCKMASTER,
TO GILBERT INCHPOT OF BRRR, OCT. 18.

The year 1961 had been inked in the margin. That date would be about right, Qwilleran figured, guessing at Nancy's age. Lena Foote was her mother and also Euphonia's longtime housekeeper. Apparently she was already employed in the Gage household before her marriage. What had Euphonia given the couple for a wedding present? A wooden nutcracker? He put the clipping in an envelope addressed to Nancy, adding thanks for her assistance with the three shows and mentioning that there might be more bookings after the holidays.

On the sixth day following the Big Snow Qwilleran was able to mail his letter. He also arranged to meet Junior for lunch at Lois's; he wanted to deliver the gold ring and two other items of interest that Koko had unearthed.

When it was time to leave for lunch, however, the jeweler's box was missing, and the desk drawer was ajar. "Drat those cats!" Qwilleran said aloud. He knew it was Yum Yum's fine Siamese paw that had opened the drawer, but he suspected it was Koko who assigned her the nefarious little task, like a feline Fagin. There was no time to search fifteen rooms and fifty closets; he hustled off to Lois's, where Junior was waiting in a booth.

The editor's first words were, "Did you remember to bring Grandpa's ring?"

"Dammit! I forgot it!" said Qwilleran, an expert at extemporaneous fibs.

"Today's special," Lois announced as she slapped two soiled menu cards on the table. "Bean soup and ham sandwich."

"Give us a minute to decide," Qwilleran said, "but you can bring us some coffee."

From an inner pocket of his jacket he produced a folded sheet of paper, ivory with age and turning brown at the creases. "Do you recognize this writing, Junior?"

"That's Grandma's!"

"It's the anonymous poem in her memorial program—the one about lovelorn butterflies."

Junior scanned the verses with the lightning speed of an experienced editor. "Do you suppose she wrote this?"

"Well, it wasn't Keats or Wordsworth. I think your sedate little grandmother had a passionate past."

"Could be. Jody always thought she had something to hide. How do women know these things?"

Lois returned with the coffee. "You guys decide what you want?"

"Not yet," said Junior. "Give us another couple of seconds."

Next, Qwilleran handed him an old envelope postmarked Lockmaster, 1929. The letter inside was addressed to "My dearest darling Cynara."

"Oh, God! Do I have to read it?" Junior whined. "Other people's love letters always sound so corny."

"Read it!" Qwilleran ordered.

Nov. 17, 1929

My dearest darling Cynara—
Last night I climbed to the roof of the horse

barn—and looked across to where you live—
thirty miles—but I can still feel you—taste you—
smell your skin—fresh as violets—After sixteen
months of heaven—it's hell to be without you—
tossing and turning all night—dreaming of
you—I want to climb to the top of the silo—and
jump down on the rocks—but it would kill my
mother—and hurt you—and you've suffered
enough for my sake—And so—my own heart's
darling—I'm going away—for good—and I beg
you to forget me—I'm returning the ring—and
thinking that maybe—some day—we'll meet in
sweetness and in light—but for now—promise to
forget—Goodbye—my Cynara—

The signature was simply "W." When Junior finished reading it, he said, "It turns my stomach."

"The content or the punctuation?" Qwilleran asked.

"How could Grandma fall for such rot?"

"She was young in 1929."

"In 1929 Grandpa was in prison. She couldn't face
the scandal in Pickax, so she went to stay in Lockmaster for two years—on somebody's farm. It looks as
if it turned out to be fun and games."

Qwilleran said, "This horse farmer was obviously
the other butterfly in the poem. She put her memories in the closet and finally paraded them at her
memorial bash: *Love's long since cancelled woes* ...
I must not think of thee ... Wouldn't it be a poetic
coincidence if her admirer in Florida turned out to
be W? But if that were the case, why would she
overdose?"

"Do you know anything about him?"

"Only that he has a magnificent head of white hair and plays the violin."

Lois advanced on their booth with hands on hips. "Are you young punks gonna order? Or do you want to pay rent for the booth?"

Both men ordered the special, and Junior said, "Grandpa got out of prison in time for the stock market crash, my mother used to say."

"That was the month before this letter was written."

"You're not putting Grandma's love life in your profile, are you, Qwill?"

"Why not?"

There was a thoughtful pause as family loyalty battled with professional principle. Then Junior said, "I guess you're right. Why not? The Gages are all dead. Where is Koko finding these choice items all of a sudden?"

Pompously Qwilleran said, "I cannot tell a lie. I picked the lock of the library closet. There are tons of papers in there. Also an empty safe. One thing Koko found was an announcement in the *Picayune* of Gil Inchpot's marriage to Euphonia's housekeeper. There was also a recipe for Lena's angel food cake with chocolate frosting that sounded delicious."

"I knew Lena," said Junior. "She was Grandma's day-help for years and years. After that, there was a series of live-in housekeepers who never stayed long. Grandma was hard to get along with in her old age."

"What about the Inchpot murder? Do the police have any suspects?"

"Haven't heard. The Big Snow brings everything to a crashing halt. Do you realize there are frozen bodies out there that won't be found until spring thaw?"

Their discussion was interrupted by the slam-bang delivery of two daily specials. They ate in silence until Junior inquired about Suitcase Productions.

"Several organizations want us after the holidays. We did three shows just before the Big Snow. The largest audience was in the basement of the Old Stone Church. Seventy-five women. Lunch at noon. Performance at one. I was supposed to use the men's restroom for exits and entrances, but there was a wedding upstairs, and the bridal party was using it as a dressing room. They said I'd have to use the women's restroom. After their lunch seventy-five women lined up to use the facilities, and it was two-thirty before we got the show on the boards. Then, just as I was describing the roaring of the wind and the crashing of burning buildings, there was a roar and a crash overhead! I thought the ceiling was caving in, but it was only the church organ upstairs, playing the wedding march full blast! I can project my voice, but it's not easy to compete with Mendelssohn on a five-hundred-pipe organ!"

Lois returned, brandishing the coffee server like a weapon. "Apple pie?" she demanded gruffly.

"I'm due back at the office," said the young editor.

"You go ahead. I'll get the check," Qwilleran told him. "And Lois, you can bring me some of your apple pie. I dreamed about it all the time I was snowbound."

"Liar!" she retorted, and she bustled away, smiling.

As soon as Nancy Fincher received Qwilleran's letter, she telephoned him. "Thanks for the clipping about my parents. It'll go in my scrapbook."

"Mrs. Gage must have had a high regard for your mother."

"Oh, yes, she relied on Mom a lot, and Mom loved Mrs. Gage. She didn't like Mr. Gage, though. When she went to work there as a young girl, he was too friendly, she told me."

"That's one way of putting it," Qwilleran said. "Why did she continue to work for them after her marriage?"

"Well, you see, Mom and Pop needed the money to get their farm started. Besides, she loved working in the big house. I took care of our farmhouse starting when I was nine years old—cooking and everything."

"Remarkable," Qwilleran murmured. "So your mother's maiden name was Foote. Did you keep in touch with your grandparents in Lockmaster?"

As before, Nancy was eager to talk. "No, it's funny, but I never saw them until they came to Mom's funeral."

"What was the reason for that?"

"I don't know. I had Grandma and Grandpa Inchpot right here in Brrr, and Mom never talked about her own parents. I thought Lockmaster was a foreign country."

"When they attended your mother's funeral, how did you react to them?"

"I didn't like them at all. They made me nervous, the way they stared at me. Pop said it was because they were surprised to see their granddaughter grown up. They were very old, of course."

Qwilleran asked, "Did it ever occur to you that your Lockmaster grandparents might have lent your father the money for his farm improvements after your mother died?"

"No way," she said. "They were only poor dirt farmers. Not everybody in Lockmaster is a rich horse breeder . . . Well, anyway, Mr. Qwilleran, I wanted to thank you and wish you a happy Thanksgiving. I'm spending it with Dan Fincher's relatives, and I'll take the kids for dogsled rides after dinner. What are you going to do?"

"Polly Duncan is roasting a turkey, and there'll be another couple, and we'll all eat too much."

"N-n-now!" shrieked Yum Yum.

It was a thankful foursome that gathered in Polly's apartment, thankful to be free after a week of confinement. The aroma of turkey was driving Bootsie to distraction, and the aroma of Mildred's mince pie, still warm from the oven, was having much the same effect on Qwilleran.

Arch Riker said, "The local pundits are saying that a Big Snow before Thanksgiving means mild weather before Christmas."

Mildred said, "I'd like to propose some ground rules for today's dinner. Anyone who mentions the Big Snow has to wash the dishes."

"What are we allowed to discuss?"

"For starters, Hixie Rice. How is she?"

"She came to the office once this week," Riker said. "Qwill drove her, and Wilfred met her at the curb with her desk chair and wheeled her into the building. She clomps around with a walker and something called a surgical boot."

"How is her substitute working out for the show, Qwill?"

"Not bad," he replied with an offhand shrug, careful not to praise too highly the petite young woman with soulful eyes.

Mildred said, "Your show has prompted a family history program in the schools. Kids are interviewing their grandparents and great-grandparents about the Depression, World War II, and Vietnam."

"Oh sure, we're sharpening their interest in history," Qwilleran said sourly as he drew a sheaf of papers from his sweater pocket. "At Black Creek School they had to write capsule reviews of the show. Would you like to hear a few of them?"

Riker said, "They'd be easier to take if I had a Scotch in my hand."

Drinks were poured, and then Qwilleran read the comments from sixth graders: "I liked the show because we got out of class . . . I liked the red light best . . . It was interesting but not so interesting that it was boring . . . My favorite part was where the guy got his arm burned off . . . It was better than sitting in English and learning . . . The man did most of the play. The woman should have more to do and not just sit there and push buttons."

"That's the spirit!" Mildred said.

He saved the rave review for the last: "It's neat how you came up with all that stuff. I would never know how to look it all up. Don't change it at all, no matter what. I'd like to see it go all over."

Riker said, "Sign that kid up! We could use a good drama critic."

Qwilleran omitted mentioning the spitball that sailed past his ear during the performance at Black Creek.

Polly carved the bird, pacifying Bootsie with some giblets, and the four sat down to the traditional feast. "Beautiful bird!" they all agreed. In deference to

Mildred the bird was never identified; there had been a star-crossed turkey farmer in her painful past.

"Now let's discuss the wedding," Polly suggested. "What are the plans so far?"

The bride-to-be said, "It'll be at the Lanspeaks' house on Purple Point, and we're all invited to stay for the three-day weekend."

Riker said, "It's black tie, Qwill, so dust off your tux."

"Black tie!" Qwilleran echoed in dismay.

"Didn't you buy a formal outfit for that weekend in Lockmaster?"

"Yes, but I never had a chance to wear it, and do you know where it is now? My dinner jacket, cummerbund, expensive shirt, three-hundred-dollar evening pumps—they're all in a closet in my barn, behind twenty feet of snow, at the end of a half mile of unplowed driveway."

"You can rent an outfit," Riker said calmly, "but what will you do about your cats? I believe they're not invited."

Polly said, "My sister-in-law will come over twice a day to feed Koko and Yum Yum as well as Bootsie."

Everyone had seconds of the bird and the squash puree with cashews. Then the aromatic mince pie was consumed and praised, and coffee was poured, during which the telephone rang.

Polly answered and said, "It's for you, Qwill."

"Who knows I'm here?" he wondered aloud.

It was Hixie. "I hate to bother you, Qwill. Are you in the middle of dinner?"

"That's all right. We've finished."

"Carol Lanspeak just called. We have a problem."

"What kind of problem?"

"Larry was scheduled to play Santa in the parade on Saturday, and he's on the verge of pneumonia," Hixie said anxiously. "Carol and I wondered if you would substitute."

"You're not serious."

"I'm not only serious, I'm desperate! When Carol gave me the news, my foot started to throb again."

Scowling and huffing into his moustache, Qwilleran was alarmingly silent.

"Qwill, have you fainted? I know it's not your choice of role, but—"

"What would it entail?" he asked in a grouchy monotone.

"First of all, you'll have to try on Larry's Santa suit. It's in the costume department at the theatre."

"I suppose you know," he reminded her, "that Larry is three sizes smaller and three inches shorter than I am."

"But Carol says the suit is cut roomy—to accommodate the padding, you know—and Wally's mother could alter the length of sleeves and pants. We don't need to worry about the beard and wig; one size fits all."

"And what happens on Saturday?"

"You get into costume at the theatre, and Carol drives you to the Dimsdale Diner, where the parade units will assemble. The parade proceeds south on Pickax Road to Main Street, where the mayor gives you the official greeting."

"And what am I supposed to be doing?"

"Just wave at people and act jolly."

"I won't feel jolly," he grumbled, "but I'll try to make an adjustment . . . I'm doing this only for your foot, Hixie . . . *ma chérie*," he added tartly.

When Qwilleran returned to the dinner table, the others regarded him with concern.

"I need another piece of pie," he said.

Later, when he returned from Polly's apartment with a generous serving of the bird, he was met by two excited Siamese. "Ho ho ho!" he boomed with simulated jollity. They fled from the room.

"I beg your royal pardons," he apologized. "I was practicing. Would you entertain the concept of turkey for dinner?"

While they devoured the plateful of light meat and dark meat with studious concentration and enraptured tails, he collected the loot under the kitchen table: an inner sole, a silver toothpick in a leather sheath, a tortoiseshell napkin ring, and . . . the jeweler's box that they had pilfered from the desk drawer.

"You rascals!" he scolded affectionately. "Where did you have it hidden?"

In the library he examined the ring once more. It was now clear that the initials entwined on the crown were W and E. There was also an intimate inscription inside the band, with the initials ERG and WBK. Then Koko leaped to the desktop and showed unusual interest in the gold memento, touching it gingerly as if it might bite. Qwilleran tamped his moustache as he questioned the cat's reaction. Was he simply attracted to a small shiny object? Or did he detect hidden significance in the ring? If the latter, it would be something more topical than the illicit affair in Lockmaster, circa 1929. But what? Koko could sense more with his whiskers than most humans could construe with their brains. Unfortunately, he had an oblique way of communicating, and Qwilleran was not always smart enough to read him.

Ring . . . gold ring . . . horse farmer . . . E and W . . . wasn't ERG a unit of energy? It seemed nonsensical, and in years gone by Qwilleran would have scoffed at such speculation, but life with Kao K'o Kung had taught him to pay attention, even though he sometimes felt like a fool.

FIFTEEN

THE DAY AFTER Thanksgiving Qwilleran was still pondering the significance of the signet ring when he went downtown to the newspaper to hand in his copy. Before leaving the house he took a roll call, as he always did. Yum Yum with graceful tail was rubbing against his ankles, and he picked her up to whisper comforting sentiments in her twitching ear. Koko was in the library closet, sitting tall and solemn in the open safe like some mythic oracle with all the answers.

Qwilleran started out to walk downtown, but the footing was precarious; the daily snowfall was packing down and turning sidewalks into minor glaciers. He drove to the newspaper office.

Junior greeted him in high spirit. "Hixie tells me you're going to be our Santa Claus! You'll be terrific! And you'll have a good time!"

"I don't know about that, but I'll give it my best shot," he replied as he handed Junior the jeweler's box.

"My grandfather's ring!"

"Guess again! Look inside the band."

"Wow!" said Junior when he read the inscription. "So WBK is the horse farmer who wanted to jump off the silo!"

"It would be interesting to know if Euphonia's recent boyfriend in Florida spells his name with a K. I thought it was C-r-o-c-u-s. I'll have to check it out."

"I haven't told you the latest," said Junior. "In probating Grandma's estate we're having trouble finding enough assets to warrant contesting the will. The bank records show huge cash deposits at the time she liquidated everything. After that there were sizable withdrawals, as if she'd invested in securities, although she didn't play the stock market. She liked something safe. But we don't find any financial documents."

"Some old people are afraid of banks," Qwilleran said. "She may have hidden them. They may be in the library closet."

"Naw, she told me to burn everything in that closet."

"Or . . . you may not be aware of this, Junior, but Gil Inchpot spent heavily on farm improvements in the last two or three years, and no one knows where he got the money. Did Euphonia lend it to him on the strength of her affection for Lena?"

"Hey! That makes sense!" said Junior. "Some time

back, Inchpot called me here at the office, asking for her address in Florida. He owed her some money and wanted to repay the loan."

"You gave him her address?"

"Sure. But if he paid her, what the devil happened to the dough! She couldn't have lost it all at the race track! Or could she?"

"When she decided to bequeath a health spa to the park, Junior, didn't she know her fortune was dwindling? Or did that happen after she wrote her new will?"

"Well, I don't know, but Wilmot hasn't given up yet. He has more possibilities to explore, but it takes time."

Qwilleran smoothed his moustache. "More and more I think the operation Down Below is shady—if not downright crepuscular. How about the lawyer who writes cheap wills? He could be in on it. How about the dealer who liquidated Euphonia's treasures? Does anyone know who he is or what he paid for the stuff? He could have robbed her blind!"

"Wow!" said Junior. "Maybe I should put a bug in Wilmot's ear."

"Not yet. Wait until I have more evidence." Qwilleran started to leave. "It just might be a well-organized crime ring!"

"Don't go, Qwill. This is getting good!"

"I have an appointment to try on my Santa Claus suit. We'll talk later."

En route to the theatre Qwilleran realized that his attitude toward the Christmas parade was mellowing. He could visualize himself riding in a sleigh behind a horse decked out in jingle bells. Sleighs were often seen on the unsalted streets of Pickax. The experience might make a good topic for his column.

At the K Theatre Carol Lanspeak and the seamstress were waiting for him, and Carol said, "We really appreciate your cooperation in the emergency, Qwill. Larry says he'll treat you to dinner at the Palomino Paddock, if he lives. Try on the pants first."

Qwilleran squeezed into the red breeches. "They're a good length for clam digging," he said.

Mrs. Toddwhistle, who worked on costumes for the Theatre Club, said, "I have some red fabric, and I can add about six inches to the length—also a stirrup to keep them down in your boots."

Carol looked critically at his yellow duck boots. "You should have black. What size do you wear? I'll bring a pair from the store."

The coat was roomy enough for two bed pillows under the belt, although snug through the shoulders and under the arms. The sleeves could be lengthened by adding more fake fur to the cuffs, the women assured him. They seemed to know what they were talking about . . . Everything would work out just fine! . . . No problem! . . . He would make a wonderful Santa!

With that matter settled he applied his attention to the situation in Florida and telephoned Celia Robinson without waiting for the discount rate. "Did you enjoy Thanksgiving, Celia?" he began.

"Oh, yes, it was very nice. About thirty of us went in the bus to a real nice restaurant. We had a reservation. It was buffet."

"Did Mr. Crocus go with you?"

"No, he didn't feel like it. He remembers last Thanksgiving when Mrs. Gage was with us and read a poem. She wrote it herself."

"I promised to send him a book of hers but got sidetracked because of the Big Snow. How does he spell his name?"

"I think it's C-r-o-c-u-s, like the flower."

"Are you sure? It could be K-r-o-k-u-s, you know. What's his first name?"

"Gerard. He has a shirt with GFC embroidered on the pocket. Mrs. Gage gave it to him, and he wears it all the time."

"Hmmm," Qwilleran murmured. Reluctantly he abandoned the long-lost-lover theory. Mr. Crocus was not WBK. "Did you ask him if he'd speak with me about Mrs. Gage?"

"Yes, I did, Mr. Qwilleran, but he said it wouldn't be in good taste to talk to the media about a dear departed friend. I don't feel that way. I'd like to see you write a beautiful article about her, and if there's anything more I can do—"

"You've been a great help, Celia, and—yes, there is more you can do. I believe I've uncovered something in the Park of Pink Sunsets that's a bigger story than Euphonia Gage."

"You don't mean it!" she said excitedly. "Is it something nice?"

Qwilleran cleared his throat and planned his approach before replying. "No, it isn't *nice,* as you say. I believe there's activity in your community that is highly unethical, if not illegal."

With sudden sharpness she said, "You reporters are always trying to dig up dirt and make trouble! This is a lovely place for retirees like me. Don't call me any more. I don't want to talk to you. You told me you were writing a nice article about Mrs. Gage! I don't want anything more to do with you!" And she slammed the receiver.

"Well! How do you like that?" Qwilleran asked the bookshelves.

"Yow!" said Koko from his reserved seat in the safe.

"Did I strike a raw nerve? Celia may be part of the ring—a simple, fun-loving grandmother, mixing with the other residents and singling out the likely victims. Now that she knows we suspect their game, what will she do?"

He thought of phoning Junior. He thought of by-passing Junior and calling Wilmot. Then he decided to wait and see.

The day of the parade was sunny but crisp, and Qwilleran wore his long underwear for the ride in an open sleigh. He assumed it would be a sleigh and not a convertible with the top down.

At the theatre, where he went to get into costume, he found the breeches lengthened and equipped with stirrups, which made them rather taut for comfort, but Carol said he would get used to the feeling. She strapped him into his two bed pillows and helped him into his coat. The sleeves had been extended with white fake fur from elbow to wrist.

"I look as if I had both arms in a cast," he complained. Trussed into the stuffed coat and taut breeches, he found it difficult to bend over. Carol had to pull on his boots.

"How is the fit?" she asked. "They run large to allow for thick socks."

"I feel as if I'm wearing snowshoes." He was hardly in a jolly mood. "Is this belly supposed to shake like a bowlful of jelly? It feels like a sack of cold oatmeal. Has Larry ever worn this getup?"

"Many times! At church and at the community Christmas party. He loves playing Santa!"

"Why does the old geezer have to look seventy-five pounds overweight? Even as a kid I doubted that he could come down a chimney. Now I question why the heart specialists don't get after him. Why aren't the health clubs coming forward?"

"Would you ruin a thousand-year-old image, Qwill? Come off your soapbox. It's all in fun." Carol powdered his moustache, reddened his cheeks, and adjusted the wig and beard before adding a red hat with a floppy pointed crown.

"I feel like an idiot!" he said. "I hope Polly won't be watching the parade from an upstairs window of the library."

They drove north in the Lanspeak van along Pickax Road, the sun glaring on the snowy roadbed and snowy landscape. Qwilleran had left his sunglasses at the theatre, and the scene was dazzling. Already the parade route was filling up with cars, vans, and pick-ups loaded with children.

"This is all very exciting," Carol said. "Pickax has never had a Christmas parade before. The welcoming ceremonies will be in front of the store, and when you arrive, Hixie's secretary will meet you and tell you what to do."

"Speaking of stores," Qwilleran said, "could you suggest a Christmas present for Polly? Jewelry, per-haps. She likes pearls, but she says she doesn't need any more."

"How about opals? I think she'd like opals, and

there's a jeweler in Minneapolis who'll send some out on approval."

They were approaching the Dimsdale Diner, where vast open fields were covered with glaring snow. "It's incredibly bright today," he said, feeling as if his eyeballs were spinning.

"Yes, a perfect day for a parade," said Carol, who was wearing sunglasses.

"What kind of conveyance do you have for jolly old St. Nick with two arms in a cast?" he asked.

"Oh, didn't Hixie tell you?" she said, eager to break the news. "We've arranged for a dogsled with eight Siberian huskies!"

Parade units were gathering around the snowy intersection: floats, a brass band on a flatbed truck, a giant snowplow, a fire truck, a group of cross-country skiers, and a yelping dogteam.

"We meet unexpectedly," Qwilleran said to Nancy. He assumed it was Nancy; the glare was distorting his vision.

"No one told me you were going to be Santa," she said with delight. "I thought it was going to be Mr. Lanspeak. There's a bale of hay in the basket for you to sit on, and I covered it with a caribou skin. I think it'll work. We won't be going very fast. Where are your sunglasses?"

"I left them in town," Qwilleran said. "Santa with shades seemed inappropriate."

"Isn't this exciting? I've never been in a parade. I wish my mom could see me now—driving Santa Claus in a dogsled! She died before I even started dogsledding. Today would have been her birthday . . . It looks as if they're getting ready to start."

The band struck up, the sheriff's car led the way,

and the parade units fell into place, with the dogsled bringing up the rear—Nancy riding the runners, Qwilleran in the basket. She drove the team with one-syllable commands: "Up! . . . Go! . . . Way!"

All along the route the spectators were shouting to Santa, and Qwilleran waved first one arm and then the other at persons he could not clearly see. Both arms were becoming gradually numb as the tight armholes hampered his circulation. When they turned onto Main Street the crowds were larger and louder but just as blurred, and he was greatly relieved when they reached their destination.

Lanspeak's Department Store was built like a castle. An iron gate raised on heavy chains extended over the sidewalk, providing a marquee from which city officials could review the parade.

As the dogsled pulled up to the store, Nancy leaned over and said to Qwilleran, "I'll take the dogs behind the store until you've finished your speech."

"Speech! What speech?" he demanded indignantly.

"Mr. Qwilleran, sir," said a young man's voice coming out of the general blur.

"Wilfred? Get me out of this contraption! I can't see a thing!"

"They're waiting for you up there," said the secretary. "I'll hold the ladder."

Only then did Qwilleran become aware of a ladder leaning against the front edge of the marquee. "I can't bend my knees; my arms are numb; and I can't see! I'm not climbing up any damned ladder!"

"You've got to," said Wilfred in panic.

Hundreds of spectators were cheering, and the officials were looking over the edge of the marquee and shouting, "Come on up, Santa!" Qwilleran walked to the foot of the ladder with a stiff-legged gait, his knees splinted by the taut breeches. He looked up speculatively to the summit. "If I fall off this thing," he said threateningly to the nervous secretary, "both you and Hixie are fired!"

He managed to lift one foot to the first rung and grasp the siderails. Cheers! Then slowly he forced one knee after the other to bend, all the while maneuvering the long-toed boots and hoisting the two bed pillows ahead of him. More cheers! There was an occasional ripping sound—where, he was not sure— but the more the rips, the easier the climb. And the louder were the cheers. Gradually he felt his way to the top of the ladder, where helping hands reached out and hauled him onto the marquee.

There was a microphone, and the mayor said a few words of welcome, his speech slurred by the fortifying nips he had taken to keep warm. "And now . . . I give you . . . Santa Claus . . . in person!" he concluded.

Qwilleran was steered to the mike. "M-er-r-ry Christmas!" he bellowed. Then he turned away and said in a voice that went out over the speakers, "Get me outa here! How do I get down? I'm not going back down that stupid ladder!"

There were more cheers from the spectators.

The store had a second-floor window through which the city officials had arrived, and Qwilleran climbed through it. Wilfred was waiting for him in the second-floor lingerie department. He said, "The dogs are being brought around to the front door."

"To hell with the dogs! I'm through! Find someone to drive me back to the theatre!"

"But they're expecting you at the courthouse, Mr. Qwilleran."

"What for?"

"Lap-sitting."

"Lap-sitting? What the devil is that?"

"They built a gingerbread house for you in front of the courthouse, and the kids sit on your lap and have their pictures taken."

"Oh, no, they don't!" Qwilleran said fiercely. "I refuse flatly! Enough is enough!"

"Mr. Qwilleran, sir, you gotta!"

They rode down on the elevator, and even before they landed on the main floor they heard a voice on the public address system: "Paging Santa Claus! Paging Santa Claus!"

"Where's a phone?" he snapped . . . "Yes?" he yelled into the mouthpiece.

"Hey, Qwill! How did it go?" It was Junior's enthusiastic voice.

"Don't ask!"

"The city desk just had a strange phone call, Qwill: Celia Robinson in Florida, calling from a pay phone in a mall. She said she had to get in touch with you secretly. What's that all about? We never give out home phones, but she's calling back this afternoon to find out how to reach you. Extremely important, she says."

"Give her Polly's number," Qwilleran said, his voice calm for the first time in two hours. "Tell her to call around eight o'clock tonight."

"Whatever you say. Are you all through with your Santa stunt?"

"No," Qwilleran said in a matter-of-fact way. "I have to go to the courthouse for lap-sitting."

SIXTEEN

IT WAS CUSTOMARY for Qwilleran and Polly to spend Saturday evening together, and this time the chief attraction was turkey leftovers, which she had prepared in a curry sauce with mushrooms, leeks and lentils. They could now call the bird a turkey.

"Do you think Mildred is still sensitive about her late husband?" Polly asked. "I hope not. She and Arch are very right for each other, and they should get on with their new life ... Tell me about the parade, dear."

"I don't want to talk about it," he said in an even voice.

She knew better than to insist.

He said, "I'm expecting a phone call around eight

o'clock, and I'd like to take it privately, if you don't mind."

"Of course I don't mind," she replied, although her lips tightened. He had not even told her who would be calling.

Exactly at eight o'clock the telephone rang, and he took the call in the bedroom with the door closed. Polly started the dishwasher.

The anguished voice of Celia Robinson blurted, "Oh, Mr. Qwilleran, I apologize for hanging up on you like that! What horrible things did you think of me? I didn't mean a word of what I said, but I was afraid somebody would be listening in. I'm making this call from a phone in a mall."

"Are you on a switchboard at the park? I thought the residents had private numbers."

"We do! We do! But Clayton thinks the whole park is bugged. I always thought he was kidding, but when you mentioned something illegal, I got worried. I thought it might be dangerous to talk to you. Is it true what you said? Are you an investigator?"

Experience warned him that she might be part of the ring, luring him to show his hand. Yet, a tremor in the roots of his moustache told him to risk the gamble. He had formulated a plan. He said, "I'm just a reporter with a suspicion that Junior's grandmother was a victim of fraud."

"Oh, dear! Are you going to expose it?"

"There's insufficient evidence at present, and that's where you can help. You thought highly of Mrs. Gage; are you willing to play a harmless trick on those who robbed her? I believe your grandson would approve."

"Can I tell Clayton about it? I write him every week."

"You're not to confide in him or Mr. Crocus or anyone else. Consider yourself an undercover agent. You'll be rewarded for your time and cooperation, of course. In Pickax we have an eleemosynary foundation that's committed to the pursuit of justice."

"I never heard of one of those," she said, "but I'm honored that you'd ask me to help. Do you think I can do it?"

"No doubt about it, provided you follow orders."

"What if it doesn't work? What if I get caught?"

Qwilleran said, "Whether it succeeds or fails, no one will suspect you of duplicity, and you'll be kept in chocolate-covered cherries for life."

Celia howled with delight. "What do I do first?"

"You'll receive your briefing along with a check to cover expenses. Where do you receive your mail?"

"It comes to the park office, and we pick it up there. It's a good excuse to go for a walk and chat with our neighbors. Sometimes we pick up each other's mail."

"That being the case," he said, "I'll send your orders to the post office in care of general delivery."

"Oh, goody!" Celia said as the elements of intrigue dawned upon her. "Is this a sting?"

"You might call it that. Now go home and say nothing. I'll put the wheels in motion, and you should receive your assignment in two days, unless we have another Big Snow."

"Thank you, Mr. Qwilleran! This gives me a real boot!"

He emerged from the bedroom patting his moustache with satisfaction. He even said a kind word to Bootsie, who was sitting outside the door, and he was very good company for the rest of the evening.

* * *

The next day, as he worked on Celia's briefing, he thought, This may be the dumbest thing I ever did in my life—sending $5,000 to a stranger who may be a double agent. And yet . . .

The document that went into the mail read as follows:

FOR YOUR EYES ONLY! Memorize, shred, and flush.

TO: Agent 0013½

FROM: Q

MISSION: Operation Greenback, Phase One

ASSIGNMENT: Your unmarried sister in Chicago has died, leaving you sole heir to a large house, valuable possessions, and financial assets. You wish to share your new fortune with your neighbors by giving a Christmas party in the clubhouse on December 11 or 12. Notify the management that you will spend as much as $5,000 on a caterer, florist, and live music. (A check for this amount, drawn on a Chicago bank, will arrive under separate cover.) Observe the management's reaction to the above and report to Q. Watch for further briefings in the mail.

Qwilleran had planned the tongue-in-cheek approach to relieve any apprehension Celia might have, and he could imagine her merry laughter upon reading the document. And if, he reflected grimly, she happened to be a double agent, her laughter would be even merrier. He still trusted the encouraging sensation on his upper lip, however, and he prepared a second secret document to go out in the mail the next day:

MISSION: Operation Greenback, Phase Two
ASSIGNMENT: Ask the management about the possibility of moving into a double-wide . . . Test them by saying that your sister wished you to adopt her cat, who has a trust fund of his own of $10,000 a year. Ask for a special permit to have an indoor cat who is quiet, and not destructive, and rich. Observe their reactions to the above and report to Q at HQ.

Qwilleran enclosed a card with his home phone number and instructions to call collect from a pay phone any evening between five and six o'clock. Then he waited. He wrote two columns for the *Moose County Something*. He signed a hundred Christmas cards for Lori Bamba to address. He looked at jewelry from Minneapolis and selected a lavaliere and earrings for Polly: fiery black opals rimmed with discreet diamonds. He read more of *Robinson Crusoe* to the cats.

One early evening, as he was beginning to doubt the wisdom of enlisting Celia, he was talking with Lori Bamba on the phone when Koko started biting the cord. "Excuse me, Lori," he said. "Koko wants me to hang up."

A moment later the phone rang, and a hushed voice said, "This is Double-Oh-Thirteen-and-a-half. Is it all right to talk?" Background noises assured him she was calling from the mall.

"By all means. I've been waiting for your report."

"Well! Let me tell you!" she said in her normal voice. "I've been having a ball! Everybody's excited about the party, and Betty and Claude are falling all over me! They used to treat me like a clown; now I get respect! They're giving me a special permit for the cat, and they're putting me at the top of the list for a double-wide!"

"You're a good operative, Celia."

"Shall I go ahead and get a cat?"

"Wait a minute! Not so fast! In the interest of realism, the cat should be shipped from Chicago."

"Clayton could bring it when he flies down for Christmas. I'd like a Burmese, but they're expensive. Maybe he could find one at an animal shelter."

Qwilleran said, "Cost is not the issue here, but let's not get ahead of the game. Wait for orders."

"I'm sorry. I'm just so excited! I feel as if I've really inherited my sister's fortune, and I don't even have a sister! What do I do next?"

"Keep checking the post office, and call whenever you have something to report."

"Isn't this *fun?*" she was squealing as he said goodnight.

Qwilleran had already plotted his next move. The following day he walked downtown to the store that had gold lettering on the window: EXBRIDGE & COBB, FINE ANTIQUES.

Susan Exbridge greeted him effusively. "Darling! You survived the Big Snow! Did you enjoy being snowbound?"

"It wasn't what John Greenleaf Whittier had led me to expect. The lucky bunch in his poem sat around a blazing fire, roasting apples and telling stories. I was alone with a kerosene stove and two cats, and all of us were bored stiff. How about you?"

"The people in my building in Indian Village played bridge for five days."

Wandering through the shop, Qwilleran lingered

over a pair of brass candlesticks a foot high, with thick, twisted stems and chunky bases the size of a soup bowl. "I like candlesticks," he remarked.

"Most men do, and I refuse to guess why," she said. "These are Dutch baroque, but I found them in Stockholm."

"I'll take them," he said. "Do you know how or where Euphonia sold her belongings?"

"I know how . . . but not exactly where," said Susan. "I wanted her to work with some good dealers in New York and Philadelphia, but someone in Florida offered her a lump sum for everything, and she fell for it. People get lazy about liquidating and want to do it the easy way."

"How much did they offer? Do you know?"

"I have no idea, but we can assume that it was well under the going price."

He paid for his purchase and asked to borrow some magazines on antiques.

On the way home he stopped at the Bushland Studio. John Bushland had transferred his commercial photography studio from Lockmaster to Pickax, and Qwilleran asked if he had any interior photos of his previous house in Lockmaster.

"I've got a complete set. Want to see 'em?"

Qwilleran had visited the photographer's century-old house and remembered the foyer with its carved staircase, stained-glass windows, and converted gaslight fixtures. "I could use a copy of this shot," he said. "Also a close-up of the marble fireplace in the front parlor and the one with painted tiles in the dining room. Don't ask me why I want them, Bushy; it's too complicated. I need them, that's all."

"Sure," said the genial young man. "How quick?"

"A.S.A.P."

"Then take these prints. I'll make more for the file."

The magazines that Qwilleran carried home contained dealer ads for choice antiques at five-digit and six-digit prices that shocked his frugal psyche. Nevertheless, he made a list of items that would fit his scheme: Jacobean chair . . . carved and gilded divan from India . . . four-poster brass bed in Gothic style . . . spiral staircase from Irish country house . . . collection of botanical plates in porcelain, eighteenth century . . . Empire desk in mahogany and ormolu . . . and more. He omitted any reference to price.

He photocopied the list at the public library. One copy would go to Susan Exbridge for appraisal; the other, to Celia Robinson with another briefing:

MISSION: Operation Greenback, Phase Three
ASSIGNMENT: Your late sister was a collector of antiques and art objects, none of which you understand or even like. There are twelve rooms of such furnishings that you wish to sell with as little effort as possible. Ask the park management if they know how to go about it. Show them the enclosed list as a sampling of the items involved. Mention also that you must sell your sister's house. Show them the enclosed photos of the interior. Report their responses as usual.

December in Pickax was a month of crowded stores, sparkling decorations, holiday parties, school pageants, and carol singing, with a picturesque snowfall every day. In the "Qwill Pen" column the veteran newsman strove to write about these perennial subjects with a fresh approach, although his mind was on

Operation Greenback. He was relieved when his agent made her second report:

"Oh, it was a wonderful party, Mr. Qwilleran! Everybody had a terrific time," she began. "All the Sunsetters congratulated me on my inheritance."

"Did Mr. Crocus attend?"

"Well, I had to coax him, but afterwards he said he had a good time. I don't know whether he meant it. He always says the polite thing."

"What do you know about his background?"

"Only that he was in some kind of wholesale business in Ohio. No one in his family ever visits him. Maybe that's why he enjoys Clayton's company. They play chess together."

Qwilleran asked, "And how did the management react to your questions?"

"They were very helpful. They have experience and a lot of connections, they said. They're going to show my list of furniture to a dealer, and he'll make an offer on the whole houseful."

"Did you show them the photographs of the house?"

"Yes, they were quite impressed and said there were things that should be removed before vandals get them. They know somebody who does that. He would pay for them, of course. And guess what! Betty and Claude invited me to the dog races! It looks as if I'm in solid! Things were going so good that I did something on my own. I hope I did right."

"What did you do?" Qwilleran asked sternly.

"I asked if my grandson could come for a whole week during the holidays, even though he's only thirteen. They said okay, but no singing dogs."

"I suppose you realize, Celia, that we're flirting with a security hazard. Clayton will want to know

why the management is buttering you up and why
the Sunsetters are raving about the big Christmas
party you gave. You'll have to tell him the truth."

"He can be trusted, Mr. Qwilleran. He won't give
me away. He'll be glad to see me putting one over on
Betty and Claude."

"Hmmm . . . Let me think about this," Qwilleran
said, cupping his moustache with his hand. "You say
he plays chess with Mr. Crocus. Perhaps he could get
the old gentleman to unburden himself about things
that are troubling him. Is Clayton smart enough, ma-
ture enough, to handle this? Mr. Crocus knew about
Mrs. Gage's bequest to the park; he might know other
things that would shed light on the matter we're investigating."

"I'm sure Clayton could do it, Mr. Qwilleran. He's a
very bright boy and much more on the ball than I am.
He reads a lot, you know. Yes, I'm positive he could
handle it. He's thirteen now."

"All right. It's worth a try," Qwilleran said. "Also,
have Clayton bring a cat with him—full-grown, because this is supposed to be your sister's cherished
pet. You'll receive a check from the Chicago bank to
cover the purchase of the cat, air transportation,
catfood, and a few holiday treats for you and Clayton."

"That's very nice of you," Celia said. "Now Clayton
can have one of those five-dollar sundaes. Is there
anything else I can do?"

"You should decide on a name for the cat and arrange to feed him or her in the manner to which a
$10,000-a-year animal is accustomed."

"I've been thinking about a name. We don't know
whether it will be a boy or a girl, but either way I

think Windy would be a good name, since it's supposed to be from Chicago."

"Do you have a second choice?" Qwilleran asked. "Windy has other connotations when applied to an animal."

After discussing this weighty subject at length, they decided to call the cat Wrigley. Celia enjoyed a few laughs, and Qwilleran was in a good mood when he hung up.

The occasion seemed to call for a dish of ice cream, and while in the kitchen he picked up Koko's current collection: a petrified stick of chewing gum, a mildewed toothbrush, a card of tiny safety pins, and other items of more than usual interest to Qwilleran. One was a purple satin pincushion embroidered ERG and obviously homemade, possibly by a child. There was a business card from Breze Services on Sandpit Road, the nine-digit zip code indicating that it was of fairly recent date. A canceled check for $100—dated December 24, 1972—had been paid to Lena Inchpot; was that the housekeeper's Christmas bonus from Mrs. Gage, or a salary check? An unpaid traffic ticket issued by the sheriff department had been issued by D. Fincher.

Of greatest interest was a yellowed envelope inscribed "Lethe" in what Qwilleran now knew to be Euphonia's handwriting, which had an exaggerated up-stroke at the end of each word. It was another poem, he assumed, Lethe being the mythical river in Hades, said to induce forgetfulness. Forgetting and not forgetting had been much on Euphonia's mind, he thought. The envelope was sealed, and he used a kitchen knife to slit it. What he found was no poem,

but an official paper, a birth certificate issued in
Lockmaster County:

> *Date of birth:* Nov. 27, 1928
> *Name of child:* Lethe Gage
> *Sex:* female   *Color:* white
> *Name of mother:* Euphonia Roff Gage
> *Name of father:*

Qwilleran rushed to the telephone. "Brace yourself
for some news, Junior!" he said when his young friend
answered. "You've got an aunt you didn't know
about!"

Junior listened to the reading of the certificate.
"Can you beat that! That's when Grandpa was in
prison! The father must have been the horse farmer."

"Here's the question," said Qwilleran. "Is Lethe
still alive? Or is she the 'dead princess' in Euphonia's
memorial program? If she's still around, wouldn't she
have come forward for a slice of the inheritance?"

"She might be living somewhere else. She might
not know Grandma's dead."

"Could be." Qwilleran thought of the foreign postcards and envelopes with foreign stamps that Koko
had dragged out of the closet. "In any case, you
should notify the attorney."

SEVENTEEN

As CHRISTMAS APPROACHED, Qwilleran accepted invitations to holiday parties, but his mind was on Operation Greenback, and he made it a point to be home between five and six o'clock, the hour when Celia might call with another report. Increasing tremors in the roots of his moustache told him he was on the right track.

One evening at five-fifteen the telephone rang, and a hollow voice said, "This is Celia, Mr. Qwilleran."

"You sound different," he said.

"I'm calling from a different mall on the other side of town, and the phones are more private. I had a scare the last time I talked to you."

"What kind of scare?"

"Well, after I hung up, I saw Betty and Claude watching me. They were waiting in line outside a restaurant. I didn't know what to do. Should I make up some kind of explanation? Then I thought, What would Clayton do? He'd play it cool. So I walked over to them and said hello, and they invited me to have dinner with them, but I'd eaten already. Whew! I was worried for a while."

"You handled it very well," Qwilleran said. "Do you have anything to report on your last assignment?"

"Only that the furniture dealer down here will give me $100,000 for the things on the list you sent me, plus $50,000 for everything else in the house. Boy! What I could do with that much money! I'm beginning to wish I'd had a rich sister."

Qwilleran made no comment. The same list of antique furnishings had been appraised by Susan Exbridge at $900,000. He said, "Good job, Celia! That's the kind of information we need."

"Thank you, chief. Do you have another assignment for me?"

"Phase Four of Operation Greenback will be mailed tomorrow."

In mailing the briefing he included a Christmas bonus with instructions to buy something exciting for herself.

MISSION: Operation Greenback, Phase Four
ASSIGNMENT: Buy an expensive Christmas plant for the manager's office . . . Tell them you'll have a surplus of cash when you sell your sister's possessions; ask if they can recommend a safe investment . . . Inquire if it's possible to place

bets on the dog races without going to the track, since you don't like crowds.

Although Qwilleran made generous Christmas gifts and ate more than his share of Christmas cookies, there was not a shred of holiday decoration in his cavernous, sparsely furnished living quarters.

"How can you stand this gloomy place?" Polly asked him.

One evening, on her way home from the library, she delivered a green wreath studded with holly berries and tiny white lights. "For your library," she said. "Just hang it up and plug it in."

The pinpoints of light only emphasized the somber effect of dark paneling, old books, and worn furniture, as they sat on the sofa sipping hot cider. The Siamese, sniffing Bootsie in absentia, applied wet noses to Polly's person, here and there.

"Out!" Qwilleran scolded, pointing to the door.

"They don't bother me," Polly protested.

"I expect them to have some manners to match their aristocratic facade . . . *Out!*"

They left the room but not immediately. First they thought about it, then scratched an ear and licked a paw, then thought about it some more, then sauntered out.

"Cats!" Qwilleran said, and Polly smiled with amusement.

They discussed cat-sitting arrangements for the Christmas weekend. Polly wanted to pick up a key for her sister-in-law. "Lynette lives only a block away, so she's happy to come twice a day. She loves cats and considers it a privilege."

Soon Koko returned, carrying in his jaws a small

square paper packet, which he dropped at Qwilleran's feet.

Picking it up, Qwilleran read the label: "Dissolve contents of envelope in three pints of water and soak feet for fifteen minutes . . . Foot powder! Where did he find that?"

Polly, ordinarily given to small smiles, was overcome with mirth. "Perhaps he's telling you something, dear."

"This isn't funny! It could be poisonous! He could tear the paper and sprinkle the powder on the floor, then walk in it and lick his paws!" He dropped the packet in a desk drawer.

After Polly had gone on her way, Qwilleran had another look at the foot powder and read the precaution: "Poisonous if ingested. Keep away from children and pets." At the same time he realized how many of Koko's discoveries were associated with feet: corn plasters, a man's sock, a woman's slipper, shoelaces, toenail clippers, an inner sole, a buttonhook, a shoe-polishing cloth—even a man's spat! Either the cat had a foot fetish or he was trying to communicate. As for his occupation with Confederate currency, canceled checks, and the *safe,* was that related to the financial skulduggery that was becoming evident?

Qwilleran pounded his moustache as a sensation on his upper lip alerted him. He glanced at his watch. It was not too late to phone Homer Tibbitt. The nonagenarian lived in a retirement complex with his new wife, who was a mere octogenarian, and they were known to observe an early bedtime.

"Homer, this is Qwill," he said in a loud, clear voice. "I haven't seen you in the library lately. Aren't you doing any historical research?"

"Hell's bells!" the historian retorted. "She won't let me out of the house in winter! She hides my over-shoes!" His voice was high and cracked, but his delivery was vigorous. "Never marry a younger woman, boy! If I drop a pencil, she thinks I've had a stroke. If I drop a shoe, she thinks I've broken a hip. She's driving me crazy! . . . What's on your mind?"

"Just this, Homer: You were in the Lockmaster school system for many years, and I wonder if you knew a family by the name of Foote."

"There are quite a few Footes in Lockmaster . . . or should I say Feete?" Homer added with a chuckle. "None of them left any footprints in the sands of time."

"You're in an arch mood tonight," Qwilleran said with a chuckle of his own. "The Foote I'm curious about is Lena Foote, who should have been a student between 1934 and 1946."

"Lena Foote, you say?" said the former principal. "She must have been a good girl. The only ones I remember are the troublemakers."

Another voice sounded in the background, and Homer turned away to say to his wife, "You don't remember that far back! You can't remember where you left your glasses ten minutes ago!" This was followed by muffled arguing and then, "Do you want to talk to him yourself? Here! Take the phone."

A woman who sounded pleasantly determined came on the line. "This is Rhoda Tibbitt, Mr. Qwilleran. I remember Lena Foote very well. I had her in high school English, and she showed unusual promise. Sad to say, she didn't finish."

"Do you know anything about her parents? Her father was Arnold Foote."

"Yes, indeed! I begged her parents to let her get her diploma, but they were poor farmers and needed the income. She went into domestic service at the age of fifteen, and that's the last I knew. Do you happen to know what happened to her?"

"Only that she died of cancer a few years ago, after a relatively short life as a farmwife, mother, and employed housekeeper," Qwilleran said. "Thank you for the information, Mrs. Tibbitt, and tell that ornery husband of yours that your memory is better than his."

"The testimonial is appreciated," she said, "and let me take this opportunity to wish you a very happy holiday."

Qwilleran was disappointed. He had learned nothing about Nancy's mother, and yet . . . Koko always had a motive for his actions—almost always. The more peculiar his behavior, the more likely it was to be important. Now there were all those references to feet!

On an impulse he called directory assistance and asked for the number of Arnold Foote in Lockmaster. There was no listing for that name. He pondered awhile. The public library was open until nine o'clock. He phoned and asked a clerk to look up Foote in the Lockmaster directory. There were fourteen listed, she said, with locations in various parts of the county.

"Give me the phone numbers of the first three," he asked.

He first tried calling Foote, Andrew. The woman who answered told him in no uncertain terms, "We don't know anything about that branch of the family. We've never had anything to do with them."

He phoned Foote, Charles. A man said, "Don't

know. Long time since I saw Arnold at the farm co-op."

Finally there was Foote, Donald. "I heard he's in a nursing home but don't know for sure. His wife died, coupla years ago."

Before Qwilleran could plan his next move, he received an excited call from Celia Robinson. "I know it's after six o'clock," she said, "but I simply had to try to reach you!"

"What news?" he asked with intense interest.

"Your check! It's so generous of you! I've always wanted a three-wheel bike. A lot of ladies have them here and ride all over the park. Is that being too extravagant?"

"That's what Christmas presents are all about, and you're deserving," he assured her. "And how about your assignment?"

"I talked to Betty and Claude and wrote it all down," Celia said. "There's something called 'bearer bonds' that would be good for me, because my heirs could cash them easily if anything happened to me. Also there are some private boxes in the office safe, and I can have one for the bonds and any cash I don't want to put in the bank. If I win at the dog races, you see, there's a way of collecting without having to report it. They have an agent at the track."

"Beautiful!" Qwilleran murmured.

"Clayton flies in tomorrow, and I'll explain Operation Greenback in the car, driving in from the airport. I can hardly wait to see Wrigley!"

"Be sure to stress the need for secrecy," Qwilleran reminded her. "Tell Clayton we're investigating financial fraud, and the victim may have had fears or suspicions that she confided to Mr. Crocus."

"Don't worry. Clayton is a regular bloodhound. If we find out anything, is it okay to call you during the holidays?"

"Of course. Have a merry Christmas, Celia."

"Same to you, chief."

As soon as Qwilleran hung up, Koko walked across the desk and faced him eyeball to eyeball, delivering a trumpetlike "Yow-w-w!" that pained the aural and olfactory senses.

"What's your problem?" Qwilleran asked. In answer, the cat knocked a pen to the floor and bit the shade of the desklamp, then raced around the room— over the furniture, up on the bookshelves, into the closet and out again, all the while uttering a rumbling growl.

When Koko staged a catfit, it was a sure sign that Qwilleran was in the doghouse. "Oh-oh! I goofed!" he said, slapping his forehead. He had told Celia she could phone during the holidays; she would drive across town through dense traffic—just to call him— and he would be in Purple Point. He had been unforgivably thoughtless.

Koko had calmed down and was grooming the fur on his underside, and Qwilleran was faced with the problem of calling her on a phone that she insisted was bugged. He gave her an hour to drive back to the park before calling her mobile home. She was surprised to hear his voice.

In a tone of exaggerated jollity he said, "Just wanted to wish you a merry Christmas before *I leave town for the weekend.* I'll be gone *for three days.*"

"Oh," she said, unsure how to respond. "Where are you going, Mr. Qwilleran?"

"To a Christmas Eve wedding out of town. I won't be back home until *Monday evening.*"

"Oh . . . Who's getting married?"

"My boss."

"That's nice. Give him my congratulations."

"I'll do that."

"Will it be a big wedding?"

"No, just a small one. It's a second marriage for both of them. So . . . you and Clayton have a happy holiday, Celia."

"Same to you . . . uh . . . Mr. Qwilleran."

Hanging up the phone, he was sure she had got the message, and he complimented himself on handling it well. He turned to say to Koko, "Thank you, old boy, for drawing it to my attention." But Koko wasn't there. He was in the closet sitting in the safe.

On the morning of December 24 Qwilleran packed his rented formal wear for the wedding in Purple Point, all the while pondering the Euphonia Gage swindle. It was now clear to him what had happened to her money. Whether or not Clayton could coax anything out of Mr. Crocus, Qwilleran believed he had a good case to present to Pender Wilmot.

He called the attorney's office, and a machine informed him they would be closed until Monday. The Wilmots were now living in the fashionable suburb of West Middle Hummock, and he tried their residence. A childish voice answered, and he said, "May I speak to your father?"

"He isn't here. He went to a meeting. They have some lunch and sing a song and tell jokes. What do you want him for?"

"It's a business matter, Timmie."

"D'you want a divorce? Do you want to sue some-body?" the boy asked helpfully.

"Nothing like that," said Qwilleran, fascinated by the initiative of the embryo lawyer. "What else does he do besides divorces and lawsuits?"

"He writes wills. He wrote my will, and I signed it. I'm leaving my trains to my sister and all my wheels to my cousins and all my videos to the school."

"Well, have your father call me, Timmie, if he gets home before three o'clock. My name is Qwilleran."

"Wait till I get a pencil." There was a long wait be-fore he returned to the line. "What's your name?"

"Qwilleran. I'll spell it for you. Q-w-i-l-l-e-r-a-n."

"Q?"

"That's right. Do you know how to make a Q? . . . Then W . . ."

"W?" asked Timmie.

"That's right. Q . . . W . . . I . . . Have you got that? Then double-L . . ."

"Another W?" Timmie asked.

A woman's voice interrupted. "Timmie, your lunch is ready . . . Hello? This is Mrs. Wilmot. May I help you?"

"This is Jim Qwilleran, and I'd like Pender to call me if he gets home before three. I was in the process of leaving a message with his law clerk."

"Pender is having lunch with the Boosters, and then they're delivering Christmas baskets, but we'll see you at the wedding tonight."

"Perfect! I'll speak with him there."

EIGHTEEN

THE MARRIAGE CEREMONY was scheduled early, so that family and friends of the couple might return home to observe their own Christmas Eve traditions. In mid-afternoon Qwilleran picked up Polly for the drive to Purple Point. It was a narrow peninsula curving into the lake to form a natural harbor on the northern shore of Moose County. Viewed across the bay at sunset it was a distinct shade of purple.

In the boom years of the nineteenth century Purple Point had been the center of fishing and shipbuilding industries, but all activity disappeared with the closing of the mines and the consequent economic collapse. Fire leveled the landscape, and hurricanes narrowed the peninsula to a mere spit of sand. Sport fishing revived the area in the 1920s as affluent families from Down Below built large summer residences, which they called fish camps.

By the time Qwilleran arrived in Moose County, these dwellings were called cottages but were actually year-round vacation homes lining both sides of the road that ran the length of the peninsula. There were few trees, and sweeping winds raised havoc with sand or snow according to season. The approach to the Point was across a low, flat, uninhabited expanse called the Flats, a wetland in summer and an arctic waste following the Big Snow. The county plows kept the road open, building high, snowy banks on both sides, while the individual cottages were walled in by their own snow blowers. It was a surreal landscape into which Qwilleran and Polly ventured on that Christmas Eve.

What the Lanspeaks called their cottage had a tall-case clock in the foyer, a baby grand piano in the living room, a quadrophonic sound system, and four bedrooms on the balcony. The only reminder of the original fish camp was the cobblestone fireplace. The bride and groom were already there, Riker assisting Larry in the preparation of an afternoon toddy, while Mildred raved about the tasteful decorations. There were banks of white poinsettias, garlands of greens, and a large Scotch pine trimmed with pearlescent ornaments, white velvet bows, and crystal icicles.

When the guests started to arrive, the wedding party was elsewhere, dressing. The first to pull into the driveway were Junior and Jody Goodwinter, carpooling with Mildred's daughter, Sharon, and her husband, Roger MacGillivray. Qwilleran, looking down from the balcony, saw Lisa and Lyle Compton arriving with John Bushland (and his camera) and June Halliburton, who sat down at the piano and started playing pleasant music. Chopin nocturnes, Polly said. Among those from the neighboring cottages were Don Exbridge and his new wife and the Wilmot family, the bespectacled Timmie in his little long-pant suit and bow tie. Hixie Rice hobbled in with her surgical boot, walker, and attentive doctor. They brought the officiating pastor with them, Ms. Sims from the Brrr church, the Pickax clergymen having declined to leave their flocks on Christmas Eve.

At five o'clock the music faded away, the tall clock bonged five times, and Mildred's daughter lighted the row of candles on the mantel. An expectant hush fell over the assembled guests. Then the pianist began a sweetly lyrical melody. Schubert's Impromptu in G Flat, Polly said. Ms. Sims in robe and surplice took her place in front of the fireplace, and—as the tender notes developed into a strong crescendo—the groom and groomsman joined her. In dinner jacket and black tie the groom looked distinguished, and the best man looked especially handsome. There was a joyous burst of music, and all eyes turned upward as Polly walked downstairs from the balcony in her blue crepe and pearls. After a moment's suspense the tender melody was heard again, and Mildred—who had lost a few pounds—moved gracefully down the stairs in apricot velvet.

For the first time in his life Qwilleran performed his nuptial duty without dropping the ring. The only ripple of levity came when Timmie Wilmot, standing in the front row, said, "Daddy, how is that lady gonna join those people together?"

After the ceremony there were champagne toasts

and the cutting of the cake. Rightfully, the bride was the center of attention. Mildred—the good-hearted, generous, charitable supporter of worthy causes—was saying, "All the restaurants have been saving their pickle jars for us, and we now have a hundred of them at cash registers around the county, collecting loose change for spaying stray cats. I call them community cats because they don't belong to anyone but they belong to everyone."

Lisa said to Qwilleran, "Who's feeding Koko and Yum Yum?"

"Polly's sister-in-law."

Polly said, "Qwill's cats get food intended for humans, and I can't convince him it's the wrong thing to do."

"If you can convince Koko," he said, "I'll gladly go along. In his formative years Koko lived with a gourmet cook and developed a taste for lobster bisque and oysters Rockefeller. If I feed the female catfood while the male is dining on take-outs from the Old Stone Mill, I'll be accused of sex discrimination."

The groom said, "We want a couple of Abyssinians as soon as we're settled."

"It's my considered opinion," said Pender Wilmot, "that the world would be a better place if everyone had a cat."

Timmie spoke up. "Oh Jay weighs twenty pounds."

The pastor said, "Whenever I sneeze, my Whisker-Belle makes a sound as if she's blessing me."

"When I was a little girl taking piano lessons," June Halliburton put in, "our cat howled every time I hit a wrong note."

"Oh Jay has fleas," said the sociable Wilmot scion.

Qwilleran caught the attorney's eye, and the two

men drifted into the library. Wilmot said, "This is the first wedding I've ever attended where the sole topic of conversation was cats."

"You could do worse," Qwilleran remarked.

"My wife says you called me."

"Yes, it's probably none of my business, but I've been researching a piece on Euphonia Gage, and a few facts about the Park of Pink Sunsets have aroused my suspicion."

"Their cavalier repurchase policy is enough to give one pause," Wilmot said.

"Right! That was the first clue. Then Junior told me about Euphonia's new will, cutting out her relatives. It was written for her by an in-house lawyer who charges surprisingly low fees."

Wilmot nodded soberly.

"There's more," said Qwilleran. "They have an associate who helps residents unload their valuables—and rips them off. One ostensibly wealthy woman was offered a lock-box in the office safe for financial documents and unreported cash. Who knows if they have extra keys to those boxes? Shall I continue?"

"By all means."

"The woman I mentioned has sent me snapshots that include the operators of the park, a couple who are chummily called Betty and Claude. Now here's a curious fact: On the weekend Euphonia died, Betty and Claude were in Pickax, attending the preview of 'The Big Burning.' Hixie Rice and I thought they were gate-crashers from Lockmaster, but they were evidently casing the place; shortly after, a dealer Down Below approached Junior about stripping the mansion of architectural features."

"Junior told me about that," said the attorney. "The

dealer indicated that Mrs. Gage was negotiating a deal before she died."

"I could go on with this," Qwilleran said, "but we're supposed to be celebrating my boss's wedding."

"Let's live with this over the weekend and then get together downtown—" He was interrupted by hubbub outdoors. "Sounds like a pack of wolves out there!"

It was a pack of huskies. Nancy Fincher and her dogteam had arrived to transport the newlyweds to the honeymoon cottage that Don Exbridge was lending them. Arch and Mildred were changing clothes, Carol said. The guests bundled into their own wraps and went out on the porch to admire the dogs and the Christmas lights. It was dark, and every cottage on both sides of the road was outlined with strings of white lights.

"A magic village!" Polly said.

The bride and groom reappeared in togs suitable for an arctic expedition and were whisked away, huddled in the basket of the sled. With Nancy riding the runners, they sped down the avenue of snow through a confetti of tiny lights, while cottagers waved and cheered and threw poorly aimed snowballs.

Then the wedding guests departed for their own cottages or the mainland, and the two remaining couples had a light supper in front of the fireplace.

"Hixie arranged for the dog-sledding," Carol said. "Nancy will be here for the next two days, taking kids for rides."

"Adults, too," Larry added. "How about you, Qwill?"

"No, thanks."

The evening passed pleasantly. From speakers on the balcony came recorded carols played on antique music boxes and great cathedral organs. At Qwilleran's request, Larry read a passage from Dickens's *Christmas Carol*—the description of the Cratchits' Christmas dinner. *"There never was such a goose!"* Then gifts were opened.

Polly was thrilled with the opals. She gave Qwilleran a twenty-seven-volume set of Shakespeare's plays and sonnets. They were leather-bound and old.

"Wait till my bibliocat sniffs these!" he said with detectable pride. He gave the Lanspeaks a pair of brass candlesticks, Dutch baroque.

The next morning began with wake-up music that Wagner had composed as a Christmas gift for his wife, and Carol prepared eggs Benedict for breakfast. It had snowed lightly, and Timmie Wilmot, with a broom over his shoulder, rang the doorbell.

"Sweep your porch?" he asked.

"All right, but be sure you do a good job," Larry admonished him. To the others he explained, "Timmie's parents want to develop his work ethic."

The snowy landscape was bright with winter sunshine, and the frozen bay was dotted with the small shanties of ice fishermen. All day the telephone jangled with holiday greetings from distant places, and the dogsled could be seen flying up and down the white canyon. After Christmas dinner—Cornish hen and plum pudding—Polly took a nap and Carol wrote thank-you notes, while Larry tinkered with his new model-building kit.

Later, they walked to an open house at the Exbridge cottage. Nancy Fincher was there, their guest for the weekend. "When are you going to run the article on dog-sledding?" she asked Qwilleran.

"As soon as the race dates are announced."

"Would you like to take a ride tomorrow?"

"I've had a ride!" he said testily.

"But the parade wasn't the real thing."

"It was real enough for me!" He remembered the discomfort of the costume and the horror of climbing the ladder while it ripped at the seams. He also remembered a conversation with Nancy. "What was the date of the parade?" he now asked her.

Her answer was prompt. "November 27."

"Are you sure?"

"I know, because it was my mother's birthday."

Qwilleran's impulse was to telephone Junior immediately, but other guests were demanding his attention. Conversation was animated until someone announced, "It's snowing, you guys! And the wind's rising! It looks like a blizzard's cooking!"

The guests said hasty farewells, and Larry guided his party home through the swirling flakes. Polly said, "I'm thankful we don't have to drive back to Pickax tonight. Crossing the Flats in a blizzard must be a horrendous experience!"

Back at the cottage Larry tuned in the weather forecast: "Snow ending by midnight. High winds continuing, gusting up to sixty miles an hour."

"If there's drifting on the Flats and the highway is buried, we'll be trapped," Carol said cheerfully, "but that's the excitement of weekending on the Point. You may have to stay longer than you intended . . . Dominoes, anyone?"

The wind howled around the cottage, making Polly nervous, and Carol sent her to bed with aspirin and earplugs. Soon she retired herself, leaving the two men sprawled in front of the fire.

Qwilleran said to Larry, "You manipulate that fireplace damper like a cellist playing Brahms."

"With this kind of wind, you have to know your stuff. Do you use the fireplaces where you're living?"

"With those old chimneys? Not a chance!"

Larry said, "I heard about Euphonia's will. Cutting off her own flesh and blood was bad enough, but throwing her fortune away at the racetrack was a crime! To be eighty-eight and suddenly broke must be tough to take. Is that why she ended it all?"

"I don't know," Qwilleran said. "They've had other suicides in the Park of Pink Sunsets."

"The name alone would drive me over the edge," Larry said. "How about a hot drink before we turn in?"

The morning after the blizzard the snowscape was smoothly sculptured by the wind, but the day was bright, and the air was so clear it was possible to hear the churchbells on the mainland.

During breakfast Larry tuned in WPKX, and Wetherby Goode said, "Well, folks, December has been mild, but last night's blizzard made up for lost time. The ice fishermen have lost their shanties. The entire westside of Pickax is blacked out. And the Purple Point Road is blockaded by ten-foot snow drifts. The plows won't be out till Monday morning, because the crews get double-time for Sundays, so you holiday-makers on the Point will have to go on drinking eggnog for another twenty-four hours. Today's forecast: mild temperatures, clear skies, variable winds—" The announcement was interrupted by the telephone.

Carol answered and said, "It's for you, Polly."

"Me?" she said in surprise and apprehension. Conversation at the breakfast table stopped as she talked in the next room. Returning, she looked grave as she said, "Qwill, I think you should take this call. It's Lynette. She's calling from your house."

He jumped up, threw his napkin on the chairseat, and hurried to the phone. "Yes, Lynette. What's the trouble?"

"I'm at your house, Mr. Qwilleran. I stopped to feed the cats on my way to church, but I can't find them! They usually come running for their food. I've searched all the rooms, but the power is off, you know, and it's hard to see inside the closets, even with a flashlight . . ."

He listened in silence, his mind hurtling from one dire possibility to another.

"But there's something else I should tell you, Mr. Qwilleran, although I don't know if it means anything. When I came over here early last evening, I drove to the carriage house first to feed Bootsie. It was dark, but I had a glimpse of a van parked behind the big house. I didn't remember seeing it before, and when I came downstairs a half hour later, it was gone. I didn't think much about it. Koko and Yum Yum gobbled their food and talked to me—"

"What kind of van?"

"Sort of a delivery van, I think, although I didn't pay that much attention—"

"I'm coming home," he interrupted. "I'll get there as fast as I can. I'll leave at once."

"Shall I wait here?"

"There's nothing more you can do. Go on to church. I'll be there in forty-five minutes." He returned to the table. "I've got to get out of here fast. Lynette can't find the cats, and she saw a strange vehicle in the yard. I won't stop to pack." He was headed for the stairs. "I'll just grab my parka and keys. Polly can drive home with you."

"Qwill!" Larry said sternly, following him to the stairway. "The road's closed! You can't get through! The highway is blocked by ten-foot drifts!"

"Could a snowmobile get through?"

"Nobody's got one. They're outlawed on the Point."

Qwilleran pounded his moustache with his fist. "Could a dogsled get through?"

"I'll call Nancy," Carol said. "She's staying with the Exbridges."

"Tell her to hurry!"

Polly said anxiously, "What can have happened, Qwill?"

"I don't know, but I have a hunch that something's seriously wrong!"

"Nancy's on her way," Carol reported. "Luckily she was harnessing her team when I called."

They were all on the porch when the dogsled and eight flying huskies arrived. Qwilleran was in his parka with the hood pulled up.

Larry asked, "Can your dogs get through ten-foot drifts, Nancy?"

"We won't use the highway. We'll cross the bay on the ice. It'll be shorter anyway."

"Is that safe?" Polly asked.

"Sure. I've been ice-fishing on the bay all my life."

Qwilleran asked, "Where do we touch land on the other side?"

"At the state park."

"Someone should meet me there and drive me to Pickax . . . Larry, try to reach Nick Bamba. Second

choice, Roger. Third choice, the sheriff . . . How long
will it take, Nancy?"

She estimated an hour at the outside. Carol gave
them thermos bottles of hot tea and coffee.

"Stay close to shore!" Larry shouted as they took off
down an easement to the bay.

Qwilleran was sitting low in the basket on caribou
skins as they skimmed across the ice at racing speed.
The high winds had left hillocks of snow and wrecked
shanties, but Nancy guided the team between obsta-
cles with gruff commands. The shoreline behind them
receded quickly.

"Where are we going?" Qwilleran shouted, mindful
of Larry's advice.

"Taking a shortcut. There's an island out there,"
she called back. "It's reached by an ice bridge."

Leaving the shore behind, they encountered a
strong wind sweeping across the lake from Canada,
and they were grateful for their hot drinks when they
stopped at the island to rest the dogs.

When they started out again, the wind changed to
offshore and was not quite as cutting. They sped
along through a world of white: ice under the runners,
wintery sky overhead, shoreline in the distance. But
soon they began to slow down, and Qwilleran could
feel the runners cutting into the ice. The dogs seemed
to find it hard going.

"It's softer than it should be," Nancy shouted. "It
rained one day last week." She turned the team farther out into the lake where the surface was firm, but
they were traveling farther from their destination.

Then Qwilleran saw a crack in the ice between the
sled and the shore. "Nancy! Are we drifting? Are we
being blown farther out?"

"Hang in there! We'll get around it!"

She headed the team even farther out, and soon they were climbing a hill of snow. She stopped the dogs with a command. "From here you can see what's happening. The north wind pushed the loose ice into shore, but the offshore breeze is breaking it up. Stand up! You can see the ice bridge."

Qwilleran peered across the bay and saw only more slush and more cracks. God! he thought . . . What am I doing here? Who is this girl? What does she know?

"Okay, let's take off! . . . Up! . . . Go! . . . haw!"

He clenched his teeth and gripped the siderails as they zigzagged across the surface. Slowly the distant shore was coming closer. At last he could see the roof of the lodge at the state park . . . Then he could see a single car parked on the overlook . . . Then he could see a man waving. Nick Bamba!

"Am I glad to see you!" Qwilleran shouted. To Nancy he said, "Dammit, woman! You deserve a medal!"

She smiled. It was a remarkably sweet smile.

"Where are you going from here, Nancy? You're not going back across the bay, I hope."

"No, I'll take the dogs home. It's only a few miles inland. I hope you find your cats all right."

"What happened?" Nick wanted to know. "What's going on here?"

"Start driving, and I'll tell you," Qwilleran said. "Drive fast!"

On the road to Pickax he summed up the situation: the missing cats, the strange van parked behind the house, the cat-sitter's frantic call to Purple Point. "I've been doing an unofficial investigation of some unscrupulous individuals, and it caused me to worry," he said. "I had to get home, but the highway is block-aded. When Nancy proposed crossing the bay on the ice, I was apprehensive. When we got into slush and started drifting out on an ice floe, I thought it was the end!"

"You didn't need to worry," Nick said. "That girl has a terrific reputation. She's a musher's musher!"

"Have you heard anything more about her father's murder?"

"Only that the state detectives are sure it wasn't a local vendetta. They think he was involved in some-thing outside the county. The cause of death," he said, "was a gunshot to the head."

When they reached Goodwinter Boulevard, Nick parked in the street. "Let's not mess up any tire tracks in the driveway . . . The power's still out in Pickax, they said on the air, so take the flashlight that's under the seat. I've got a high-powered lantern in the trunk."

They walked to the side door under the porte cochere, where wind currents had swept the drive clear in one spot and piled up the snow in another.

Qwilleran said, "The tire tracks leading to the car-riage house are Lynette's. They were made this morn-ing after the blizzard. She saw the van in the rear last evening before the blizzard. If they broke into the house, it would be through the kitchen door." He was speaking in a controlled monotone that belied the anxiety he felt in the pit of his stomach.

"The van has been back again since last night," Nick said. "I'd guess it was here during the blizzard and left before the snow stopped."

Qwilleran unlocked the side door and automatically reached for a wall switch, but power had not been restored. The foyer with its dark paneling and dark parquet floor was like a cave except for one shaft of light slanting in from a circular window on the stair landing, and in the patch of warmth was a Siamese cat, huddled against the chill but otherwise unperturbed.

"Koko! My God! Where were you?" Qwilleran shouted. "Where's Yum Yum?"

"There she is!" said Nick, beaming the big lantern down the hall. She was in a hunched position with rump elevated and head low—her mousing stance— and she was watching the door of the elevator.

At the same time there was pounding in the walls and a distant cry of distress.

The two men looked at each other in a moment's perplexity.

"Someone's trapped in the elevator!" Qwilleran said in amazement.

Nick peered through the small pane of glass in the elevator door. "It's stuck between here and the basement."

There was more pounding and hysterical yelling, and Qwilleran rushed to the lower level. "Call the police!" he shouted up to Nick. "The phone's in the library!"

The beam of his flashlight exposed a ravaged ballroom. Electrical wires were hanging from the ceiling and protruding from the walls, and canvas murals, peeled from their backgrounds, were lying in rolls on the floor.

NINETEEN

THE THWARTED BURGLARY on Goodwinter Boulevard was the subject of a news bulletin on WPKX Sunday afternoon. It was a newscaster's dream: breaking and entering, vandalism, attempted theft, and four big names: the *Gage* mansion owned by Junior *Goodwinter* and occupied by James *Qwilleran,* the *Klingenschoen* heir.

After the broadcast, Junior was the first to call. "Hey, Qwill! Is there a lot of damage?"

"The ballroom's a wreck, but they didn't get around to anything on the main floor, thanks to the blackout. The light fixtures are still on the elevator. The murals are rolled up on the ballroom floor; I hope they can be salvaged."

"I'd better buzz over and take a look. Is the power back on?"

"It was restored while the police were here. I'll plug in the coffeemaker."

Minutes later, when Junior viewed the dangling wires and stripped walls, he said, "I can't believe this! Who did it? He wasn't named on the air, and our reporter couldn't get anything at police headquarters. The suspect won't be charged until tomorrow."

"Suspect! That's a laugh! He was caught red-handed when the cops arrived—trapped in the elevator with his loot. Brodie himself was here . . . Come into the kitchen." Qwilleran poured coffee and said, "It's my guess that he's the dealer who phoned you and wanted to buy the stuff. He's from Milwaukee."

Junior unwrapped a few slices of fruitcake. "What made him think he could help himself?"

"It wasn't his own idea—or so he swears. He had a partner, an electrician, who decamped with the van when the power failed. It was the dealer's van, and he was madder'n hell! He was glad to name his accomplice, thinking the guy had thrown a circuit breaker in order to steal the vehicle. He didn't know it was a general blackout."

"How do you know all this?"

"I talked to Brodie afterward. The state police are tracking the van. And listen, Junior: Anything I tell you is off the record. If you jump the gun and I lose my credibility with Andy, your name isn't Junior anymore; it's something else."

"Agreed," said the editor.

"That isn't good enough."

"Scout's honor! . . . So if the neighborhood hadn't

blacked out, the rats would have gotten away with it. That's some coincidence!"

"And if I hadn't come home when I did," Qwilleran said, "the suspect, as he is charitably called, wouldn't be in jail."

"What brought you home, Qwill? I thought you were staying till Monday. And how did you get off the Point? The highway's still blocked."

"Regarding the latter question, read my column in Tuesday's paper. The other question . . ." He related the cat-sitter incident: the missing cats, the frantic phone call, the strange vehicle, the alarming possibilities. "But when I walked in, there they were! Both cats! Acting as if nothing had happened! Where were those two devils hiding when Lynette was looking for them, and *why* were they hiding? I'm convinced that Koko can sense evil, but did he know that their absence would bring me home in a hurry?. . . This is good fruitcake. Who made it?"

"Mildred . . . But how did the thieves know you wouldn't be home?"

"That part of the story gets complicated." Qwilleran smoothed his moustache, a familiar gesture. "With Celia Robinson's help, I've been collecting evidence about those con artists down there. She's been reporting to me from a mall, thinking her home phone is tapped. Just before Christmas I took a chance on calling her at home—about a small but urgent matter— and that's the only way those crooks could find out I'd be gone for the weekend. Her phone really was tapped, and they'd connect my name with the Gage mansion. Betty and Claude were here, you remember, for the preview of our show. They're no dummies! They're real professionals!"

Junior said, "Wait till Wilmot hears your story!"

"I discussed my suspicions with him at the wedding, but now that it's become police business, it puts a new face on the matter. There's some hard evidence."

"It'll make a hot story," the editor said, "especially with the cats involved."

"Leave the cats out of it," Qwilleran said sternly.

"Don't be crazy! That's the best part!"

"If you want a hot story, get this, Junior: Your aunt Lethe was born on the same day as your grandmother's housekeeper and in the same place. In a county as small as Lockmaster was in 1928, how many girl babies would be born on November 27? It's my contention that Euphonia paid a farm family to take Lethe and change her name to Lena Foote ... That would make Nancy Fincher your cousin."

Junior gulped audibly. "That's a wild guess on your part."

"Okay. Send a reporter to Lockmaster to search the county records for a Lena Foote and a Lethe Gage born on the same day. I'll bet you a five-course dinner there's only one ... unless ... your esteemed grandmother bribed the county clerk to rig the books."

"That's a possibility," Junior admitted. "We all know how corrupt they are in Lockmaster."

"Don't you find it significant that Lena dropped out of school at the age of fifteen and entered the employ of the Gages—where she remained for more than forty years? Don't you think Nancy has your grandmother's genes? Euphonia was tiny, and so is she—"

"And I'm vertically challenged myself," Junior interrupted.

"Now you're getting it! Also, a deceptively young

countenance is characteristic of all three of you. Nancy even has Euphonia's sweet smile. Sorry I can't say the same about you ... More coffee?"

"No, thanks. I'll amble home and break the news to Jody that we have a pack of Siberian huskies for first-cousins-once-removed."

"And don't forget that the murdered potato farmer was your uncle-by-marriage," Qwilleran added.

Junior wandered out of the house in an apparent daze.

The Siamese were under the kitchen table, waiting for crumbs, and Qwilleran shared the last slice of fruitcake with them. They slobbered over it eagerly, being careful to spit out the nuts and fruits.

On Monday the snowbound Purple Pointers were able to return to town. An electrical contractor sent a crew to the Gage mansion to restore the ballroom fixtures. An installer from Amanda's design studio prepared to rehang the murals. Qwilleran wrote a column about his experience on the frozen bay, with paragraphs of praise for the musher's musher. And at five o'clock Celia Robinson called.

"Did you enjoy Christmas?" he asked.

"Yes, we had a good time," she said in a subdued manner that was unusual for her. "We splurged on dinner at a nice place, and Clayton had a real steak, not chopped."

"Did he bring Wrigley with him?"

"Yes, Wrigley's a nice cat. Black and white. But something odd is happening here, Mr. Qwilleran. Pete, the assistant manager, went to Wisconsin to spend Christmas with his parents, and he hasn't come back. Betty and Claude haven't been seen since yesterday noon. There's no one in charge of the office. Clayton and I went in and sorted the mail today, but everybody's upset."

"What is Claude's last name?"

"I think it's Sprott. Another thing, Mr. Qwilleran. I've decided to leave Florida. Too many old people! I'm only sixty-eight."

"Where would you go?" he asked.

"Someplace back in Illinois, where I can get a part-time job and be closer to my grandson."

"Excellent idea!"

"But I'm babbling about myself. How was your Christmas? That was a funny phone call I got from you, but I figured out why you did it. Was it a nice wedding?"

"Very fine."

"Did Santa bring you something exciting?"

"Some books, that's all, but that's better than a necktie. Was Clayton able to carry out his assignment?"

"Didn't you get his tape recording? We mailed it Friday afternoon. When I told him what you wanted, he went right out and bought a little tape recorder to wear under his cap. He wore it when he visited Mr. Crocus."

"Did you listen to the tape?"

"No, we wanted to get it into the mail before the holiday. I thought you'd have it today."

"Mail is always slow in reaching Moose County. Meanwhile, Celia, I have a question for you, if you can think back to the day you discovered Mrs. Gage's body. It was a Monday noon, you told me. She'd been dead sixteen hours, the doctor said, meaning she died

Sunday evening. Did you see anyone go to her home on Sunday?"

"Oh dear! Let me think . . . You think someone might have given her disturbing news that made her take those pills?"

"Whatever."

"I can't recall right off the bat, but maybe Mr. Crocus will know. He's the kind that notices things."

"Well, give it some serious thought, and I'll watch the mail for Clayton's tape."

"And Mr. Qwilleran, I put something in the package for you personally. It isn't much. Just a little holiday goodie."

"That's very thoughtful of you, Celia. I'll keep in touch."

When Celia's package arrived on Tuesday, Qwilleran sank his teeth into a rich, nut-filled, chewy chocolate brownie, and he had a vision. He envisioned Celia transplanted to Pickax, baking meatloaf for the cats and brownies for himself, catering parties now and then, laughing a lot. Then he abandoned his fantasy and listened to Clayton's tape. What he heard prompted him to phone Pender Wilmot immediately.

"I'd like to hear it," the attorney said. "Would you like to bring it to my office tomorrow afternoon?"

"No. Now!" Qwilleran said firmly.

The law office in the new Klingenschoen Professional Building was unique in Pickax, where dark mahogany and red leather were the legal norm. Wilmot's office was paneled in light teakwood, with chrome-based chairs upholstered in slate blue and plum.

Qwilleran noticed a black iron lamp with saucer shade. "That looks like a Charles Rennie Mackintosh design," he said. "I saw his work in Glasgow last September. My mother was a Mackintosh."

"I have Scots blood myself," said the attorney. "My mother's ancestors came out in the 1745 Rising." He showed Qwilleran a framed etching of an ancestral castle. "Now, what is the new development you mentioned?"

"The attempted burglary," Qwilleran began, "confirms my theory about the Pink Sunset management, and news of the arrest has obviously reached them through their assistant. He's undoubtedly the electrician who removed the light fixtures and then stole the other fellow's van. All three of them have disappeared, according to my informant at the park. She has also sent me a taped conversation that warrants further investigation."

"Who made the tape?"

"Her grandson. He's friendly with an elderly resident who was a confidant of Mrs. Gage. The young man secreted a recording device under his cap when he went to see the old gentleman. I had a hunch that this Mr. Crocus might know something enlightening about her last days." Qwilleran started the tape. "The preliminary dialogue is irrelevant but interesting. He was probably testing the equipment."

As the tape unreeled, it produced the charming voice of a young woman and an adolescent baritone with falsetto overtones.

"Are you Betty? My grandma sent you this plant. She's Mrs. Robinson on Kumquat Court."

"A Christmas cactus! How sweet of her! And what is your name?"

"Clayton."

"Tell her thank-you, Clayton. We'll put it right here on the counter, where all the Sunsetters can enjoy it when they come in for their mail."

"Last year she gave a Christmas plant to the old lady next door, but she died."

"We say *elderly*, not *old*, Clayton."

"Okay. What was her name?"

"Mrs. Gage."

"What happened to her, anyway?"

"She passed away in her sleep."

"She looked healthy last Christmas."

"I'm afraid she accidentally took the wrong medication."

"How do you know?"

"The doctor said so. We really don't like to talk about these things, Clayton."

"Why not?"

"It's so sad, and at this time of year we try to be happy."

"Was it written up in the paper?"

"No, this is a large city, and they can't report everything."

"But my grandma says she was rich. They always write up rich people when they die, don't they?"

"Clayton, this is an interesting conversation, but you'll have to excuse me. I have work to do."

"Can I help?"

"No, thank you, but it's kind of you to offer."

"I could sort the mail."

"Not today. Just tell your grandmother that we appreciate the plant."

"I know computers."

"I'm sure you do, but there's really nothing—"

"You're a very pretty lady."

"Thank you, Clayton. Now please . . . just go away!"

Wilmot chuckled. "His ingenuous performance is ingenious. How old is he?"

"Thirteen."

After a few seconds of taped silence, the adolescent voice alternated with the husky, gasping voice of an elderly man.

"Hi, Mr. Crocus! Remember me?"

"Clayton! I hardly recognized you. . . . No beard this year."

"I shaved it off. How're you feeling, Mr. Crocus?"

"Moderately well."

"What are you doing? Just sitting in the sun?"

"That's all."

"Grandma sent you this plant. It's a Christmas cactus."

"Very kind of her."

"Where'll I put it?"

"Next to the door. Tell her thank-you."

"Okay if I sit down?"

"Yes . . . yes . . . please!"

"Been doing any chess lately?"

"No one plays chess here."

"Not even your grandkids?"

"My grandchildren never visit me. Might as well not have any."

"I don't have a grandpa. Why don't we work out a deal?"

(Slight chuckle.) "What terms do you propose?"

"We could play chess by mail, and I could tell you about school. I just made Junior Band."

"What instrument?"

"Trumpet. Do you still play the violin?"

"Not recently."

"Why not?"

"No desire. I've had a very great loss."

"That's too bad. What happened?"

"Mrs. Gage . . . passed away."

"She was a nice lady. Was she sick long?"

"Sad to say, it was . . . suicide."

"I knew somebody that did that. Depression, they said. Was she depressed?"

"She had her troubles."

"What kind of troubles?"

"One shouldn't talk about . . . a friend's personal affairs."

"Our counselor at school says it's good to talk about it when you lose a friend."

"I have no one who's . . . interested."

"I'm interested, if you're going to be my grandpa."

"You're a kind young person."

"Do you know what kind of troubles she had?"

(Pause.) "Someone was . . . taking her money . . . wrongfully."

"Did she report it to the police?"

"It was not . . . She didn't feel . . . that she could do that."

"Why not?"

"It was . . . extortion."

"How do you mean?"

"She was being . . . blackmailed."

"That's bad! What was it about? Do you know?"

"A family secret."

"Somebody committed a crime?"

"I don't know."

"Did she say who was blackmailing her?"

"Someone up north. That's all she'd say."

"How long did it go on?"

"A few years."

"I'd go to the police, if it was me."

"I told her to tell Claude."

"Why him?"

"She was leaving her money to the park, and . . . she was afraid . . . there wouldn't be any left."

"Is he Betty's husband?"

"Something like that."

"What did he say?"

"He told her not to worry."

"That's not much help."

"He said he could put a stop to it."

"What did she think about that?"

"She worried about it. In a few days . . . she was gone."

"Did she leave a suicide note?"

"Not even for me. That grieved me."

"You must have liked her a lot."

"She was a lovely lady. She liked music and art and poetry."

"I like music."

"But what kind? You young people—"

"Would you like a game of chess after supper, Mr. Crocus?"

"I would look forward to that with pleasure."

"I have to go somewhere with my grandma now. I'll see you after supper."

The attorney said, "So we know—or think we know—what happened to Mrs. Gage's money."

"We know more than that," Qwilleran said. "We know that she gave birth to a natural daughter in 1928 while her husband was in prison. In those days, and in a community like Pickax, that was an intolerable disgrace for a woman with her pride and pretensions. It's my contention that she gave her daughter—with certain stipulations and considerations—to a Lockmaster farm family, who raised her as Lena Foote. In her teens Lena went to work in the Gage household and remained there for the rest of her life. I'm guessing that Euphonia continued to pay hush money to the foster parents. Lena lost contact with them, but they came to her funeral a few years ago. Shortly afterward, Lena's widower began spending large sums of money for which there was no visible source. I say he's your blackmailer. The foster parents, being very old, may have passed on their secret to him—a kind of legacy for his daughter."

Wilmot had been listening intently to Qwilleran's fabric of fact and conjecture. "How did you acquire your information?"

"It's remarkable how many secrets you uncover when you work for a newspaper. When Mrs. Gage moved to Florida, the man I suspect of being the blackmailer obtained her address from her grandson, saying he owed her money which he wished to repay. He continued to hound her, until she confided in Claude Sprott. A few days later, Gil Inchpot was murdered, and the state detectives have neither a motive nor a suspect."

Wilmot was swiveling in his chair, a rapt listener.

"Sprott had a vested interest in Mrs. Gage's estate, of course."

"What was left of it," Qwilleran added. "His sticky fingers had already been in the pie, one way and another."

"If he arranged for Inchpot's murder, who could have pulled the trigger?"

Qwilleran was ready for the question. "When you and I talked about it at the wedding, Pender, I told you that Sprott and his companion were in Pickax, incognito, for the preview of 'The Big Burning.' Now it occurs to me that they had flown up here not only to appraise the rare chandeliers. That was the weekend Inchpot disappeared. They probably rented a car at the airport and knocked on the door of his farmhouse, saying they were out of gas—after which they dropped his body in the woods and left his truck at the airport."

"Odd, isn't it, that they chose the Klingenschoen woods?"

"Not odd. Virtually unavoidable. Do you realize how many square miles of woodland belong to the Klingenschoen estate around Mooseville and Brrr? . . . And here's something else I've just learned," Qwilleran told the attorney. "As soon as their Milwaukee associate was arrested in my elevator and their Florida assistant was fugitive in a stolen vehicle, they skipped the Park of Pink Sunsets."

"We should see the prosecutor fast," Wilmot said. "Let's try to catch him before he goes to lunch."

TWENTY

AFTER A LONG session with the Moose County prosecutor, Qwilleran telephoned Celia Robinson. "I called to sing the praises of your chocolate brownies," he said. "I assume no one is listening to our conversation."

"Nobody ever came back," she said in a tone of bewilderment. "The police have been here, asking questions. Clayton and I have sort of taken charge of the office. We're trying to keep people calm, but the oldsters at the park get very upset."

"I also want to compliment your grandson on the tape. He's a smart young man."

"Yes, I'm proud of him."

"Have you been able to recall anything about the Sunday that Mrs. Gage died?"

"Well, Mr. Crocus and I put our heads together," she said, "and we remembered that the electricity went off around suppertime. There was no storm or anything, but every home on Kumquat Court lost power, and Pete came looking for a short circuit. He went to every home on the court."

"Including Mrs. Gage's?"

"Everybody's. We never found out what caused it. The power wasn't off for long, so it wasn't serious. That's the only thing we can remember."

"Good enough!" Qwilleran commended her.

"Is there anything else I can do for you, Mr. Qwilleran?"

"I may have an idea to discuss with you later on . . . Excuse me a moment. The doorbell's ringing."

"That's all right. I'll hang up. Happy New Year!"

It was Andrew Brodie at the door. "Come on in, chief," Qwilleran said. "Is this a social call, or did you come to talk shop?"

"Both. I'll take a nip of Scotch if you've got any. I'm on my way home." He followed Qwilleran into the kitchen. "A little water and no ice. What are you gonna drink?"

"Cider. Let's take our glasses into the library."

Brodie dropped into a large, old, underslung leather chair. "Feels like a hammock," he said.

"You'll sag, too, when you're that old."

"That's some Christmas tree you've got." The chief was looking at Polly's wreath.

"Have a good Christmas, Andy?"

"The usual. Did you get your lights fixed downstairs?"

"Good as new."

Something was on Brodie's mind. His staccato small

talk was a kind of vamp-till-ready until he came to the point. "What's happening on Goodwinter Boulevard?" he asked. "A lot of property's changing hands."

"Is that good or bad?" Qwilleran asked.

"All depends. There's a rumor that the Klingenschoen money is behind it."

"Interesting, if true."

Brodie threw him a swift, fierce Scottish scowl. "In other words, you ain't talkin'."

"I've nothing to say."

"You had plenty to say to the prosecutor's office today. I hear they even sent out for roast beef sandwiches from Lois's."

"Your operatives don't miss a thing, Andy."

"I knew Inchpot," the chief said, "and I'd never figure him for a blackmailer."

"Perhaps he had professional advice," Qwilleran suggested slyly. "Extortion consultation and one-stop money-laundering would be the kind of services George Breze might offer. His business card was found in Euphonia's files. Was he an intermediary?"

Brodie brushed the jest aside. "He serviced her Mercedes . . . How come you came up with all those clues in the Inchpot case when the state bureau was stymied? Did your psychic cat work on it?" He had learned about Koko's unique capabilities from a city detective Down Below.

"Well, I'll tell you this: Koko and his sidekick collaborated to catch the thief in the elevator. I don't know how many hours he'd been trapped in pitch darkness, but claustrophobia had made him a screaming maniac by the time Nick Bamba and I walked in . . . Freshen your drink?"

"A wee drop."

Qwilleran brought in the bottle and a jug of water. "Help yourself."

"By this time I thought Koko would come up with a clue to Euphonia's suicide."

"Well, let me tell you something that's just occurred to me, Andy. I think she was not the first victim of fraud at the mobile home park, and I know for a fact she was not the first suicide. I have a hunch . . ." Qwilleran combed his moustache with his fingertips. "I have a hunch they were all murders. The management profited by a quick turnover. Rob 'em and rub 'em out!"

"You didn't tell that to the prosecutor!"

"I had nothing to support my suspicions when I was at the courthouse, but a phone call from Florida filled in some blanks."

"You know," said the chief, "I never thought that feisty woman would cash in like they said she did. Overdose, they said."

"It could have been a drop of poison in her Dubonnet. She always had to have her apéritif before dinner, I'm told. The medical examiner who wrote it off as suicide could have been one of those overworked civil servants you hear about, or he could be another useful link in the crime ring. At any rate, I'm going back to the courthouse tomorrow." The telephone jangled, and he let it ring.

"Answer it!" Brodie snapped, tossing off his drink. "I'll let myself out."

It was Junior on the line, getting straight to the point with his usual impetuosity. "Hey, Qwill! I just heard a terrific rumor! They say we're getting a community college in Pickax! And Goodwinter Boulevard is gonna be the campus! How d'you like that? All those white elephants are made to order for administration offices, classrooms, dorms— I hope it's true!"

"I don't see why it shouldn't be true," Qwilleran said calmly. "Lockmaster has its College of Animal Husbandry. Pickax could have an Institute of Rumor Technology, with courses in Conspiracy Theory, Advanced Gossip, and Media Leak."

"Very funny," Junior said sourly. "I'll call Lyle Compton. He'll know what's happening."

Qwilleran lost no time in phoning Polly. "Have you heard the rumors about Goodwinter Boulevard?"

"No, I haven't. What are they saying?" she asked anxiously.

"The police have heard one rumor, and the newspaper has heard another," he said, "and they're both true. I merely want you to be assured, Polly, that your carriage house won't be affected."

"Are you involved, Qwill? Aren't you going to tell me what the rumors are?"

"No. At the rate gossip travels in Pickax, you'll find out soon enough."

"You're cruel! I'm going to phone my sister-in-law."

Within hours, Betty and Claude were picked up in Texas near the Mexican border. Pete was arrested at an airport in Kentucky, having abandoned the stolen van. All three suspects would be arraigned on murder charges.

For Qwilleran the case was closed, and he entertained himself with speculations: If he had not rented the Gage mansion for the winter, Koko would not have discovered the historically important scrap of paper that led to "The Big Burning of 1869," and if the cat had not become a closet archaeologist, the mysterious deaths of Euphonia Gage and Gil Inchpot might have gone unsolved, and if Oh Jay had not infuriated Qwilleran by spraying the back door, Pickax would not be getting a community college. Would it be named after the Goodwinters, who founded the city? Or the eleemosynary foundation that was funding it? Or the orange cat with fleas and bad breath?

They were fanciful thoughts, but Qwilleran was feeling heady from too much caffeine. It was shortly before New Year's. He plugged in the lighted Christmas wreath in the dingy library and relaxed in the hammock-contoured lounge chair with yet another cup of coffee. With refurbishing, he reflected, the library would make an impressive office for the president of the college. Yum Yum was lounging on his lap, her chin resting heavily on his right hand, forcing him to lift his coffee cup with his left. Koko was sitting on *Robinson Crusoe* in the warm glow of a table lamp. It was a strange coincidence that the cat had chosen that title for their winter reading; it would be even stranger if Celia Robinson were to move to Pickax and become a purveyor of meatloaf to their royal highnesses.

The Robinson Connection was not the only coincidence that aroused Qwilleran's wonder. There were three desk drawers filled with pipe cleaners, used emery boards, half-empty matchbooks, pencil stubs, and other junk destined for the trashcan. Yet, among them were articles clearly associated with the recent investigation: the chess piece, for example . . . someone's denture . . . the 1928 birth certificate . . . a great deal of *purple* . . . and many items related to financial affairs. And then there was the safe! All these were obvious. It required a great leap of imagination, however, to link shoelaces and corn plasters with the Foote family. Nevertheless, Qwilleran had learned to give his imagination free rein when Koko telegraphed his messages. After all, it was a gold signet *ring* that finally suggested a ring of criminals in the Pink Sunset case. Was it all happenstance? he wondered.

"YOW!" said the cat at his elbow—a piercing utterance with negative significance.

If Qwilleran had any further doubts about Koko's role in the investigation, they were dispelled by the cat's subsequent behavior: He never sat in the safe again . . . He lost interest in *Robinson Crusoe* . . . He completely ignored the fifty closets.

The case was closed, he seemed to be indicating. Or was it only feline fickleness?

Cats! Qwilleran thought; I'll never understand them.

For the remainder of the winter Koko was content to watch falling snowflakes from the window of the library, meditate on top of heat registers, chase Yum Yum up and down the stairs, and frequently bite her neck. She loved it!

*And now, a special excerpt from
the newest mystery starring
Qwilleran, Koko, and Yum Yum . . .*

THE CAT WHO CAME TO BREAKFAST

The locals call it "Breakfast Island"—a cozy
place known for peace and quiet. But the peace
is shattered when plans for a resort complex get
under way . . . and a series of deadly "accidents" follows. Is it sabotage? It's up to
Qwilleran and the cats to find out . . .

*Available in hardcover
from G. P. Putnam's Sons*

It was a weekend in June—glorious weather for boating. A small cabin cruiser with *Double-Six* freshly painted on the sternboard chugged across the lake at a cautious speed. Stowed on the aft deck were suitcases, cartons, a turkey roaster without handles, and a small wire-mesh cage with a jacket thrown over the top.

"They're quiet!" the pilot yelled above the motor noise.

The passenger, a man with a large moustache, shouted back, "They like the vibration!"

"Yeah. They can smell the lake, too!"

"How long does it take to cross?"

"The ferry makes it in thirty minutes! I'm going slow so they don't get seasick!"

The passenger lifted a sleeve of the jacket for a surreptitious peek. "They seem to be okay!"

Pointing across the water to a thin black line on the horizon, the pilot announced loudly. "That's our destination! . . . Breakfast Island, ahoy!"

"YOW!" came a piercing baritone from the cage.

"That's Koko!" the passenger yelled. "He knows what 'breakfast' means!"

"N-n-NOW!" came a shrill soprano echo.

"That's Yum Yum! They're both hungry!"

The cabin cruiser picked up speed. For all of them it was a voyage to another world.

Breakfast Island, several miles from the Moose County mainland, was not on the navigation chart. The pear-shaped blip of land—broad at the south end and elongated at the northern tip—had been named Pear Island by nineteenth-century cartographers. Less printable names were invented by lake captains who lost ships and cargo on the treacherous rocks at the stem end of the pear.

The southern shore was more hospitable. For many years fishermen from the mainland, rowing out at dawn to try their luck, would beach their dinghies on the sand and fry up some of their catch for breakfast. No one knew exactly when or how Breakfast Island earned its affectionate nickname, but it was a long time before the economic blessing known as tourism.

Moose County itself, 400 miles north of everywhere, had recently been discovered as a vacation paradise; its popularity was developing gradually by word of mouth. Breakfast Island, on the other hand, blossomed suddenly—the result of a seed planted by a real-estate entrepreneur, nurtured by a financial institution, and watered by the careful hand of national publicity.

Two days before the voyage of the *Double-Six,* the flowering of Breakfast Island was the subject of debate on the mainland, where two couples were having dinner at the Old Stone Mill.

"Let's drink a toast to the new Pear Island resort," said Arch Riker, publisher of the local newspaper. "Best thing that ever happened to Moose County!"

"I can hardly wait to see it," said Polly Duncan, head of the Pickax Public Library.

Mildred Riker suggested, "Let's all four of us go over for a weekend and stay at a bed-and-breakfast!"

The fourth member of the party sat in moody silence, tamping his luxuriant moustache.

"How about it, Qwill?" asked Riker. "Will you drink to that?"

"No!" said Jim Qwilleran. "I don't like what they've done to Breakfast Island; I see no reason for changing its name; and I have no desire to go there!"

"Well!" said Polly in surprise.

"Really!" said Mildred in protest.

The two men were old friends—journalists from "Down Below," as Moose County natives called the population centers of the United States. Now Riker was realizing his dream of publishing a country newspaper, and Qwilleran, having inherited money, was living a comfortable bachelor life in Pickax City (population 3,000) and writing a column for the *Moose County Something.* Despite the droop of his pepper-and-salt moustache and the melancholy look in his heavy-lidded eyes, he had found middle-aged contentment here. He walked and biked and filled his lungs with country air. He met new people and confronted new challenges. He had a fulfilling friendship with Polly Duncan. He lived in a spectacular converted apple barn. And he shared the routine of everday living with two Siamese cats.

"Let me tell you," he went on to his dinner partners, "why I'm opposed to the Pear Island resort. When I first came up here from Down Below, some boaters took me out to the island, and we tied up at an old wooden pier. The silence was absolute, except for the scream of a gull or the splash of a fish jumping out of the water. God! It was peaceful! No cars, no paved roads, no telephone poles, no people, and only a few nondescript shacks on the edge of the forest!" He paused and noted the effect he was having on his listeners. "What is on that lonely shore now? A three-story hotel, a marina with fifty boat slips, a pizza parlor, a T-shirt studio, and *two fudge shops!*"

"How do you know?" Riker challenged him. "You haven't even been over there to see the resort, let alone count the fudge shops."

"I read the publicity releases. That was enough to turn me off."

"If you had attended the press preview, you'd have a proper perspective." Riker had the ruddy face and paunchy figure of an editor who had attended too many press previews.

"If I ate their free lunch," Qwilleran shot back, "they'd expect all kinds of puffery in my column . . . No, it was enough, Arch, that you gave them the lead story on page one, three pictures inside, and an editorial!"

The publisher's new wife, Mildred, spoke up. "Qwill,

I went to the preview with Arch and thought XYZ Enterprises did a very tasteful job with the hotel. It's rustic and blends in nicely. There's a shopping strip on either side of the hotel—also rustic—and the signage is standardized and not at all junky." This was high praise coming from someone who taught art in the public schools. "I must admit, though, that you can smell fudge all over the island."

"And horses," said her husband. "It's a heady combination, let me tell you! Since motor vehicles are prohibited, visitors hire carriages or hail horse cabs or rent bicycles or walk."

"Can you picture the traffic jam when that little island is cluttered with hordes of bicycles and strollers and sightseeing carriages?" Qwilleran asked with a hint of belligerence.

Polly Duncan laid a hand softly on his arm. "Qwill, dear, should we attribute your negative attitude to guilt? If so, banish the thought!"

Qwilleran winced. There was some painful truth in her well-intended statement. It was his own money that had financed, to a great degree, the development of the island. Having inherited the enormous Klingenschoen fortune based in Moose County, he had established the Klingenschoen Foundation to distribute megamillions for the betterment of the community, thus relieving himself of responsibility. A host of changes had resulted, some of which he questioned. Nevertheless, he adhered to his policy of hands-off.

Polly continued, with sincere enthusiasm. "Think how much the K Foundation has done for the schools, health care, and literacy! If it weren't for Klingenschoen backing, we wouldn't have a good newspaper and plans for a community college!"

Riker said, "The Pear Island Hotel alone will provide three hundred jobs, many of them much-needed summer work for young people. We pointed that out on our editorial page. Also, the influx of tourists will pour millions into the local economy over a period of time. At the press preview, I met the editor of the *Lockmaster Ledger*, and he told me that Lockmaster County is green with envy. They say we have an offshore gold mine. One has to admire XYZ for undertaking such a herculean project. Everthing had to be shipped over on barges: building materials, heavy equipment, furniture! Talk about giving yourself a few problems!"

The man with a prominent moustache huffed into it with annoyance.

"Why fight it, Qwill? Isn't the K Foundation a philanthropic institution? Isn't it mandated to do what's best for the community?"

Qwilleran shifted uncomfortably in his chair. "I've kept my nose out of the operation because I know nothing about business and finance—and care even less—but if I had offered more input, the directors might have balanced economic improvement with environmental foresight. More and more I'm concerned about the future of our planet."

"Well, you have a point there," Riker admitted. "Let's drink to environmental conscience!" he said jovially, waving his empty glass at a tall serving person, who was hovering nearby. Derek Cuttlebrink was obviously listening to their conversation. "Another Scotch, Derek."

"No more for me," said Mildred.

Polly was still sipping her first glass of sherry.

Qwilleran shook his head, having downed two glasses of a local mineral water.

Everyone was ready to order, and Riker inquired if there were any specials.

"Chicken Florentine," said the server, making a disagreeable face.

The four diners glanced at each other, and Mildred said, "Oh, no!"

They consulted the menu, and the eventual choice was trout for Mildred, sweetbreads for Polly, and rack of lamb for the two men. Then Qwilleran returned to the subject: "Why did they change it to Pear Island? I say that Breakfast Island has a friendly and appetizing connotation."

"It won't do any good to complain," Riker told him. "XYZ Enterprises has spent a fortune on wining and dining travel editors, and every travel page in the country has hailed the discovery of Pear Island. Anyway, that's what it's called on the map, and it happens to be pear-shaped. Furthermore, surveys indicate that a sophisticated market Down Below finds 'Pear Island' more appealing than 'Breakfast Island,' according to Don Exbridge." He referred to the X in XYZ Enterprises.

"They like the pear's erotic shape," Qwilleran grumbled. "As a fruit it's either underripe or overripe, mealy or gritty, with a choice of mild flavor or no flavor."

Mildred protested. "I insist there's nothing to equal a beautiful, russet-colored Bosc with a wedge of Roquefort!"

"Of course! A pear needs all the help it can get. It's delicious with chocolate sauce or fresh raspberries. What isn't?"

"Qwill's on his soapbox again," Riker observed.

"I agree with him on the name of the island," said Polly. "I think 'Breakfast Island' has a certain quaint charm. Names of islands on the map usually reflect a bureaucratic lack of imagination."

"Enough about pears!" Riker said, rolling his eyes in exasperation. "Let's eat."

Mildred asked Qwilleran, "Don't you have friends who've opened a bed-and-breakfast on the island?"

"I do indeed, and it disturbs me. Nick and Lori Bamba were about to convert one of the old fishing lodges there. Then the Pear Island resort hoopla started, and they got sucked into the general promotional scheme. They would have preferred leaving the island in its natural state as much as possible."

"Here comes the food," Arch Riker said with a sigh of relief.

Qwilleran turned to the young man who was serving the entrées. "How come you're waiting on tables, Derek? I thought you'd been promoted to assistant chef."

"Yeah ... well ... I was in charge of French fries and garlic toast, but I can make more money out on the floor, what with tips, you know. Mr. Exbridge— he's one of the owners here—said he might give me a summer job at his new hotel. You can have a lot of fun working at a resort. I'd like to be captain in the hotel dining room, where they slip you a ten for giving them a good table."

"As a captain you'd be outstanding," Qwilleran said. Derek Cuttlebrink was six-feet-eight and still growing.

Polly asked him, "Now that Pickax is getting a

community college, do you think you might further your education?"

"If they're gonna teach ecology, maybe I will. I've met this girl, you know, and she's into ecology pretty heavy."

Qwilleran asked, "Is she the girl who owns the blue nylon tent?"

"Yeah, we went camping last summer. I learned a lot ... Anything else you guys want here?"

When Derek had ambled away, Riker muttered, "When will his consumption of French fries and hot dogs start nourishing his brain instead of his arms and legs?"

"Give him a break. He's smarter than you think," Qwilleran replied.

The meal was untainted by any further argument about Breakfast Island. The Rikers described the new addition to their beach house on the sand dune near Mooseville. Polly announced that her old college roommate had invited her to visit Oregon. Qwilleran, when pressed, said he might do some free-lance writing during the summer.

In pleased surprise Polly asked, "Do you have something important in mind, dear?" As a librarian, she entertained a perennial hope that Qwilleran would write a literary masterpiece. Although the two of them had a warm and understanding relationship, this particular aspiration was hers, not his. Whenever she launched into her favorite theme, he found a way to tease her.

"Yes ... I'm thinking ... of a project," he said soberly. "I may undertake to write ... cat opera for TV. How's this for a scenario? ... In the first episode we've left Fluffy and Ting Foy hissing at each other, after an unidentified male has approached her and caused Ting Foy to make a big tail. Today's episode starts with a long shot of Fluffy and Ting Foy at their feeding station, gobbling their food amicably. We zoom in on the empty plate and the wash-up ritual, frontal exposures only. Then . . . close-up of a cuckoo clock. (Sound of cuckooing.) Ting Foy leaves the scene. (Sound of scratching in litter box.) Cut to female, sitting on her brisket, meditating. She turns her head. She hears something! She reacts anxiously. Has her mysterious lover returned? Will Ting Foy come back from the litter box? Why is he taking so long? What will happen when the two males meet? . . . Tune in tomorrow, same time."

Riker guffawed. "This has great sponsorship potential, Qwill: catfood, cat litter, flea collars . . ."

Mildred giggled, and Polly smiled indulgently. "Very amusing, Qwill dear, but I wish you'd apply your talents to belles lettres."

"I know my limitations," he said. "I'm a hack journalist, but a *good* hack journalist: nosy, aggressive, suspicious, cynical—"

"Please, Qwill!" Polly remonstrated. "We appreciate a little nonsense, but let's not be totally absurd."

Across the table the newlyweds gazed at each other in middle-aged bliss. They were old enough to have grandchildren but young enough to hold hands under the tablecloth. Both had survived marital upheavals, but now the easy-going publisher had married the warm-hearted Mildred Hanstable, who taught art and homemaking skills in the public schools. She also wrote the food column for the *Moose County Something*. She was noticeably overweight, but so was her bridegroom.

For this occasion Mildred had baked a chocolate cake, and she suggested having dessert and coffee at their beach house. The new addition had doubled the size of the little yellow cottage, and an enlarged deck overlooked the lake. Somewhere out there was Breakfast and/or Pear Island.

The interior of the beach house had undergone some changes, too, since their marriage. The handmade quilts that previously muffled the walls and furniture had been removed, and the interior was light and airy with splashes of bright yellow. The focal point was a Japanese screen from the VanBrook estate, a wedding gift from Qwilleran.

Riker said, "It's hard to find a builder for a small job, but Don Exbridge sent one of his crackerjack construction crews, and they built our new wing in a jiffy. Charged only for labor and materials."

A black-and-white cat with rakish markings walked inquisitively into their midst and was introduced as Toulouse. He went directly to Qwilleran and had his ears scratched.

"We wanted a purebred," said Mildred, "but Toulouse came to our door one day and just moved in."

"His coloring is perfect with all the yellow in the house," Polly remarked.

"Do you think I've used too much? It's my favorite color, and I tend to overdo it."

"Not at all. It makes a very spirited and happy ambiance. It reflects your new lifestyle."

Riker said, "Toulouse is a nice cat, but he has one bad habit. He pounces on the kitchen counter when Mildred is cooking and steals a shrimp or a pork chop, right from under her nose. When I lived Down Below, we had a cat who was a counter-pouncer, and we cured his habit with a spray bottle of water. We had a damp pet for a couple of weeks (that's spelled d-a-m-p), but he got the message and was a model of propriety for the rest of his life—except when we weren't looking."

The evening ended earlier than usual, because Polly was working the next day. No one else had any Saturday commitments. Riker, following his recent marriage, no longer spent seven days a week at the office, and Qwilleran's life was unstructured, except for feeding and brushing the Siamese and servicing their commode. "My self-image," he liked to say, "was formerly that of a journalist; now I perceive myself as handservant to a pair of cats—also tailservant."

He and Polly drove back to Pickax, where she had an apartment on Goodwinter Boulevard, not far from his converted apple barn. As soon as they pulled away from the beach house he popped the question: "What's all this about going to Oregon? You never told me."

"I'm sorry, dear. My old roommate phoned just before you picked me up, and the invitation was so unexpected, I hardly knew how to decide. But I have two weeks more of vacation time, and I've never seen Oregon. They say it's a beautiful state."

"Hmmm," Qwilleran murmured as he considered all the aspects of this sudden decision. Once she had gone to England alone and had become quite ill. Once she had gone to Lockmaster for a weekend and had met another man. At length he asked, "Shall I feed Bootsie while you're away?"

"That's kind of you to offer, Qwill, but he really needs a live-in companion for that length of time. My sister-in-law will be happy to move in. When I return, we should think seriously about spending a weekend on the island at an interesting bed-and-breakfast."

"A weekend of inhaling fudge fumes could be hazardous to our health," he objected. "It would be safer to fly down to Minneapolis with the Rikers. You and Mildred could go shopping, and Arch and I could see a ballgame." He stroked his moustache in indecision, wondering how much to tell her. He had an uneasiness about the present situation that was rooted in the old days, when he and Riker worked for large newspapers Down Below. They kept a punctilious distance from advertisers, lobbyists, and politicians as a matter of policy. Now, Riker was getting too chummy with Don Exbridge. XYZ Enterprises was a heavy advertiser in the *Moose County Something*; Exbridge had lent the Rikers a cottage for their honeymoon; and he had expedited the building of an addition to their beach house.

To Qwilleran it looked bad. And yet, he tried to tell himself, this was a small town, and everything was different. There were fewer people, and they were constantly thrown together at churches, fraternal lodges, business organizations, and country clubs. They were all on first-name terms and mutually supportive. And there were times when they covered up for each other. He had met Don Exbridge socially and at the Pickax Boosters Club and found him a hearty, likable man, ever ready with a handshake and a compliment. His cheerful face always looked scrubbed and polished; so did the top of his head, having only a fringe of brown hair over the ears. Exbridge was the idea man for the XYZ firm, and he said his cranium could sprout either ideas or hair but not both.

Polly said, "You're quiet tonight. Did you have a

good time? You looked wonderful—ten years younger than your age." Under his blazer he was wearing her birthday gift—a boldly striped shirt with white collar and a patterned tie.

"Thanks. You're looking pretty spiffy yourself. I'm glad to see you wearing bright colors. I assume it means you're happy."

"You know I'm happy, dear—happier than I've ever been in my life! . . . What did you think of Mildred's decorating?"

"I'm glad she got rid of all those quilts. The yellow's okay, I guess."

They turned into Goodwinter Boulevard, an avenue of old stone mansions that would soon be the campus of the new community college. The Klingenschoen Foundation had bought the property and donated it to the city. Currently there was some debate as to whether the institution should be named after the Goodwinters, who had founded the city, or after the original Klingenschoen, who was a rascally old saloonkeeper. Polly's apartment occupied a carriage house behind one of the mansions—within walking distance of the public library—and she was assured of a leasehold.

"Things will get lively here when the college opens," Qwilleran reminded her.

"That's all right. I like having young people around," she said, adding slyly, "Would you like to come upstairs and say goodnight to Bootsie?"

Afterward, driving home to his barn, Qwilleran considered the hazards of letting Polly out of his sight for two weeks. She was a perfect companion for him, being a loving, attractive, intelligent woman of his own age, with a gentle voice that never ceased to thrill him.

Anything could happen in Oregon, he told himself as he turned on the car radio. After the usual Friday night rundown on the soccer game between Moose County and Lockmaster, the WPKX announcer said:

"Another serious incident has occurred at the Pear Island Hotel, the second in less than a week. An adult male was found drowned in the hotel pool at eleven-fifteen this evening. The name of the victim is being withheld, but police say he was not a resident of Moose County. This incident follows on the heels of the food poisoning that caused fifteen hotel guests to become ill, three of them critically. Authorities have given the cause as contaminated chicken."

As soon as Qwilleran reached the barn, he telephoned Riker. "Did you hear the midnight news?"

"Damn shame!" said the publisher. "The island's been getting so much national coverage that the media will pounce on these accidents with perverse glee! What concerns me is the effect the bad publicity will have on the hotel and other businesses. They've gambled a helluva lot of money on these projects."

"Do you really think the incidents are accidents?" Qwilleran asked pointedly.

"Here we go again! With your mind-set, everything's foul play," Riker retorted. "Wait a minute. Mildred's trying to tell me something." After a pause he came back on the line. "She wishes you'd reconsider the idea of a weekend on the island—the four of us—when Polly returns from vacation. She thinks it would be fun."

"Well . . . you know, Arch . . . I don't go for resorts or cruises or anything like that."

"I know. You like working vacations. Well, sleep on the idea anyway. It would please the girls . . . and since you're such a workaholic, how about writing three columns a week instead of two during the summer? Staff members will be taking vacations, and we'll be short-handed."

"Steer them away from Pear Island resort," Qwilleran said. "I have a hunch the ancient gods of the island are frowning."